Also by Trey Ellis
Platitudes
Home Repairs

Right Here, Right Now

Trey Ellis

SIMON & SCHUSTER

SIMON & SCHUSTER
Rockefeller Center
1230 Avenue of the Americas
New York, NY 10020

SIMON AND SCHUSTER and colophon are registered trademarks of
Simon & Schuster Inc.

Designed by DEIRDRE C. AMTHOR

Manufactured in the United States of America

Library of Congress Cataloging-in-Publication Data

Ellis, Trey
Right here, right now/Trey Ellis
    p.   cm.
    I.Title
    PS3555.L617R54   1999
813'.54—dc21   98-34786
            CIP

ISBN 0-684-84592-X

For Ava,
Welcome.

Acknowledgments

I would like to give special thanks to my amazingly tireless and brilliant staff, in particular Mary Anne Rothberg, who first alerted me to Ashton Robinson and his self-help seminars so many years ago; Jackie Barth, my assistant producer, who never learned the meaning of the word "No"; and of course the inimitable Mr. Bruce Shulman-Handy. I'd also like to thank voice-recognition experts Erika Joi, Fletcher Robinson, Guy Reidel, Eli Workman, Jill Ricketts, and Craig Preston for their exhaustive and excellent work; and Brett King and the others at Transcon Transcripts for their speedy transcriptions of the hundreds of hours of tapes. Finally, this book would never have seen the light of day without the help of my agent, Lisa Bankoff, and I thank her for that.

Introduction

Believe those who are seeking the truth.
Doubt those who find it
                              –André Gide

The day before they came for the house
I'd fake my own death and disappear
(the regular kind, lowercase).
                              –Ashton Robinson

I'm a very popular guy at cocktail parties these days. As soon as the other guests discover I produced the original *60 Minutes* investigations on Ashton Robinson, I am quickly pinned in a corner and peppered with questions.

Early on I had been contacted by various publishers about writing a book, but so much had already been written about him, about the cult, about the trial, about his parents that I didn't feel there was anything more to say. (And after his amateur pornographic videos were uncovered and broadcast on pay-per-view, I'd had it up to here with the whole thing!)

Then the so-called Boron Incident happened and Deputy

Introduction

Sheriff Victor Cabrera discovered, at the base of a Joshua tree in the middle of the Mojave Desert, the most exhaustively analyzed microcassette recorder in the world.

A week later a package arrived at *60 Minutes*'s Manhattan offices. I for one was convinced it was a bomb and immediately contacted the NYPD. The bomb squad gingerly transferred it to its demolition site on the Hudson River. They were about to detonate the package by exploding a hand grenade next to it when my curiosity got the better of me and I pleaded with the police captain to at least try peeking inside with his remote-controlled robot. I had to sign a form promising CBS would pay the NYPD $116,000 if their precious robot were blown to bits. It was maybe the happiest day of my life. Inside, neatly stacked, were 135 microcassette tapes, logged and labled, the audio diary of one of the world's most-wanted men.

If you still do not believe the conclusion of the majority of the audioengineering experts hired by both the FBI and my news organization, that Robinson was always alone when he said he was conversing with his Brazilian "guardian angel," then this exhaustive record of his most private thoughts probably won't change your mind. However, for the rest of you this edited transcript of hundreds and hundreds of hours of his compulsively recorded audio diary will provide a chilling glimpse into the twisted soul of a con man–turned–madman–turned–con man again.

I've begun Robinson's transcripts from the beginning, months before his "conversion," so we will all remember how "sane" he and his organization used to be before that fateful July 4 two years ago.

As to the identity of the brave person who turned over this

amazing audio library, I have my suspicions but I must respect the individual's desire for anonymity.

Finally, when some well-meaning soul comes up to me with tears in her eyes (usually fresh from one of the dozens of Robinson-inspired Now House meditation centers sprouting up all over the United States, Canada, and now the Netherlands) and says, "How can you still be such a skeptic after all that has happened?" I remind them that throughout history seemingly miraculous things happen that are eventually explained by good old-fashioned logic. I am convinced that Interpol will eventually catch up to him and put to rest forever all this reckless speculation of the supernatural. I think one of the special agents at the FBI still assigned to his case said it best: "Just 'cause his footsteps disappeared in the desert don't mean that Robinson can walk on water."

Part One

St. Barths, French West Indies

May 15th

Until I think up a better system, we'll do it like this. I'll play the recording of the day's lecture on the little boom box here in my hotel room, hovering over the *pause* tab to chime in with edits, additions, and clarifications. I wish there were a way to directly patch the boom box right into you, Mr. Microcassette Recorder, but I don't see any extra holes on you. Anyway, the sound quality should certainly be good enough for a transcript.

I want this next book to dig deeper than the last two, to really give my fans—my follow— I want to give the people that buy my books and audiotapes a better sense of Ashton Robinson the man. They'll buy the book and make it a best-seller like the first two, almost no matter what I put in it, so I might as well stretch out this time and give them a few surprises.

I get a sense from so many of their letters that they think of me as being as divorced from their reality as Santa Claus. Wouldn't it be nicer if they just thought of me as their faraway friend? The one who left their hometown and made good, but who's still there for them when they're needed? So, along with the transcripts of the lectures I'm delivering these days, I'll be throwing in behind-the-scenes moments of my everyday life. At least for this first draft, that is. I'll have plenty of time to edit later.

This morning's lecture was a variation on the one I gave last year in Maui, but I think this one had a tad more zing.

[Sound of cassette player buttons clacking, then very loud calypso music. Robinson curses unintelligibly. One minute, forty-five seconds of silence before the recording of the lecture.]

—The DeHavilland Otter, dropping nose-first toward the six hundred meters of runway, the second-shortest in the Caribbean, scared the dozen of us pleasantly until a shrill alarm sounded that I would later learn was the indicator of a stall. But you didn't need to know its exact function to realize that it was trying to tell us something extremely important. Suddenly, the humorous anecdote about this tiny and funny-looking prop-driven plane that I was at that moment revising in my head to relate to you now exploded into the headline of a small article on the front page of the *San Jose Mercury News*, my local paper . . .

—Then, just as suddenly, the heavy plane bounced itself upward to level, then again descended, less steeply now, and we soon touched Tarmac with a happy bleat from the tires, then an angry whinnying engine yell of reverse. The family of bathers knee deep in the pretty water at the beach just off the runway's far end closed their open mouths, and the videotaping father lowered his camera, seemed almost disappointed—visions of money and a free trip for all to *Rescue 911*'s production facilities in Orlando when they aired our crash seemed to have swelled within him, then left just as suddenly, as we safely rolled to a stop. Even our copilot clapped, I think . . .

—That is just the sort of experience I make myself have. Let me repeat, *make myself have*. Now, of course, you are all thinking, Did he will the plane to stall? Did he telepathically increase the wind shear over the mountains? Of course not, you all say. Is there no end to this man's egotism? you must be thinking. And I say unto you, No, sirs and madams, there is not.

[Audience laughs.]

This laughter from my students temporarily distracted the French waiters and waitresses, all in their twenties, good looking, and ponytailed. My students jiggled their pens quickly through their notebooks. Each binder has *PES, Inc.* stamped in silver on the deep grain of the chocolate-colored leather. And each one cost me thirty-five bucks, even bought in bulk. When some muckraker complains about how much I'm worth, they never seem to bring up how much I spend.

—You are my master class. You are no longer just listening to me on your commutes: "This is the end of side seven. Please fast-forward and turn the tape over to side eight."

This made them laugh again. An inside joke. The best kind. They were no longer three or four hundred crowding the rickety folding chairs in the Lindbergh Room of the Dallas–Ft. Worth Airporter Days Inn. This time they are just thirty-one, the chosen few.

—So, as participants in my master class, you're all going to get to go behind the scenes, as it were, and really see how full of myself I really am! How high on myself I am. Literally and figuratively. I love me so goddamn much! And it's from here that my success springs! How many of you have ever told yourselves you love yourselves? Well, I do, five to fifteen times a day! How many of you have ever called themselves "stupid," a "jerk," or an "idiot," or worse . . . ? Hands. Come on, I want to see hands . . . Now, how many of you have already called yourselves that this morning . . . ? Good . . . Excellent. Thank you for your honesty. I won't ask, but I am sure there's at least one of you here whose first words to themselves immediately after opening their eyes this morning were something like "Damn," or "Shit, I forgot to . . ."

—But you know what was the first thing I said to myself? "Good morning, good looking." I'm not a zombie; it's not what I always say; it's just what immediately came to mind. And you'll all get a kick out of this. I awoke with the very pleasant buzz of an erection. Last night I probably dreamed the recurring dream I've had since the fifth grade: I'm the star running back for the Buffalo Bills. It's the day of the Super Bowl and right before the game the Dallas Cowboy cheerleaders kidnap me and have their way with me. I know, I know. I'm thirty-four years old. I should get over it already. But my inner child, you see, he has a will of his own.

—Anyway, the point is, I wake up loving myself and ready for bear. Do you think it is a coincidence that I have that attitude, work for myself, smile all the time, and have more money in the bank than many medium-sized companies?

—Was I born with such an outsized ego? Yes, I was. Were you? Damn straight. All of us were. But your parents, your teachers, television, that juvenile delinquent a couple years older who chased you around the playground, held you down, and farted on you in front of Darla Kincaid all unknowingly conspired to beat the love of self right out of you. Write this down, ladies and germs. Write this down in your expensive leather-bound notebooks: "I am going to get it back."

Woman's voice: "On its own separate page?"

She didn't say that as a devoted fan. More as a gentle jibe. And instantly, I liked her even more. I had noticed her last night, from the mezzanine, as they were all checking in down below. Strappy, high-heeled sandals. Gucci, maybe, but definitely bought just for this trip. This morning her auburn hair curled behind her ears under her floating straw hat. A jug of sunblock squatted beside her portfolio, but still her arms were practically freckling right before my eyes, like bubbles on cooking pancakes. Pale as she was, I could still tell she was at least part black. I shot my eyes down and over the seating chart, then up and into her eyes.

—Nikki Kennedy, Hyde Park, Chicago, hello. The size, punctuation, and layout of the phrase is completely up to you. Good question, though. Because how you just wrote it down speaks volumes about how much you really want it. Now, I'm not saying capitalize and triple-underline everything like a serial killer. I'm just saying roll up your sleeves and let's get ready to work.

I met Lenny Gilroy, of the Gilroy Memory System, at last year's Infomercial Industry Leader Super Summit, and he gave me a set of his tapes, free. (Mine retail for a lot more than his, but I felt I had to give him a free set. But I really shouldn't complain. Now that I bought out the cassette-duplicating company, my price per unit's dropped to just forty cents.) Anyway, Gilroy teaches that words themselves are very difficult to remember but pictures are hard to forget. So, to remember Nikki's name I pictured Nikita Khrushchev shaking hands with JFK.

—So, let's get back to loving ourselves. There was a time, folks, when not ten minutes would pass where I wouldn't curse myself, doubt myself, make myself as miserable as possible. It was my dark period, and you might have heard me talk about it before. I was a junior at Yale and just couldn't take it anymore. The mental straitjacket I was in, in that institution! I thought it was me. I blamed myself for not fitting in, despite having tried for three lonely years. I cried, people. There were nights when I cried like a baby. My grades weren't miserable; they just weren't stellar. My relationships were superficial and all of them dead ends. I'd allowed the self-love and self-confidence I'd enjoyed up until high school to be absolutely exhausted by a bunch of skinny East Coast pseudointellectual fops in capes! So I quit that venerable institution of higher learning, traveled the world, and dedicated myself to rebuilding the love of myself that I knew still lay dormant somewhere deep inside me.

Waves coming apart noisily on the sand, vacationers' children screaming just to hear themselves. I remember these sounds entering the space behind my question. I tell these stories of myself almost every time I lecture, but here, on such a magnificent island, the difference between where I've been and where I am startles even me.

Later May 15th

I've got to hurry up and get this all down before dinner with Jill. I'll start with what Rom said. I'm told I do a good impersonation of his gravelly voice:

"Let's get Ashton on the beach before we lose the fucking light. No, he doesn't need no fucking makeup. It's a long shot, his fucking face's away from us, and it's dark. If I were six-six and could suck in my gut, we could shoot the fucking back of my head and none would be the wiser."

"Rom, you don't have little dreadlocks. You can spot Ashton's a mile away." Jill, on tiptoes, smoothed my collar, then pushed me onto the sand. The sun was already strongly orange and more than half flattened. She has been working with me since I started in paid-promotional television. I've known her as long as I've known Rom Casciato, the director. He, Terry the cameraman, and their quiet soundman who doesn't seem to have a name were swinging their steel suitcases of equipment through the restaurant and onto the patio, their knees and thighs walking the heavy containers forward corner by corner. Dragging the cases across the terra-cotta pavers left long scratches like the lines around objects in cartoons that indicate speed.

"Ash, just walk up and down, up and down slowly, like you're thinking of something important, some wonderful bon mot."

This Rom yelled, pronouncing "mot" like *maht* and pleased with himself. Barefoot honeymooners, walking hand in hand, first trotted out of frame, then turned back to stare. I kicked at the waves after they'd finished with an effervescence but before they shrank back into the Caribbean.

"Got it."

"Rom, let's try it over here by the rocks."

It was hard to converse across fifty feet of beach, even when the air was as still as it was right then.

"Hey, Ash, look, we're losing the light. Besides, I'm here another two days. We can try again tomorrow."

"Let's try it over here by the rocks."

I smiled falsely. I didn't want to make a big deal about it, but I started as his production assistant and I feel, sometimes, that in his mind, as his P.A. I have stayed.

"It's your nickel, mister. Maybe stand on the rocks, maybe look out to sea. We might get something we can use."

After the sun had truly gone, I moved to the patio with Jill. Chains of tiny electric lights like frozen white fireflies stretched in a long sag overhead.

"*Est-ce que vous avez de pastis?*"

"*Bien sûr, Monsieur Ashton. Et pour madame?*"

"Jill, would you like a pastis too?"

"What's that?"

"It's like Pernod, or ouzo. Kinda licoricey."

"Is it good?"

"Why else would I drink it?"

Right Here, Right Now

Jill seemed to think about this, then tilted her head past me and up to the looming waiter. *"Oui, oui. Même chose."* He smiled, nodded, and left. She twisted the elastic out of her hair and shook her head and scratched her scalp till the blond strands all fell to curving piles over her shoulders. Her white blouse was unbuttoned over her bikini top and knotted over her stomach till she undid it and buttoned it properly against the breeze in the dark, against the mosquitoes.

"So, Jill, what do you think of this batch?"

"Maybe not as interesting as last year's."

"You mean, no recently separated professional baseball players?"

"Shut up! If you ever tell Alan anything, I swear I'll— Look. Shut the fuck up. This is one game I don't think you can win."

"Sorry! I'm not throwing any stones, believe me. This is a Personal Empowerment Systems master class, not the priesthood. We're all adults here and in control of our own orgasms."

"I can't believe I told you about that."

"If I remember right, I just took a wild guess and you took a swing at me."

The waiter showily landed the tall glasses filled with only a few fingers of thick clear liquid, the miniature white carafes of water, and the small glass bucket of ice. He quickly whipped two long spoons off his tray, but slowly laid one beside each glass.

"Voilà."

"Merci."

And he disappeared back into the restaurant. Other guests, not all of them with the seminar, drifted to tables all around us and talked, quietly, under the noise of the sea. I pinched one irregular ice cube at a time, dropped each into Jill's glass of clear syrup, dribbled water from her carafe over her cubes, and the pastis's transparence magically precipitated into a gray cloud. Her eyes widened. I prepared my own. She started to lean her glass to mine to toast, but I was already sipping. Quickly, she did too.

"Yuck! Do you really like this stuff?"

"I like its unexpected magic. Two things combine and—*poof!*—something altogether new. It's like life. See—"

"Hey, Boss? Save it for the paying customers."

"What? Why all the needling? You don't believe in me anymore?"

"Do you?"

"Yow!"

Then just a little later . . . "Am I interrupting?"

Nikki Kennedy already stood over our small table. Already she was smiling at me. I've found they're often the class beauties, the ones who doubt.

"I hope you're being careful about the sun, uh, Nikki, isn't it?"

"This shows you how serious I am about this seminar, doesn't it? I mean, this sun'll be the death of me."

"I hope not."

"I have to keep track of every freckle. If they're still there after a month or two, I'll get them checked out. But I'm black, you know, on both sides."

"I didn't know. But I suspected."

"Well, I had no idea." Jill scanned Nikki's face, her skin; she tracked over her body, moving her whole head, not just her eyes.

"People usually don't. Black or white. It's no biggie, though, really."

I turned my palms up to her in welcome and she slid a white chair to our table, and then prettily, she sat.

"Did you naturally remember my name, or did you use some kind of trick?"

"Um . . ."

"It doesn't matter, I guess. But we met at the Days Inn, Hyde Park, last summer? The free, introductory clinic you did? I asked you about the no-money-down real estate seminars. What you thought of those guys? You said they were the pornographers of the personal-improvement business."

"Oh, yes! Nikki! Of course I remember. Right after the talk we . . . ?"

"Nope. I think you're thinking of my girlfriend, Dorothy."

"Dorothy. Of course. Works for an airline . . . *Delta*. How is she?"

"Fine."

The silence was one of those bad ones.

"Oh, it doesn't matter. You can't remember everybody who comes up to pester you every day. But what you said made a lot of sense. And I'm not usually, you know, one of these kind of people."

"Neither am I."

"I'm sorry, but you know what I mean."

"I know exactly what you mean, and neither am I."

She was still as she looked at me, then the top of her dress rose with her breath. Soon after almost anyone comes to me they tell me how different they are from the losers and lunatics they think I attract, but Nikki really just might be. Jill seemed a little worried about my "Neither am I," as if I were about to confess something unseemly to this stranger. Usually she leaves me alone the minute any other pretty woman shows up.

"Ashton, our reservations are for nine. I'll meet you in the lobby just before? Enjoy the seminar, Nikki."

"Thank you. Good night."

In the silence I could feel Nikki wanting to ask the question. I delighted in not answering it directly.

"Jill has been with me since the beginning."

"Since the Novel Café, in Venice, California?"

"I didn't think I ever mentioned the exact place in a lecture."

"A friend of mine—Lindsey Bolt—used to listen to you there every Sunday."

"Oh, yes! She and her husband were some of my first listeners."

"I know. They're the first ones that told me to watch you on TV."

Then another silence.

"I would ask you to join us for dinner, but I've found over the years that anything that smacks of favoritism destroys the cohesion of the group."

"Don't worry about it. Since we've already paid for the meals here, I can't really afford eating out. Especially not on this island. I read about this restaurant here where lunch for two is more than two hundred and fifty dollars."

"The Lafayette Club. It's worth it."

"Well, maybe after the seminar I'll be able to bop down here once a month."

Nikki laughed. Her hair, her skin, her freckles were a sunset of reds.

"Maybe?" I reinforced the words with a seriousness that almost always has the desired effect.

"Uh-oh. Was that a test? Then let me try again: If I want to come down here once a month, then I will make it one of my LifeGoals. I will write it in ink in my Manifest Manifesto, and every morning before I get out of bed, I will spend three minutes thinking about how, today, I will push myself one step closer to my goal."

"Do you always mock techniques whose only goal is your happiness?"

Right Here, Right Now

"No! I wasn't! How do you think I got myself here on my measly salary?" She blushed yet another hue of red.

I've never been formally trained in psychology, theology, anything. I first had the idea for the Manifest Manifesto on a beach on Goa. I'd been traveling for over three years, but ten days after that day on a beach in India, surrounded by drug-addled international hippies, I was back in the States working as an extra on a TV series about mountain-bike-riding cops for the USA Network. I'd decided on manifesting an acting career and needed to log I forget how many hours to get my SAG card. For four weeks I lived in the International Youth Hostel on Venice Beach, the only American there.

May 16th

After breakfast they hurried to their seats. I strode to my white rattan armchair and sat, leaned my elbows on my knees and my chin on my laced fingers. Here goes the tape:

—Before I was different. I mean, before, I was different. Timid and internal. Self-pitying. But now I am—wait. What I was just about to tell you today, under this already angry sun, would have been a lie. I am no different than I was before. I am still, like most megalomaniacs, hiding a fragile, frightened wimp within me—Hemingway being the most overanalyzed example. Great actions, for many of us, burst from us only because we believe that is what great people do. And by portraying that great character long enough, we pray that it will someday seep into and permanently stain our scared and chattering soul. As a lonely, overweight, pseudointellectual twelve-year-old in Flint, Michigan, I had a nightly routine. I would vault onto my top bunk without aid of any ladder just to make it harder, just to build my character, because I always knew that it was as weak and flabby as my body. And each night, up there on the top bunk, close to the pebbly plaster of the ceiling, I'd read the fattest books in the house. An eight-hundred-page biography of Hirohito I remember not only reading but, more importantly, wanting everyone to know I was reading. You can imagine I was not the most popular kid in a working-class factory town obsessed with just three things: the Lions, Motown, and the latest layoffs over at GM. If my big brother hadn't been the fastest high school tailback in the city, my life would have been a living hell.

—Then I picked up one of my sister's college psychology books. *The Significance of Sleeping,* it was called, by B. Louis Sandweiss, Ph.D. He'd interviewed hundreds of people, videotaped them sleeping, and concluded that there were four sleeping positions, and for each, a particular psychology. The first he called Fetuses, of course. Can anyone guess what type of person sleeps like that? Of course you can, but back then, to me, it all seemed so very profound. The others were called Left Siders, Right Siders, and Kings. Left Siders, according to Sandweiss—and remember, this was 1974 and pop psychology was the new religion—Left Siders were interesting, dynamic, artistic people, though sometimes a bit soft and lazy. Right Siders, on the other hand, were reliable, middle-management people, not quite as wimpy as Fetuses, but could go there if they suddenly lost their job or one day caught their wife in the back of the neighborhood drugstore blowing the balding pharmacist.

—Finally, Kings: men and women who slept on their backs and were the masters of all they surveyed. Even before reading Sandweiss I'd been impressed by how my brother slept on his back and snored like a very old man. So the little twelve-year-old me closed the big book and with two hands hefted it off the bunk to the pile of dirty clothes on the floor like a sick carrier pigeon. Suddenly I could not remember how it was that I slept. I knew I was no King, but beyond that . . . ? I turned my head to the left and raised my left knee. It felt strange. Hyperextended. I turned my head to the right, raised my right knee, and instantly felt so terribly comfortable.

—I lifted the broom handle I kept by the side of the bed, stretched, and jabbed at the light switch by the door a few times before hitting it off. It was important to me back then not to have to get back out of bed to turn off the light. I lay back on my light blue sheets with the logo of every NFL team scattered across the cotton. On my back. I'd be damned if I was going to remain a wimpy Right Sider one more night, and as long as I was making the change, I might as well go all the way to King, right? So, flat on my back, I closed my eyes . . . I waited for sleep to creep upon me, but only anxiety came. I adjusted and readjusted my brittle shoulder blades so they would lie flatter on the mattress . . . Still waiting . . . I forced more air into my lungs, though it crossed my mind that perhaps I was missing a gene, or something, that allowed one to sleep on their back. Perhaps nonnatural Kings *physically* could not sleep on their backs without suffocating during the night. But I forbade myself to turn like the commoners, the Right Siders, the Left Siders. By three-fifteen in the morning I was crazed—so conscious of my own breathing I was convinced the moment I stopped willing air into my lungs they would permanently collapse. I flipped myself over, hugged the pillow, and nearly instantly slept the sleep of a Fetus . . .

—For sixteen nights I squirmed and whimpered and considered suicide on my back till near dawn, then caved in and rolled and napped but an hour or two. Finally, after a month, I could finally fall asleep on my back at a decent hour, but each morning I'd open my eyes—and damn!—my face would somehow be back buried in my pillow! As soon as I'd fallen asleep, it seemed, my wimpy subconscious deposited me back in my natural, lowly state. It took another five months before I'd find myself still on my back the next morning . . .

—So, did all this hard work turn me into a King? Hell, no. It was an adolescent waste of precious time. Except for the possible benefits in the name of clear skin (your pores get more clogged with your face in a dirty pillow all night) and the definite benefits to my lower back (less pressure on the lumbar region), the change in my sleeping position in no way changed me as a person. I was just as neurotic and self-doubting, just as insecure and internal and teen suicidal.

Rom Casciato pushed his cameraman past the first row of my students. I remember being suddenly conscious of acting casually, of smiling sincerely.

—I guess what I am attempting to impart is that in some way, we are all false. We are either who we are afraid we are, or who we hope to be, depending on whether we are losers or winners.

Not everyone copied that down, so I repeated it.

—I said, we are either who we are afraid we are, or who we hope to be—depending on whether we see ourselves as losers or winners. Losers act like the losers they fear they truly are. Winners act like the winners they hope to be. Inside each are similar neuroses, fears, triumphs, hatreds, lusts. We each just pick the role we choose to play—or passively accept the default value set for us at the factory . . . Yes . . . ?

Cleavon Smalls then raised his hand. He reminds me of my father. "So, it's that simple?" he asked. "Like Captain Jean-Luc Picard says, 'Make it so'?"

—Precisely . . . if we were computers. Unfortunately, as biological computers, our wiring is a little more stubborn.

Most of them wrote that down. Once in a while, when I get a little bored, I play a little game with them and see how many I can get to write down something trivial like the name of my elementary school.

— So our job together is to close the inevitable gap between awareness and action. That is why you are here. When we get to the one-on-one sessions in a few days, I'd like all of you to be able to tell me precisely the nature of your past ruts and precisely how and when you intend to change.

I could almost feel the sudden tension that seized them. Homework. They'd stopped listening to the rest of the lecture, too busy sweating over what they'd tell me when they got me alone. What a bunch of—

[Tape ends.]

May 17th

—Raise your hand if you've ever said, "Things happen for a reason." . . . Now, keep your hands up if you still believe that . . .
You three, what the hell are you doing here?!! Flushing your
hard-earned money down a toilet, because around here we believe that things happen because . . . ? Anyone? Because we
make it happen. Fortune-cookie philosophy, to be sure, but true
nonetheless. I believe what most all theoretical physicists believe,
that entropy and inertia rule this universe. Concepts diametri-
cally opposed to you three Things-Happen-for-a-Reasoners. "Entropy: a tendency for the universe to attain a state of maximum
homogeneity in which all matter is at a uniform temperature;
a.k.a. heat death." Just as the moon tugs the oceans away from the
shore, the universe tugs us all to homogeneous mediocrity, heat
death, if you will. We should all know this to be true. Inaction is
always easier than action. And the longer we are inactive, the
harder it is to reactivate ourselves. It is like the seven-hundred-
pound man. Was he born that way? Hell, no! He just stopped
combating entropy until it consumed him in a cocoon of fat . . .

—Newton's Law of Inertia is a related concept: "A body at rest tends to stay at rest. A body in motion tends to stay in motion." In other words, nothing changes without a reason. The ball doesn't move till you kick it. It doesn't stop till the force of rolling friction overcomes the ball's momentum. If you hate your job, and your husband hates you, and you spend your days clawing your way to a retirement that is still fifteen years away, that situation will not change on its own . . .

—I'll give you a rather spicy example of what I mean. Kathryn Moi was a friend of mine at Yale, a Kenyan as brown and luminous as polished wood and generally considered the most beautiful woman at school. When I say friend, I really mean, I loved her madly while she loved someone else. She just tolerated my constantly straggling after her like a banner of toilet paper fixed to her shoe. Sound familiar to anyone yet . . . ? Good. For three years I trailed behind her—dating other women, sure, perhaps even a lot of them—but I never stopped dreaming of Kathryn. Unfortunately for me, like me, she had a reputation for mainly dating whites . . .

—It was one of the last nights of my junior year, but I was already thinking about leaving school for good. I was disgusted by the small minds surrounding me in that supposedly elite institution and knew that my destiny lay far beyond those ivy walls. Anyway, I was in the midst of some pretty agonizing soul searching. It must have been one in the morning. She knocked. "Would you care to go walking with me, Ashton?" Even after three years I never got used to this regal, dark black woman speaking the English of Diana Rigg from *The Avengers*. Immediately I rose . . .

—When she told me she wanted to pick up some cocaine from a friend of hers across campus so she could stay up all week to finish all her papers, and the friend with the cocaine had a crush on her, so would probably try to coerce her into staying the night, so she needed me, her best friend, to come with her, still my disappointment did not outweigh my excitement. Outside his room she asked me to wait, then she knocked and quickly twisted herself around the edge of the opening door. And I waited. And waited. Was that a moan I just heard? But I could hear little over the rattling of my heart. Finally she reappeared, twisting herself back around the door's edge and smiling. "What took you so long?" I asked. "I told him you and I were in love," she said. What a strange laugh I then gave . . .

—Back in our dorm she skipped and leapt onto my noisy, thin bed, offered me some coke, but I declined. As I have said, I was in the midst of some pretty serious soul searching and was sorely tempted. But cocaine is powdered courage and I knew even then that buying courage does very bad things to the soul. I sat next to her, the sag of the bed tilting us closer still. I rose and played Grover Washington's makeout album *Winelight*, then returned to my slouching bed. Still, I was paralyzed by something even more profound than fear: indecision. Fear, at least, is a definite point of view: "Hell, no." "Stop!" "Don't do it." Indecision, on the other hand, is like playing Red Light, Green Light with the devil. There's no way you can win. Diverse factions in my brain were rioting: "If I try to kiss her, does our friendship crumble?" "Do I lose a best friend?" "Yet, how blissful if I succeed!"

—So, as we sat there, and both fidgeting, Kathryn from cocaine, me from indecision, I had an epiphany. Use your brain, I said to myself. Look into the future. So I assessed the situation using the decision tree I had just learned in a logic class. If I do not try to kiss her, we remain as before, that is, I lose. If I do try to kiss her, I am either *(a)* pushed away or *(b)* kissed back. But aha! As a woman she is smarter about these things than I am, already knows I want to kiss her, and has long been ready for it with either *(a)* "Ashton! I'm sorry, but I like you as just a friend" or *(b)* "What took you so long?" In fact, if I don't try to kiss her, she will think I am either *(a)* homosexual or *(b)* not interested in her in that way . . .

—Suddenly my indecision fell away from my body like a robe dropped to the ground. I wore a madman's grin. I wanted to phone my parents, wake them up, and say, "See! You did get your money's worth from my education." I finally realized that Kathryn was my final exam. "What the hell are you grinning about?" she asked me. Now was the time to act. I had figured out the answer to the problem but had not yet written it down in the blue book. So I kissed her, and she said, "Finally."

They smiled at the punch line. They always do.

What I didn't tell them was I was so nervous about Kathryn and so preoccupied by the thought of possibly dropping out of school that the sex was awful, clumsy, and vague. She even had to ask if I came. I didn't tell them she left three days later for a year abroad in Paris, where she promptly fell in love with a married advertising exec. I didn't tell them that years later she moved in with and has a child by her friend with the cocaine, an acne-scarred Russian, and together they own Thai Me Up!, a South-western chain of Thai restaurants famous for the exotic beauty of its waitresses.

The true story is too messy. It's amazing that I bring it up at all, even this sanitized version. These middle managers really don't want anything thornier than the sort of anecdote they might hear from a supermodel on a late-night talk show. Why on earth do they give me so much of their money if they aren't really prepared to dig deep? I'm not saying they're suckers; I'm just saying they're weak. I should know. I was weak once myself.

Obviously, this last little bit won't make it into the final manuscript.

Later May 17th

I just got back in from surfing for Rom and his cameras. Decent waves.

"Hey, Rom, tell me these bags under my eyes didn't show up on camera this morning? And don't forget to loop 'No-Doz' over the two times I said 'cocaine.'"

"I was wondering what the fuck you was gonna do about that."

"But leave it in the home video. Gives more punch to the story. And I assume you're shooting a lot of singles, especially of that light-skinned black woman in row three."

"Nikki Kennedy. Have no fear, Chief. Remember, before the infomercials I came out of CBS Sports. For eight years my job was popping off singles of pretty broads in the stands, maybe fifty, maybe a hundred yards away. I'm telling you, I've got great inserts of her nodding her head, and one terrific one of her laughing. But I'll say one thing for her, she's no fucking zombie, not like some of the rest of them freaks."

"Fuck you and shut the fuck up."

"Aw, come off it, Ash. We go way back. I remember when you was running around the set trying to find Dale extra packets of Equal."

"That's very true. I don't deny it. And you were trying to talk me into becoming a boom operator."

"Hey, they make good money. And you're tall and got long arms. I bet you could hold that mike steady for hours."

"We'll never know now, will we?"

"Unless *60 Minutes* goes after you again."

I almost jammed my board right down his bearded, sweaty throat. He knows how to get to me, and sometimes I don't know why the fuck I keep taking it. It was all I could do to grab my board and press through the dry sand along the beach. Rom waddled quickly to keep up.

"Rom. Buddy. You're such a skeptic. Ed Bradley and his bloodhounds didn't dig up a thing against me. I don't know why they even aired that fucking segment."

"Hmmm."

"Hmmm, what? You know what your problem is? You keep confusing me with Dale. My operation is a helluva lot different and a helluva lot bigger than his ever was. You keep forgetting that. Besides, it's not like what he was selling didn't work. Many guys did get women's phone numbers in under six minutes. It was just the 'Or your money back' part he was a little slow on. And about that other thing, how old did *you* think she was? But listen, the waves aren't blown out for once, so let's do this. Hurry back with your crew."

After Dale was released for time served, he moved to Arizona. Last time I heard from him, he was doing something with cable radio and trailer homes. For a while he had too much pride to ask me to help him out, but last year I loaned him ten grand. I mean, he did teach me everything I know about this business and I did kind of buy out his operation for ten cents on the dollar.

Anyway, I had the board made especially for the trip. I gave my friend Todd the PES logo and he airbrushed it onto the blank before glassing it. The candy smell of wax is almost my favorite experience in surfing. And unlike in Santa Cruz, the water here is hot and shark-unfriendly. The air was so warm my fingers dented the puck of wax and it caked on my board easily, but coated my fingertips, so they were soon breaded with sand. Some French kids were already out at the point, and they didn't surf too badly either. The peaks were clean and almost shoulder high, which they say is big for St. Barths. My first retreats were in Hawaii, mainly for the surf but also because, after working for Dale, I knew the palms to grease to get the best rates. But Maui is now littered with camps of shrill-voiced, greasy-haired buffoons hawking self-hypnosis, no-money-down real estate, or 900-number resell scams. (Who the hell'd want to make a million off 1-900-966-PEEE, "Where the extra *E* is for extra pee"?)

St. Barths sets me apart. When I am corralled with those low-rent snake-oil salespersons in some six-months-too-late *Time* magazine trend article, I burn. And fucking Ed Bradley. Bastard ogled an Emmy over my corpse, or the corpses of my "followers." That's what he called them. My lawyers got them to nix the references to Koresh and Applewhite, thank God, but that first shot! If the energy was low in the room, I would occasionally ask them to stand and clap, first arhythmically, then rhythmically, but never for any more than three minutes or four minutes. It's just an old tent-revival technique to perk up a crowd. I must have seen my mother's pastor do it hundreds of time. As the clapping finds a rhythm and builds, a collective current of energy hovers above the crowd. If you are lucky, scalps will start tingling. It's not magic and I never said it was, but if one has never been to church, the experience can be a bit overpowering. The damn *60 Minutes* spy with a camera hidden under his baseball cap caught this freckle-faced yuppie woman with the craziest grin on her face, while behind her, out of focus, stood row upon row of grinning, clapping zombies. Fucking Leni Riefenstahl couldn't have found better images at Nuremberg.

"Come on, Rom, let's do this. The waves are breaking pretty far out. Will you be able to get me from the beach?"

"I brought a lens that could get a close-up of your nuts from a fucking weather balloon."

"Big deal. I've got big nuts."

"Fuckin' comedian. That's why I like you, Ash."

This Dutch guy at the youth hostel had the bunk under mine, and he'd found out that this production company just down the street was paying twenty bucks and lunch just to sit in the audience and watch a TV show. We all ran down there, hippie travelers from all over Europe and an Argentine and I. They made porno films in the same studio at night. Flimsy scenery flats for a hospital room set were propped against the wall as we all filed into our seats. Rom was yelling at a grip to straighten the fake windowpane at the back of the kitchen set. Then Dale himself came out and thanked us for coming and asked us to be as delighted with this fantastic new product as he was. The Wrap-a-rizer was supposedly a revolutionary new concept in food, apparel, and collectibles preservation. You wrapped thin plastic sheeting around the desired object, then pierced the plastic with the special attachment that fit most standard vacuum cleaners, turned on the machine, and presto! Anything you wanted sealed tight enough for a time capsule. A preternaturally perky blonde in a matching blazer and short skirt like a European stewardess circa 1965 came out and asked us to notice the lights above the stage. Each time they flashed she instructed us to ooh and aah like children watching fireworks. I still tease Jill about it and it still gets a rise out of her.

I loved the beehive of activity, and even the cheesiness of that week's product somehow appealed to me. (Dale was hawking some new contraption every few weeks till he hit upon How to Get a Woman's Phone Number in Six Minutes or Less. That's what bought him the Ferrari, and I think it's the Ferrari that really brought the FTC down on his ass.) I found Rom after the show, told him I'd been a production assistant for years in Europe, and he hired me on the spot. I needed a steadier source of income than extra's work to tide me over till I landed a regular gig on a TV series.

May 18th

When I decided to raise my prices half a grand for this intensive, I knew I had to offer more bang for their bucks. The one-on-one sessions were Jill's idea. She briefly flirted with scientology during college and said the one smart thing they did was personally interview each and every person who came through the door. She said sensing that a huge international institution was focusing, even briefly, on her needs made it not quite so painful forking over thousands of her mother and father's dollars. Say what you want about those scientologists, they do an amazing job of turning everybody who comes near them into a cash cow.

Mr. Smalls was my first.

"Mr. Smalls! Sit down! First off, I would like to thank you for joining us down here on this intensive."

"Thank me? I thank you! Every day! You see, I built my firm up from scratch, but that was twelve years ago—I'm an executive minority headhunter—but we've been stuck in a rut for the last three or four years at least. I needed a kick in the pants (back when I was growing up we'd call it a foot up your ass), so that's why I'm here! I watched your infomercial last year by mistake! I thought a game was coming on, but it was blacked out. The wife thought I was out of my mind at first, but then I got her listening to the tapes—I just stuck them in the tape deck in her Caddy— and bam! Now she's hooked as I am. Wanted to come but she had to have this little surgery—woman's thing—and she's sick about missing you."

He looked so like my papa, his eyes especially, bright and younger than the rest of him, that I was just waiting for him to shout, "Boy, give them peoples back they money." That's exactly what papa said the first time I told him how much the Pittsburgh Steelers were paying me for a seminar. The fact that they reached the play-offs that year didn't seem to impress him at all.

"Um . . . wow . . . thanks, Mr. Smalls."

"Cleavon. Could you call me Cleavon, please?"

"Of course. So, your business is in a rut. What are you going to do to jump-start it?"

"Well, I've been taking real careful notes, and it seems to me the keys to everything are blame and responsibility, right?"

I had to nod before he continued.

"I can't blame the Republicans for taking on affirmative action; hell, I am a Republican, been one since seventy-six. There was no such thing as a minority recruiter twenty-five years ago, and there probably won't be one left ten years from today! So I'll just have to diversify my database with a couple of high-profile white clients."

"Will they be stigmatized by signing with a black head-hunter?"

"I-I-I guess so."

He is a round man, so when he deflated he seemed to shrink several sizes.

"Well, do you have a particular expertise in placing people in a specific industry?"

As simply as that, he inflated again. No, he bloomed.

"You mean instead of specializing in minorities, specialize in something else! Remain small, focused, like you talk about, but specialize in, say, the insurance industry, where I worked for the better part of a decade!"

Jerking his notebook from the floor, he paged through it so quickly he noisily mashed many of the pages. Forests of exclamation points, boxcars of all-cap words flashed by till he'd found the first empty page and cramped his hand into a hook to chisel "IN-SURANCE!!!" into the paper. If Papa'd ever listened to me like that he'd've been the biggest electrician in central California.

As Mr. Smalls backed out of the anteroom to my suite, bobbing his head with each "I'll be goddamned" and "Thank you," Jill turned sideways and on tiptoes to stretch past him and into my room. Her skin was a matte gold and her breasts skittered inside her sleeveless blouse.

"You know, if your hair weren't so blond you could almost look mixed."

"Flattery will get you nowhere, Boss."

"Flattery pays your salary and mine."

"Touché. So that's what you did to that guy?"

"I'll be damned if I know what I did to that guy. All I know is, there goes another satisfied customer."

"Shame Rom didn't catch his look for the new show."

"So, how many more to go?"

Suddenly I had to stop talking and cough and clear some gunk out of my throat. It's been irritated since last month's lecture tour of the Midwest. I think it's a combination of talking so much and too much dairy.

"If you can do seven before lunch, we'll be pretty much on schedule."

"Maybe I should leave a cup by the door for tips."

"At these prices, gratuity is included. Speaking of pricey, are you still taking me to the Lafayette Club? I still dream about that foie gras we had last year."

"Consider it your Easter bonus."

■　■　■

"Dennis, have a seat. I won't bite you."

"I-it's not that. See, I just don't really know what to say."

"You mean you don't know what you are doing on this retreat? Why you have spent so much money to listen to me prattle?"

"I-it's not that. Not that at all. I-I'm here more generally than specifically, is all."

"So, how do you expect to *generally* readjust your life without taking any specific first moves?"

Dennis Rothberg is, in every way, my typical student. A mid-thirties white man who stumbled into success early but for some years now has stalled and watched people he had early on competed with and vanquished suddenly overtaking him. His Movado watch, at least five years old and striped with deep scratches, speaks volumes.

"Uh. I guess I . . ."

"You stumbled into success early, but for some years now feel in low gear. People you had once competed with and felt smug in having vanquished are now threatening to—no, are overtaking you daily. There's someone specific, isn't there? It is that person's unlikely success that has precipitated your presence here."

"Holy shit!"

"I am no mind reader. It's obvious. Sane people do not shell out thousands of dollars *generally*. That is a decision that is only made *specifically*. So your specific goal is . . ."

"To sell more commercial real estate than that fucking Stu Siefel so my girlfriend stops nagging me about not winning that fucking week in Puerto Vallarta."

"So, is it more important that she stops nagging, or that you sell more?"

"I want to sell more, don't get me wrong. But this nagging stuff is pretty fucking unreal."

"When you were successful, she didn't nag."

"Are you kidding? She was my fucking geisha."

"Hmmm . . ."

"Hmmm, what? Are you saying I should dump her? You ain't seen her. She looks like that exercise lady—what's her name, Kathy Smith—a lot, only younger. Stu Siefel's wife has pimples on her neck."

The dress hung in such a brittle way with its oversized blue flowers and skinny shoulder straps that it could not have been on her body for more than the time it took to leave her room and come here to mine. No. Wrong. I am forgetting the long moments of indecision when she twirled in it barefoot before the long mirror and the smoking French boutique owner earlier this afternoon. She marched to me on clapping sandals, right hand boomed forward stiffly to shake.

"Good afternoon, Nikki. Please, have a seat."

"Thank you. You know, I've been thinking a lot about our little talk, uh, Ashton, and I guess what it is that I want is my own company. That is what I want."

"Is that true?"

"What do you mean? Who wouldn't want their own agency? I mean, in your TV shows you don't have testimonials from *vice presidents* of Fortune 500 companies, *runners-up* for Miss Universe."

"Nikki, do you know about SPH?"

"*Smiles Per Hour*, tape seven of *Right Here, Right Now*, right?"

"So you know I have traveled the world and studied dozens of different cultures and that many, in fact most, cultures other than ours put vastly less emphasis on material gain. We call the !Kung people of the Kalahari primitive, yet they only work about three hours a day, and alcoholism and suicide are almost unheard of. We see in their faces, by clocking their smiles per hour, that on the whole their levels of general happiness are vastly superior to our own."

"God, that's so true. My boss, for example, is miserable. Divorced once, and his second marriage, to one of our old temps, is already on the rocks. But he makes me miserable, so I was thinking, if I had my own agency I could, I don't know, at least be out from under his thumb."

"Good! So you're starting to think about happiness and how to get there, rather than societally prescribed goals!"

She jumped a bit when I raised my voice. Often they need that. Then her cheeks dropped as she really thought about it. Then she uncrossed and recrossed her legs, and the outline of her quads swam inside the smooth skin of her thighs. Her sandal dangled from her toe. A woman's pretty foot in a sexy shoe is my cryptonite. And since, as I've said, I'm not a priest or psychiatrist, their ethical regulations don't apply. Tony Robbins and I haven't yet created any International Association of Motivational Speakers. We're still free, ungoverned by charter or bylaw. On the road, especially in Texas, for some reason, women often follow me upstairs from the hotel ballrooms we're renting. I am in a town only one night, so the complications are minimal. But Nikki is here two more days. But I haven't really stopped thinking about her since our session. But wait. I'm getting ahead of myself.

"Doesn't everyone want to be happy?" she said. "I mean, what should I do?!"

I should have seen it coming. She widened her already immense black eyes to try to keep the wetness suddenly sheening them from spilling. I had the hardest time trying to figure out what was really inside her. Then . . .

"You were engaged, weren't you? That's what made you come."

"No, Ashton. Bahhh. Wrong. You can't always be right, you know . . . I was married. Two years. But as soon as we settled on the alimony, I wrote the check for this trip."

"I'm sorry, but believe it or not, I've found that divorces, deaths, and losing your job are about the only times most people are receptive enough to redirect their lives. These big events are markers by which we measure the history of our selves. Almost always people report that catastrophes, with time, were the best things that ever happened to them. So, please, do not squander this pain. Use it to propel you to where you would like to be . . . By the way, have you made it to the Lafayette Club yet?"

I don't know why I asked her, especially why then. It just sort of came out.

"Maybe next trip. The food here at the hotel is just great."

"And like you said at drinks, prepaid."

"That too."

"I apologize for making you cry . . . That wasn't my intention."

So why didn't you tell her your fucking intention?

"I have reservations for lunch there for two, but Jill has some business to finish up with the hotel."

The words worked on her physically and slowly; her posture straightened. I promise I'll take Jill there tomorrow.

"I . . . I . . ."

"I have to see four more people till then, but what if I meet you in the parking lot at a quarter to two?"

"Of course, but . . ."

"It is a horribly expensive restaurant, yes. We have already discussed that. But it is what you want, is it not? It is something you will always remember, correct? That must be factored into the price. Your desire."

Still, she frowned, looked off at nothing as she debated, but finally she relaxed into this amazing smile. Of course I will treat her. Yet it was important I didn't tell her just then. She had to commit to paying herself, thirty-five-dollar appetizers be damned.

"What about what you said about favoritism? Should I—?"

"Hide in the bougainvillea? No."

May 19th

Perhaps she was a little too loud for the repressed rich surrounding us, her sighs while dipping the thick shreds of lobster meat into the small glass cup of *sauce vierge*—olive oil, clarified butter, and chopped tomato.

All the tables are right on the beach. How wonderful was the way the legs of our chairs settled deep between the grains of sand with a pleasing, gentle crunching, the lazy surf barely breaking and slipping up the slope of the beach, while over our heads lines of grass mats gently sagged between wooden poles silvered by the sea air. Sunlight sifted through the weave, dappling us.

A few hours afterward, as I was going down on her, her legs pedaled around my ears, her toes fanned and fisted to a rhythm.

Club Lafayette's model was new this year. Last year she looked like Jane Fonda in her Vadim period. This year's could double for Romy Schneider. Nikki was amazed by her beauty and the novelty of a scowling model prowling between tables in the sand, showing off a succession of bathing suits and wraps, stiffly holding large cards embossed with the names of the islands' boutiques where the overpriced beachwear came from. Actually, though I had seen it before, I was a little amazed myself. In my adolescence in the central Californian working class, I obsessed on imagining what the rich were at that very moment doing while I was double-checking my pockets for change for a corn dog on the pier. And watching models parade around eighty-dollar lobsters was exactly what I feared they might be doing.

In my bed she was close again to coming, but she had been close before. If she had just relaxed, trusted herself and me, I could have worked another finger inside. Just as my neck started cramping I realized it was too late to order a massage until the morning. I needed to move, but every time I repositioned myself she cooled down just enough to delay her even more. Then I felt it. A rumble from her core. Muffled and faint still, but promising. I felt like a medicine man with his ear to the base of a volcano. Well, not his ear . . .

The wine diluted some of Nikki's nervousness, so after lunch, by the restaurant's pool, the fact that Stephen Baldwin asked her to pass our ashtray did not seem to faze her. She then purred on her stomach, her suit top unhitched as I lotioned her shoulder blades without asking. "Thank you," she said as my fingers read the small hard muscles on her back. Lotioning the back of a woman is as trite as a knock-knock joke, yet that is exactly what makes it so comfortably exciting. Like trimming a Christmas tree, or suffering a hangover the morning after a bachelor party, it is one of America's last rites, and the weight of time-honored tradition only increases the thrill.

Chynna Phillips and the rest of the women around the restaurant's pool preened topless in the sun. I could see by the darting of her eyes that Nikki was tempted, yet when she turned over she held her top to her breasts and awkwardly refastened her straps.

"Urrrrr-RAAAAA!" That's the sound she made when she finally came. Her hard thighs clamped my head, instantly giving me a headache, clamped so hard it seemed it was all she wanted to do in life, clamp my head till it popped. Cleavon Smalls was in his room next door; I heard the shower. Nikki shoved my head away and rolled into a ball like a potato bug. A gorgeous potato bug, she undulated to the rhythm of my ghost between her legs still.

By her bent knee I rotated her back on her back as gently as if she were wounded. Then I saw her face! Breathe! I couldn't breathe; my heart was suddenly too big; her face was a flushed angel's face, enlightened. Did I do that? I had to kiss her, so I fell on her. Ahhh! I was inside her, wasn't even aiming, but there I was and my balls were glowing. I—

[Tape ends.]

May 20th

—My father is an electrician from Greenwood, Mississippi. My mother, before she retired, was an elementary school teacher. Both the children of sharecroppers who were the grandchildren of slaves. They migrated to Flint, Michigan, in the fifties, then in January of seventy-five while watching the U of M get creamed by USC once again in the Rose Bowl, they finally realized that it was seventy-eight degrees in California while the insides of the windows in our den were spiderwebbed with frost! By March we had moved to California, to Santa Cruz, because my dad liked the sound of the name . . .

—So, what does a young, bookish, and solitary black boy from a dying industrial city do when he arrives in a town where the mayor drives a hot pink VW microbus? [Cough.] He adapts or dies . . .

—We moved into a modest neighborhood of working-class Chicanos and whites. The Chicanos, just one generation away from migrant workers, the sharecroppers of the West, now worked the canneries, while the whites, for the most part, worked in construction. My folks still live in that same little house, will not let me buy them a new one.

—In this new town no one knew me as the obnoxious wiseass little brother of the local football hero, so I could and did reinvent myself. I changed myself not only to better adapt to my new environment but into something that would thrive in that new soil. Of course I couldn't become Chicano or white, but I could learn Spanish and how to surf. I could invent an exotic past for myself of urban bravery, college-aged girlfriends, and semiprofessional skateboarding. In four months I had more friends in Santa Cruz than in my lifetime in Flint.

—You see, ladies and gentlemen—and this is important, so put down your orange juices—life is acting. It's a perpetual theater whose only script is one we either inherit or invent. A successful sex therapist friend of mine tells her frigid female patients to try acting as if they were having the time of their life. Scream, yell, claw at your partner's back. Really overdo it. It sounds crazy, I know, but guess what? With time, something clicks inside the troubled women. By acting, they get a glimpse of how they might possibly feel in the future, and one day—bing!—a real orgasm starts rumbling from deep inside them like a freight train from the dark.

An air-filled, explosive laugh shot from Dennis Rothberg. He tried to gasp it back in before it had completely left his lungs. The others smiled at him indulgently as he burned red and withdrew into his chair.

Then her pretty, freckled arm, flowing in the warm air as elegantly as a tower of kelp in the ocean, reminded me that I was still sore, pleasantly. I had been trying throughout the lecture and with very little success to avoid her eyes. I pretended to look up her name on the seating chart.

What the hell. I smiled at her and felt something, maybe, open, a little.

Women have always been my best listeners. That's actually how this whole thing began. Every day after running around fetching pints of vodka and the phone numbers of the trashiest girls in the studio audience for Dale, I used to hang out at the Novel Café trying to find my own romance. I used his How to Get a Woman's Phone Number in Six Minutes or Less techniques but added my own spin. The café had one nice leather club chair right by the phone, and I'd install myself in it with a thick French novel. Proust was a little too on the nose and frankly too hard for me to understand, but Flaubert's *Trois Contes* was just the ticket. While some very cute UCLA grad student was fishing in her backpack for change for the phone I'd let out a loud "God, what a genius!" then pretend to be embarrassed and nose back into the book. I'd feel her eyes stray my way and I'd devise some way to flash her the cover.

Six minutes later I might not have her phone number but we would be very close and talking very, very fast. The batter for all these dime-store pep talks I dream up (and that now pay the mortgage on my ten-thousand-square-foot seaside home) might have been mixing during my years of traveling, but the only thing that baked them into a cake was my fervent desire to get laid. I found that the women were actually hanging on my every word, so even if it turned out they had a boyfriend, they'd just bring him along the next time. In a few months I became known as "that guy at the café." Jill started coming around, and she's the one who brought Dale. He put up the dough but also scalped 78 percent of the profits from my first broadcast. Four months later he was both in Chapter 11 and doing eighteen to twenty-four months in Boron.

As my mama would say, "God don't like ugly."

Later May 20th

"So, is she now your eternal love slave? Is she having *PES, Inc.* tattooed onto her upper thigh?"

Jill's blue eyes mocked and her white teeth grinned above and below the black sunglasses she slid down her tiny nose.

"Are you finished?"

"Don't you dare try and pretend nothing happened, not with me you don't. I could read that look on her face a mile away."

"Like looking in a mirror?"

She was already opening her mouth when she got it.

"You'd feel proud of yourself if you made me slap you, wouldn't you, Boss? And I thought you were a gentleman. Look, I don't even remember much of that drunken night, what is it now, six years ago? Just that it angles upward."

"It does?"

"Ask Miss Windy City if you don't trust me."

I'd never noticed. I wanted to dash into the bathroom right then and double-check.

"I swear I didn't want to touch her. It was a mistake. But it was an intense one."

"So, she gave as good as she got?"

"You know, no one would guess that such a proper-looking WASP could be such a great channeler of the spirit of an eighteenth-century drunken sailor."

"Thank you. But seriously, don't forget: before the IRS, Dale was already in trouble about that girl."

"He made his living teaching guys how to pick up women! So he picked up one. I mean, I saw her. She looked like a woman. When her parents said she was still in junior high, I made them show us her birth certificate. You know what she is doing now don't you?"

"Don't try and change the subject, Ash."

"She's one of those bikini'd fitness trainers on ESPN."

"You're joking."

"If I'm lying, I'm flying."

"All I'm saying is our market research shows your look and demeanor are sixty-four percent of why women take your course in the first place. That's why you have to keep your zipper shut. Your doubters and detractors assume the worst anyway. One scandal will bring all of this down, and I just put a bid on a three-bedroom Spanish with a pool."

"Our empire, swallowed by the sea like Atlantis. I know. I know. If you would just fix me up with somebody, your worries would be over."

"I wouldn't fix you up with Ellen VanEwick, the bitch who stole Charlie Michaelovitch from me in the tenth grade, then our senior year freaked out on crystal meth, smashed her parents' Saab, and ended up a quad."

"Sounds like you really loved him."

"I'm just saying you need another model, anchorwoman, or actress. Someone who can start to compete with your ego."

"You think?"

Later Still May 20th

If one more yuppie sap tells me all they want out of life is to become regional parts manager by some birthday that ends with a zero, I swear I'll douse their Hawaiian shirt with brandy and shove them at the nearest tiki torch. Though they seem to enjoy the one-on-ones, though they have been gushing at me their everlasting appreciation, several times I have been just an instant's loss of reserve away from screaming, "You are absolutely interchangeable with the rest of the people who have been whinnying at me all morning. You have sucked all the wonderful, imaginative possibilities you were born with right out of your psyche and left yourself nothing but a plastic husk, a human piñata somebody forgot to fill with candy."

So Ed Bradley found some chump dopey enough to spend the money he'd set aside for his kid's corrective surgery on one of my seminars. Believe me, I suffer myself.

Sometimes I get really, really sad.

Part Two

Santa Cruz, California

July 3rd

After finally finding the house keys that I had zipped into an obscure pocket on the bag at the beginning of the trip, I pushed the door in with the weight of the luggage and the force of my knee. The alarm toned and I marched to it and quickly fingered in my code. "Alarm . . . is . . . disarmed," said its voice synthesizer. At the opened door I left my bags, then roamed the house, quickly mashing every light switch I passed. When I'd first returned to the States, after living at the youth hostel, I moved to this residence hotel over Cheap Sunglasses right on the Venice Beach boardwalk. I'd unlock the door and shove it open quickly, then hook my hand inside and paw for the light before stepping inside. The good thing about the room being so small is that one glance would assure me that all was clear.

God knows, it takes longer now. I entered the library first, lit the atrium—something I normally do only for parties—found the wall panel, and started up the CDs. They are programmed to shuffle, and the first song that randomly seeped out of the walls, warming this cave, was Clifford Brown's version of "Laura." The muted trumpet calmed me so I could patrol more slowly. The den, the first living room, the dining room all looked unfamiliar to me. I have lived here a year, been on the road almost half that, and am realizing I have probably not spent more than twenty minutes total in my own dining room. Jill's cousin was my interior designer and sometimes I think the house looks more like hers—she is a blonde ex–flight attendant, ex-wife of an Israeli arms merchant—than the home of a black surfer who grew up five miles away in a home fifty square feet smaller than this place's garage.

In the kitchen I had to use both hands to pry open the main refrigerator. I don't know how little Rosamaria does it. I bought the house because of the two Sub-Zeros. One of my first clients—he met me at the Novel Café in Venice—is an extremely well known actor. His kitchen was like this, as large as a jewelry store and with twin Sub-Zeros side by side, like weapons of mass destruction.

Out of the refrigerator I took the last Yoo-Hoo and wrote "Yoo-Hoo" on the pad in the breakfast nook. Out the window I could see the moon lighting the waves after they broke and foamed white to shore. I should have gone out there; night surfing is a kick. Yet I'm convinced that one time, while I am surfing alone at night, a shark will see my feet dangling above him and get as excited as I am when I see KFC honey barbecue wings at a picnic. For some reason I don't think he will eat all of me, just my feet.

My home office is between the kitchen and the pool, and tonight my desk was crowded with rubber-banded statuettes of mail stacks. Lawrence, my assistant, sorts out the crap, gives the bills to Geoffrey, my business manager, and the letters covered in crayoned knives and machine guns dripping blood to the FBI, so ideally all I have left on my desk is fan mail and marriage proposals (often accompanied by a photograph of the woman naked or, better yet, naked in heels).

I remember that first autumn after leaving Yale, I was living in Milan, fruitlessly trying to earn spaghetti money modeling. Besides my not being handsome enough, the only bookings for black men seemed to be as set dressing for women's shows. Once they wanted me in a leopard-print Speedo, another time in a butler's tie and tails. Instead, I sold cheap leather jackets to tourists outside the *Last Supper*. Yet it was a wonderful time. In the four months between my birthday and Christmas, I received not a single piece of mail. It was as if I'd been witness-relocated. It was exactly what I needed back then. [Cough.]

My letter opener I got in Uganda. It is really a Tutsi circumcision knife, made of mahogany. I traded it with a cabdriver in Kampala for my tape of Michael Jackson's *Thriller*. I told him the tape was so stretched Michael sounded like a Swiss yodeler, but he insisted.

The first letter was typical. She was a housewife, used to make fun of personal-improvement infomercials, but something about mine struck her, so on a whim she called up and ordered. She's now recently divorced and just gone back for her nursing degree, and if I ever happen to find myself in northern Wisconsin . . . Like 72 percent of my pen pals, she is white. The next letter was from Ben Lurkman. He says he went to junior high with me. I think he might have been this triple-jumper with a sharp Adam's apple and a sexy sister a year younger—Felicia, I think it was. Now he's a VP at some corporation back east called Dyno-Wyn. It seems, after listening to my tapes going to and from work, he realized he hated his job and would like nothing better than to come work for me. Six or seven of these offers float in a week. I'll pass on his résumé to Jill. You never know.

Then there was this letter from a teenager from Akron who says I helped him increase his SATs three hundred points. Another from a realtor who claims she just sold her first office park thanks to me. And one from my friend Vanni in Milan. His wife just had another baby.

I have been telling you all of this from up here in my bedroom. The wave that just smashed down on the beach must have been the king of the set. I wonder if you're sensitive enough to pick up its explosion.* [Cough-cough-cough.] Damn, I have been on the road talking for four weeks and my throat is perpetually irritated. Hey, speaking of irritating my throat . . .

I bought the pipe in Bali. It masquerades as a statuette of a naked and cross-legged Balinese woman. The bowl rests in her lap and I release a pinch of Humboldt weed into it. Her clay hands collar the top of the bowl, her mouth smiles, and her eyes are happily thin. I hold a match over the bowl and inhale out of the back of her head. Let's go back downstairs.

Twisting the handles simultaneously, I open the French doors and step through to the terrace. The wind is familiar, and I am smiling before I realize I am smiling. Vapors curl over the blue light of the pool like Arabian magic, and the water's reflections are projected across the stone facade of the house in dreamy overlapping rows of trembling lines. The house was on the market for two years before I bought it, and several film companies rented it out. Always it was the home of an acne-scarred villain surrounded by reclining women in swimwear and bodyguards with ponytails.

I can't believe I have to go back on the road in two days.

---

* The recorder was not.

Right Here, Right Now

At least it's only one shot, Chicago, and not another monthlong tour of the whole upper Midwest. Yet it's piggish of me to complain.

It is the tours that bought me this house, not the books, not the tapes. Like the Dead when Garcia was alive, it is not the records that keep me going, but the concerts. The Dead, they picked the name by dropping a Bible on its spine and picking the first phrase their finger poked. Chance, we ascribe so much to it. "There is a destiny that shapes our ends, rough-hew them how we will." *Macbeth*, if memory serves, Shakespeare anyway, but bullshit no matter. I mean, who can honestly breathe on this planet and not realize that the only principles at work are gravity, randomness, and greed, real estate being the unholy nexus of all three? Wait. The waves have stopped suddenly; something happened; I can't hear them at all. No, wait a minute, here they go again; waves don't stop. I am so fucking horny I wish that Nikki were close by. We were really wonderful together, unlike that concierge at the hotel after the group left. Marie-France. Sure, she looked a little bit like Emmanuele Beart and let herself right into my room that night, but the sex I can't even remember. I don't know; it's just so hard, I see why movie stars marry their own. The lifestyle is so particular, only another one would understand. That's why I once asked Barbara DeAngelis out; her infomercial is tasteful and pretty good, but she's married. Susan Powter said in an interview once she'd like to lick syrup off my butt, but please, Stop the Insanity. I've always been a loner but never so lonely before. In a youth hostel or a college dorm you can always just roam the halls till you find a conversation. If they wouldn't hassle me I'd drive down to Starbucks before they close. But the last time, I got stared and whispered at so much I felt like a burn victim. When I poured a sugar substitute into my cappuccino I could almost hear them saying, "Oh look, that infomercial guy, he uses Equal."

God, how long have I been shaking? Let me go inside and get to bed. My business manager's coming by in the morning, then Jill. I can't do this crap forever. I can't keep this up for the rest of my life. [Cough.] My throat feels like a road under construction.

July 4th

"You mean if I sell this house to the newly founded Ashton Robinson Foundation for a dollar, the loss will almost cut my tax load in half?"

"Just about. Over five years."

Geoffrey, my business manager, and I went to Santa Cruz High at the same time, yet we hardly ever spoke. The two of us and Shandra Raddock were the only blacks in the senior class, yet I don't think we even once ate lunch together.

"Where do I sign?"

"Here, here, and here, along with your Social Security number. This one has to be notarized, so I'll need your thumbprint."

A thin tin case was pulled out of his briefcase. It opened with a pop, and the black cake of ink inside was subtly decorated with the overlapping impressions of hundreds of thumbs. I pressed mine in and the ink was cool. Geoffrey opened a ledger and swooshed it around in a circle on my desk to face me. I pressed my thumb onto a blank square.

"Now roll it from side to side, then lift straight up."

"If you're wrong about all these creative-accounting ideas, the next time I do this will be in jail."

"Then think of this as practice."

"Funny. I didn't know you were so funny back in high school."

"You were too busy chasing after the white girls."

"They were chasing after me. I was chasing the Mexican girls. What choice did I have? The twins loved lowriders and Shandra was a lesbian."

"No!"

"I thought you knew."

"I asked her out about every damn weekend for three years!"

"Well, at least that gave you a lot of time to study and get into Stanford."

"Aw, man . . . Oh, before I kill myself, sign this too. It's that SEP/IRA we were talking about."

"So, when can I retire and start spending it?"

"As long as PES keeps shipping those tapes, you could retire today and never know what to do with all your money."

"Don't tempt me."

Bong-bong-bong . . . and chimes as mellow as notes from a vibraphone spread through the house like an aroma.

"That must be Jill."

"I'm done anyhow."

I walked Geoffrey to the front door, and the hard heels of his brown shoes clacked against the granite. Just before the door he suddenly stopped and turned to me, but in the abrupt silence my ears kept hearing his shoes.

"You know, most of the guys in high school can't believe how far you've come, but I always tell them I always knew. Remember that girl—what was her name—Carolyn Pinda? Everybody knew she was anorexic; she looked like a damn coat hanger. But nobody was really her friend, so nobody said nothing till that one day on the south stairs, practically the whole damn school was in the halls for fifth period, and you grabbed her and shook her and said, "What the hell's the matter with you? Can't you see you're shriveling up and dying! Jesus Christ! You and me are cutting out early and I'm getting you a couple of strawberry shakes at Jack in the Box . . . !"

As Geoffrey snorted he shook his head and smiled.

"It was no big deal. I just couldn't stand to see her wasting a perfectly good life like that. She still calls me every Christmas."

I was opening the door before I'd finished my sentence, and there was Jill in tennis whites, smiling.

"Geoffrey, hello! Hey, Boss."

"See you later, Ashton. Jill, my office just finished your tax return, if you could come in sometime this week to sign it . . ."

As Geoffrey walked past the fountain in the middle of the driveway to his car, I saw Alan, Jill's husband, waiting in the driver's seat of their BMW.

"Doesn't he want to come in? This might take a second."

"He, uh . . ."

"Hates my guts."

"He doesn't. He didn't used to. Not in the beginning. Can we go in now?"

"You didn't tell him about Maui . . . ?"

"No! But he imagines it."

"Probably turns him on."

I stepped past her, arced around the fountain, barefoot on the red tiles. I snuck up to Alan at the wheel, his shoulders as shapeless as if he'd been deboned. He and Jill were some of my very first listeners down in Venice. They were just friends then;

she was living with a woman and having an affair with Dale, but it was obvious Alan had a big crush on her. When I met him he was the assistant manager of a one-hour photo lab and five years overdue on finishing his master's in electrical engineering. Now he's some junior executive at a small software firm in Los Gatos. He even did a taped testimonial for my first infomercial. Then about a year after Jill started traveling with me on some of the lecture tours, he turned on me.

The windows were up, the car idled quietly, and as I got nearer I could hear the rush of the air-conditioning. My waist was right outside his window when I heard him jump. As I crouched down, the greened glass was powering down and he was recoiling from it.

"Didn't mean to scare you, Alan. Long time no see."

"Hello, Ashton."

"I apologize for having Jill work on the Fourth, but I promise not to keep her very long. Won't you come in for a drink? Rosamaria can squeeze you some o.j. You need to fill up before you get out on the courts."

"Really, no."

Too late. I was already opening his car door. He waited a beat, admitted defeat, and stepped out of the car. He stretched to his full height, about six foot two, and frowned as he always does when he has to look up the three inches to my eyes. I smiled at him.

"Alan, you must be, what, six-four?"

"Six-two."

"Are you sure? I am usually a good judge of height."

"I haven't been measured since college, but—"

"I bet you gained a couple of inches. Anyway, thanks again for letting Jill come over on a Saturday like this. After we come off an intensive it takes a few days to get the machine here at home back up to speed. You know Dave Kalkstein called while we were gone. Seems he would like us to set up a corporate retreat."

"My boss!"

"I do a little consulting with him on the phone from time to time. I am sorry. I thought you knew. Jill, you didn't tell your husband Dave Kalkstein is one of our clients?"

"It slipped my mind."

An erection snuck up on me, grew down my pants leg. That one night in Maui she was so sexually vibrant and inventive. What a waste. I bent to tug my jeans down at the knee so I could walk, tilted my head to give Alan another smile. Then into the house I led them.

"Alan [cough], if you would like to watch television in the den . . ."

I swept my arm toward the den in a slow-motion backhand as my other hand reached for his wife's attaché, our hands mingling awkwardly during the transfer. I led her down the hall to my office, the granite pleasantly freezing the soles of my feet.

Later July 4th

I love recording while I drive. There's a cubbyhole above the car stereo seemingly tailor-made for you, Mr. Microcassette Recorder. In these days of car phones with built-in speakers, people don't think you're a nut for talking while driving. Fortunately for me they don't realize I'm talking to myself.

I am in the Jaguar and not the Land Cruiser because my mother always says it is the prettiest car she has ever seen in all her life. I keep meaning to get the license plates changed, but I don't want to offend my staff. For my birthday a year ago, the plates were wrapped in tissue paper, lying on my desk. Jill, Lawrence, and the rest huddled around me as I pulled at the paper and it ripped noisily. *MPROV*, just the five letters, on each plate.

"Improv?" I said.

"IMPROVE," they shouted.

"I told you we needed the *E*," grumbled Jill.

" 'Improve' with an *E* was already taken," said Lawrence.

I calmed them all, smiled, and lied that I loved it. Of course the last shot in the *60 Minutes* hatchet job last year was me driving away in the Jag, top down, and waving to a neighbor like a pasha, then a close-up and freeze-frame of *MPROV*. And now, as I am rolling up Water Street, a few people point, a few heads turn. UCSC upperclassmen tell freshmen, "There goes that infomercial guy. You know, *60 Minutes* did a thing on him."

Not yet on the level of Clint Eastwood, just down the coast in Carmel, I am currently, believe it or not, Santa Cruz's most famous citizen.

When did the junior high get new windows? Though it is just a couple of miles away, if I am not visiting the folks, I almost never find myself back on this side of town.

Our next-door neighbors must be back home for a few weeks. The flag is jammed into the flag holder by their front door and their white Winnebago fills their driveway like a prefabricated wing of their small house. Since he retired from the post office a few years ago, they are almost always in San Miguel de Allende, Mexico, or Yellowstone National Park, or Sarasota, Florida, with other Winnebagans (none without the smiling Good Sam decals on the vinyl spare-tire covers on the backs of their vehicles, right next to the lacquered wood plaques with their names burnt in cursive, or maybe spelled out in shellacked rope).

Talk to you later. Here comes my mother.

Mrs. Robinson: "Why, if that isn't the prettiest car I've ever seen in all my life!"

■ ■ ■

She pivoted herself through the squawking steel screen door, rotating around her cane and making sure her thick ankles and beige orthopedic shoes were stable before swinging all that weight again. Perpetually dieting, perpetually visiting from Dr.

Watson, she still refuses to cut out the fried chicken and the breakfast meats. She is the only one of her seven brothers and sisters yet to have a stroke, and one of only three still living.

"Oh, baby, if you don't get better and better looking . . ."

Her fingers stretched up to my face, and I bent for her. Her fleshy hand cupped my cheek and my eyes closed on their own. Her lips warmed my other cheek and her skin smelled like cooking.

"Mommy, hello."

She turned herself around, huffing, in the doorway, hung her arm from my waist instead of the cane, and I walked her through the living room. We passed the knickknack hutch, shaped like a triangle to fit in the corner. It's stuffed with leis, figurines made of coconut husks, and photos of their forty-fifth-anniversary trip to Hawaii, the most Papa has ever accepted from me. The walls on each side of the hutch hold our photos. My brother on the football team in high school, in the army; his first wedding; his three daughters all in rigid, three-quarter profiles and all grinning sweetly in front of a painted backdrop of pale clouds. My sister's college graduation; her first marriage. My model U.N. certificate, student body president certificate, National Merit Scholar certificate (my sister's ex burned hers during the divorce); a framed original of my high-school salutatorian speech; the cover of a favorable story on me in the *San Francisco Chronicle Magazine*; the covers of my books; photos of me shaking hands with Clinton, with Dudley Moore, with Teddy Pendergrass.

"As much money as you've got, you still can't comb your hair to see your mama."

My father stood in the kitchen and instantly crowded the

room. Just an inch shorter than I am and sixty-five next month, he's still thick and immovable wherever he stands.

"Hi, Papa. I've told you. They're dreadlocks. You can't comb them out."

"If I were a roach or a water bug, I'd look at that rat's nest of yours and think I'd died and gone to heaven. Come on over here, boy, I've got a hacksaw in the garage."

He pushed my head down into the vise of his bent arm and pantomimed sawing off my locks. Everyone laughed, including Avon and Allison, who'd appeared in the back door. Avon, my big brother, is forty-five years old and now as thick as he is tall. Allison is forty. She must have just ironed her hair because the room suddenly smelled of distant toast.

"Papa, you say that every time you see me."

"And I'll keep saying it till you chop off them little monkey dicks."

"Virgil!"

"Well, that's what they look like. You've said so yourself."

"I never did no such thing! I think they look just fine, baby, if that is what you want sitting on top of your head."

"All y'all just leave my little brother alone . . . Ashton, don't listen to them. You know your TV show is on channel fifteen just about every night."

"I sure do know. I write the check."

"How much does something like that cost?"

"It depends on the time and the channel, but maybe somewhere around ten grand."

Avon whistled. He used to carry me on his shoulders into the locker room before football games. But ever since last year, when I gave him $26,000 to pay off his second wife, he nervously stares my way, studying me to anticipate my laughter, then rushes awkwardly to laugh with me.

"Why couldn't you sell something useful, like the Ab-Blaster®?"

"Hush, Allison."

Then I coughed. A bad one, so throaty it sounded like chunks of esophagus were coming up with it. My father petted my back.

"Boy, you sick?"

"I've just been on the road too long. Hotel food, and sometimes I'm lecturing six hours a day. My throat is a little raspy, is all."

"Well, take care of yourself. Verna, don't we have some cough syrup in the back?"

Mama was in the middle of sprinkling celery seed into the yellow mountain of potato salad jutting out of the green Tupperware bowl on the counter but stopped in midshake to obey my father and go look. I wanted to say something, to defend her, but did not want us to fight today. Soon she and her cane were back with a purple bottle so old the label had disappeared.

"Thanks, Mommy."

I took it and my fingers stuck to the outside. The cap was sugared to the bottle and crunched when I finally turned it free. I filled a big spoon with the purple water and loaded it into my mouth, careful not to spill it down my silk shirt. I could feel it coating my throat on its way to my stomach. The alcohol in it made me open my mouth and exhale purple breath. I poured another load into the spoon.

"Keep it, boy, we don't need it."

"Thank you, Papa."

"Ashton, Allison, Avon, ribs won't be ready for another half an hour, but if y'all're hungry I can thaw some hamburger patties in the microwave."

"No thank you, Mama."

"There's slaw, and this potato salad's almost done."

Those generic outdoor chairs, now faded and frayed green nylon webbed onto scaly and dented aluminum frames, came with the house when we moved in. My father never found an outdoor table that he liked, so we never had one. Instead, we laid plates on our knees and beers at our ankles. Papa caught all our eyes with his and we all remembered to shut up and bow.

"Most merciful Father, we are truly thankful for the food we are about to receive on this, our Fourth of July family picnic. We would like to say a prayer for Avon's and Allison's children, our grandchildren who are with their other parents this holiday season but, next year, we hope, will be celebrating again with us. For Christ's sake. Amen."

We all mumbled amens and soon Allison was complaining that all her physical plant workers at the university were threatening another strike. My father promised he would retire this year if Avon and the Paquito twins can ever go a month without electrocuting themselves. My mother just kept stealing flirtatious glances at me, sly smiles forced out by inner thoughts.

"What are you thinking about, Mommy?"

"Only good things, baby."

"Mama, he's thirty-four years old."

"I call you baby too, Ally-girl."

Mr. Hernandez knocked on the back fence between our yards before stretching on tiptoes and stretching his neck to peek over.

"Happy Fourth of July, everybody."

"Happy, happy, Hector."

That is all the encouragement he needed from my father, and he suddenly looked back behind the fence, hissed and snapped to someone, and then the heads of all his kids, cousins, and in-laws started popping up on the fence next to him. It was funny how the heads of the children and the very short grandmother wobbled, so I guess they'd rushed a picnic bench to the edge of the fence and all clambered up. In high school I would hop this fence and cut through his yard when I did not want my folks to know when I was leaving or coming back—until Mr. Hernandez started leaving his cousin's German shepherd back there on nights when he thought I'd be coming through.

"Ashton, we keep seeing you on TV. Say hello to the president and that guy on *ER* the next time you see them."

He laughed alone. Yet the entire family was grinning at me creepily, as if they had not watched me grow up.

"I mean it, Ashton. When are you gonna give your old neighbors a free copy of the tapes?"

When that dog's bites disappear from my ass, I craved to say. But instead, I played nice.

"I keep forgetting, Mr. H. Sorry."

As the silence lengthened, most of the family had the sense to go back to their own picnic, but Mr. Hernandez just steadied himself against the grayed peaks of the wooden fence.

"That's one helluva ride you got."

"Thank you."

"Wanna trade?"

He drives a '78 Monte Carlo that, in 1978, was the nicest car on our block.

"I'd like to, Mr. H., but I'm leasing."

His laughter nearly toppled him. Behind me I heard my brother laughing loudly as well. I thought I would try to stay there till late. I had not seen any of them in months, and it is the Fourth of July and I had nothing better to do, but I had to get away from there as soon as my mother would let me.

My mother was nearly at the back door before I noticed her and rushed to help. She was balancing the dirty plates—one atop the other but cockeyed from the gnawed bones—in one hand, her cane in the other. I lifted the plates from her, jerked open the screen door.

"Why, thank you, baby. You know, I miss having you around the house."

I tilted the plates into the double-paper bags under the sink, then turned to head back outside for the rest when her hand clamped my forearm, trembling. Her age makes me sad.

"Are you happy, baby?"

"Are you happy, Mommy?"

"When I see you. When I see my other babies."

"Well, I'm happy when I see you too."

"Then why isn't that hardly ever at all?"

"I travel. A hundred thousand miles last year."

"So, that big old museum of a house of yours is nearly always empty? Boy, you should save your money, move back in here with us."

"Sometimes I'd like that."

"And how's your little old white girl?"

"Jill? She's just my friend. She's married."

My mother's grunt came from somewhere deep past her throat. I remembered my lifetime of hearing it and smiled. It is as disapproving as she ever gets with me and used to steal my breath.

"Lord knows there aren't too many of us around here, but in all your travels, haven't you met a nice black girl?"

"When did you stop saying 'colored'?"

"Don't you get smart with me."

"I did meet a nice girl in the Caribbean. She's black, too, cousin Charmaine's color."

"That's all right now. We're a rainbow people. Your grand-mama had gray eyes and Choctaw hair to the middle of her back. Well, what's her name?"

"Nikki. Nikki Kennedy. From Chicago."

"Is she related to that Leon Isaac Kennedy?"

"I don't know, Mommy. I doubt it."

"Good. After what he did to that poor Jane girl. Pretty as she was. Isn't she on your TV program?"

"No. She is on the psychic something network."

"Well, she's a big girl now. Probably still traumatized from that marriage. You should give her a call and help her like you did that rich man who went blind and paralyzed and wanted to kill himself. Whatever happened to him, anyway?"

"Oh, I don't know. You sure you don't want me to go get the rest of the things from outside?"

[Loud street noises. Shouting.]

Let me stop for a minute, till I get past this block.

[Tape stops. Restarts.]

Anyway, Allison was already coming in from outside with the green plastic tubs of potato salad and cole slaw and baked beans, pages of wrinkled aluminum foil, browned from the heat, splattered red with barbecue sauce.

"I've got to pick up the boys from their father, Mama."

"Kiss the babies for me, baby."

"You all right, little brother?"

"Yeah. Fine. Thanks."

Right Here, Right Now

"No more of those problems you had back in school?"

"Allison! Hush! My baby's just fi—"

"That was a long time ago, Allison."

"But it was a big problem."

I faked a long, wet cough.

"I should be going too. I'd like to sleep off whatever it is that's got my throat."

"You children are always in a hurry to move on. Well, I'm just happy y'all stayed as long as you did."

"Awww."

I kissed her cheek, and this time it was her eyes that closed sweetly.

Later Still July 4th

I'm still driving home, but I've finally gotten through the very worst clots of the holiday crowds. It seems like the entire city is drunk, stoned, or pitching lit firecrackers at the feet of their friends. I rolled through them slowly, like a cowboy through a herd, and a few drunks pointed, and one rushed my car and tried to tilt his beer-and-a-half-long beer can to my lips. First I flinched, then I collected myself and burned him with my eyes.

"Sorry, man! Jesus H. Christ, if you don't fucking drink, why didn't you say the fuck so?"

He loped back to his friends on the curb, then turned to me and raised his sinewy arms out and up, shrunk his head into his body.

"'Scuse me for fucking living, you rich fuck."

The road home now is suddenly empty and dark, and the memory of Nelson Bing resurfaces. Damnit. Somehow I thought my mother had heard. Thank God it was after the *60 Minutes* show. It is exactly the kind of story they would have liked to have led with. Self-made software millionaire by twenty-five. Married to a gorgeous ex–*Price Is Right* spokesmodel named Jenny. And besides cocaine, he was also addicted to thrill sports, particularly shooting class five rapids in his kayak. He and some friends flew down to Costa Rica to be the first to navigate a thunderous stretch of the Corobici. It had six-foot-tall standing waves and two fifteen-foot waterfalls. He shot the first falls fine, but on the second he got pinned under an underwater shelf, held there for two minutes before his kayak broke apart and loosed him down the rest of the river with just his paddle.

They found him six miles downstream. One leg and one arm were broken, but he crawled onto a rock and waited. His spine must have already been cracked, because when they tried to lift him off the rock they heard a loud *pop* and suddenly all feeling went out of his body. It was like someone had just turned off a switch, he later told me on camera.

He suddenly went from being one of the most dynamic men in America to one of the most static. He ran through ten personal nurses in a year because he tried to bribe each one of them to end his life. The tenth tried and gave him a shot of something. His wife saved him, but not before the drug had destroyed his optic nerve, leaving him almost completely blind.

It was Jenny who bought him my audiocassettes. A month later she wrote me the nicest letter. Though before that I had always refused, on my next trip through southern Florida I made my first house call. I was so nervous as Jenny opened the door and led me into his room. But he smiled when he heard my voice. He's the first person I ever wanted to confess to that I didn't know what the hell I was talking about, that he should seek professional therapy and not stake all his hope on anybody who buys cheap airtime on late-night independent television stations. I wanted to tell him I'm just like the psychic networks, "For Entertainment Purposes Only." But we hit it off immediately, two loud and arrogant wunderkinder. We swapped stories about our adventures around the globe. We had both fallen in love with Panajachel on Lake Atitlán, Guatemala; had both gotten drunk with the same old German hippie/anarchist video-bar owner there. I was this close to telling him what I know about suicide.

Anyway, we would talk the first Sunday of every month. He was making amazing progress and soon was dictating software programs into a state-of-the-art, voice-activated PC, and once in a while even cracking a joke. It was his idea, not mine, to tape a testimonial for my next show. Cassette sales zoomed 18 percent. My office forwarded great canvas bags of mail to his home. He had his doctor remove sperm from his testes to artificially inseminate Jenny.

When I got her call, that he had choked himself by biting off and swallowing hunks of his foam pillow, it took the rest of the day and into the next to believe it.

I desperately wanted to go to the funeral. I already had my ticket. But my attorneys forbade me. After the 60 Minutes piece they said I had to immediately disassociate myself from any more bad press. Yet I talked with Jenny on the phone for two hours. I told her I was swamped in several crises here at the office and just couldn't possibly get away. She said she understood and that I'd be there in spirit. [Cough.] Damn, the syrup's worn off.

I am still warily impressed by the eerie silence of my gates as they fan apart as elegantly as the hands of a geisha to let me up my driveway. I feel like James Bond arrogantly walking right into his bald-headed, heavily-accented-English-speaking villain's lair.

Except, of course, I'm the good guy. Oops, running low. Let me change the tape.

I'm in the den now, packing the pipe tight with the rest of my stash; light her up and inhale slowly not to irritate my throat any more than it already is. I hold. Wait . . .

I just held my breath for at least a minute, and when I finally exhaled, almost no smoke clouded out of my mouth. Repeat. [Cough. Cough. Cough.] Damn. Let me find that cough syrup before I won't be able to find anything. Then I'll sit by the pool in my sweater and watch the night and strategize the next bend in the snaky road of my life. Maybe a Snapple lemon-flavored iced tea too, only I don't think it will go to goo—too well, with cough syrup. I should have had a party here for the Fourth, invited the staff, my family, and the guys I grew up with who still live around here. The realtor gushed that this cavern was "absolutely ideal for entertaining!" [Cough. Cough.]

It'll be nice to see Nikki in Chicago next week. Am I always talking about her? Weird. I love Chicago in the summer, but I have never known anyone there who could show me around, except our local officiators. What're their names, anyway? Oh yeah, the Dawbridges. Kiss-assy middle managers, the both of them, interested only in showing me restaurants and parts of the city that reflected well on them. Did I leave the cough syrup in the car? I could've sworn I carried it inside . . . Oh, here it is. On the island in the kitchen. Where I put everything.

Hmmm! Tasty! Even thinner than I remembered back at Mommy's. It must be the alcohol. Like *I Love Lucy*, this could be my Veg-a-Mit-a-Mix. [Cough.] But seriously, it works, but the reason it wears off so quickly must be it's so old. Probably expired in the eighties. Probably not much stronger than grape juice, and my mouth is so damn dry . . . There, the warmth spreads nicely to the four corners of my body. I wonder if I could chug the rest. What's the worst that could happen? I'll go outside and stay there a while. First let me get my sweater . . .

I feel good, but not so good. My brain is a little fogged in, but not unpleasantly so, and my stomach distantly rumbles like the napping god who dwells inside the volcano looming in the mist over the Polynesian village. Uhhh-HUUUH! No jokes now, it could go either way, but sooner or later, my stomach's contents are gonna go somewhere, north or south, front door or basement. It felt like it took hours to find the perfect sweater, the one that fit my mood, but I could swear the one I'm wearing now isn't the one I put on upstairs. [Singing.] Look at the pool like a giant jewel, you fool. I'm never silly anymore, of course. I don't think I ever was, not even in the third grade. It was back then that I remember being more serious, more driven than anybody else, including the teachers. I remember telling one really dull teacher back in Flint who leaned over me grinning so paternalistically while my guts were boiling inside me like they are now, but back then it was because I snuck downstairs after dinner and ate the entire casserole dish of candied carrots, then tilted a curved corner of the Pyrex to my mouth and slid the rest of the sweet juices down my little throat till it goateed me in brown syrup, so the next day I wasn't feeling too hot at all, and this loser's leaning over me and I tell him my tummy ached 'cause I thought he'd have to look up "stomach" in the dictionary.

Do these thoughts make any sense? I should get out the videocamera and record not just my words but my expressions too, sell the tapes at Blockbuster, *The Other Side of Ashton Robinson*, *The Many Moods of Ashton Robinson*, *A Very Special Evening with Ashton R*. But if getting whatever sweater it is that

Right Here, Right Now

I'm wearing now was such a production, imagine finding the videocamera, loading in a tape, and taping myself? Just thinking about it makes me want to take a nap, but no, jumping in the pool with my clothes on would be cool, memorable. No one around, so it's not like you're doing it to show how wild you are. So am I gonna take off my clothes and live a little, for once practice an iota of what I teach? But on the other hand it's cold. But I don't feel it right now. But it's California, on the coast, nearish to midnight. It is always cool. See, here comes a cool breeze somehow invading my long pants to lightly electrify my balls. Somehow I knew my brain would wander back to the neighborhood of sex; it always does. But I truly would pay one hundred grand right now for a woman. Nikki Kennedy and the officiator in Dallas; the assistant officiator in Phoenix; Jill—what if they were all right here right now and all I had to do was lay back in this lounge chair and they would take turns squatting over me as if I were a fountain and their sexes thirsty for drink?

I like pulling a sweater off, the way it bumps over your chin then finally comes free of your head. I always do it quickly 'cause for that moment when I am blinded, the wool hooding my eyes, it is exactly then that I'm sure God is going to visit, or a kidnaper. As soon as I can see again I always quickly look around to try and catch up on what I just missed. CAN YOU STILL HEAR ME, MR. RECORDER MAN? But this pricey linen shirt I'm now unbuttoning holds no philosophy. My pants and my boxers I push off my thighs together, they drop to a puddle around my ankles. The grid of red tiles, big squares, surrounding me must be so pleasantly cool. Let me step out of my loafers and touch one with my foot . . . Yes, it feels wonderful. Almost as pleasant as a first kiss.

[Scraping noise.]

Trey Ellis

I'm dragging a chaise longue to the pool's lip and here rest you on the chair's white vinyl tubes of strapping so I can go into the water, but gently, so I won't splash you. I HOPE YOU CAN STILL HEAR ME. A breeze angles the mist off the pool, past my shoulders, my head, and it dissolves dancing into the night. My every step and arm sweep make the water around me chatter, push away the magic of the silence until I freeze again and let the noiselessness catch up again. [Unintelligible] would come the assassin, behind me, with a silencer, the azure reflection of the pool tattooing his body, stylishly noir. I would sag into the water and as the hemoglobin reacted with the chlorine, the blood billowing from my wounds would turn some interestingly unexpected color.

[Splashing sound.]

Butterflying, I crash like cymbals in the water, yet hardly advance at all for all the splashing, so surrender and corkscrew onto my back and backstroke more softly, now comically erect. My cock a submarine's conning tower . . .

[Eight and a half minutes of silence.]

My God, I am frozen in place, aren't I? My arms and legs refuse my commands, but my lungs . . . !? Good. At least they still move. And I can blink. Will I drown? Thank God I'm faceup. I hope you're still getting all this. Jesus, keep air in your lungs, breath deep to keep your head buoyed on the surface till this passes. Steady now, don't get too paranoid, though this paralysis is real and you're awake and in your pool and that erection is gone, thank God, so when they find you drowned in this goddamn pool at least that won't be another thing to ridicule your corpse about. Let's try it again; maybe a pinkie will budge . . . ? Nope.

Why, oh why, Mr. Microcassette Recorder, can't you call the

police? You're my black box flight data recorder! So, Officers, that's it. The dope and the cough syrup killed me. No foul play at all. Oh. One more thing. What science can't recycle, cremate.

[Three minutes and thirty-five seconds of silence.]

Wait! Perhaps it's passing. All sounds so weird in my underwater ears. Maybe the neck can twist, but no. Weird how my lips and lungs can move but just barely, and nothing else at all. I can't hear the world, but I see the stars over my head. I can't move but I feel the cold. So that's how I'll die. I won't drown, but all the heat from my being will drain into this chemically blue water, blue like a novelty drink, and my gums will go blue as I die. Rosamaria comes to clean four days a week. She'll be the one who'll find me.

What was that! They are swimming now, the stars, shifting colors, breaking and falling. It must be my eyes; maybe they play tricks, put on a show before they shut off. Do researchers already know this? Will this audio recording of my passing be fodder for some young researcher's dissertation? Are the stars now noisy? Underwater I can't really hear them, but something is popping and . . . Fireworks! Idiot, fireworks are going off, or have been going off, but they seem to have stopped. No! Here explodes another cluster; shrapnel of light drift landward yet wink off well before landing. I wonder if high school kids are down on the beach, smoking and fucking like they did in my day on the Fourth. If I don't thaw soon, I'll start yelling for help. Tell them to ignore the *Armed Patrol* and *Go Ahead, Make My Pit Bull's Day* stickers on the seawall on my stretch of beach. I'd have to bribe them not to tell the police or *Hard Copy*. What did Richard Gere do if he really did have that gerbil up his ass? When did the bleeding or the, I don't know, the weight gain get so bad that he said to himself, Fuck it, I'm going to the hospital, scandal be damned. That's what I want to know. I'd rather live and lose my empire than die naked in my pool.

There goes the fireworks finale. Booms barely reach through the water to my ears; overlapping blossoms of light crowd part of the sky. I hear cheering in the distance.

Wait! I am moving now. Or something is moving me. Wild shaking, vibrating like a custom color in a paint mixer. I can hear myself shaking, hear the water slapping. Is someone slapping my face?

Ahhh! My hands move suddenly; my knees, they bend. Ow! They hit the pool's pebbly bottom, leaving some skin. I must be in the shallow end, two feet of water. Ideal place to drown on drugs. The blue water's surface is suddenly, prettily, brown and orange. Dead flowers and leaves blown into the pool. My throat burns, my sinuses burn. Hendrix died in a pool of vomit. Vomit! That's what coats the water, that's what burns my nose; let me swim away from it carefully, dive down and wash it out of my dreads, off my arms. There is an outside shower somewhere around the pool; the realtor kept mentioning it, but I have never used it and can't quite remember where it should be.

Oh God! He scared me so that I slipped and took flight for an instant, landed back on my feet with a wet foot slap in a cartoon-ish miracle.

"Who the fuck are you? Get out of here before I call the cops!"

*Unknown voice: "Nao se perturbar. Eu sou um amigo."**

---

* "Don't be afraid. I am a friend." We hired a team of internationally renowned voice-recognition experts, and four of the seven concluded that the voices heard speaking Portuguese on the tapes, though extremely cleverly disguised, were Robinson's own. The majority of the FBI's experts examining the Boron desert

Right Here, Right Now

Why is this tiny fucking Brazilian in my backyard? And why the fuck is he naked? I have no idea where I left my own clothes. And where are those panic buttons the alarm guy hid all over the house? I wasn't really listening when he showed me where they are. Who'd want to attack me?

Unknown voice: "You have to change your life. You are a very important man in the history of the world, so why the hell are you wasting your vast talent?"*

"Who are you? *O que é que é você?* Look, I'm recording this whole conversation. You're in big trouble. Did I meet you when I was down in Brazil? Are you a friend of Jorge?"

Oh, God. He was just telling me I've got to change my life, I'm important to the life and history of the world, so why am I wasting my talents? I'm pretty sure I didn't meet him when I was down in Brazil. Certainly not ever naked. His skin looks as dark as burnt wood, but something about the configuration of his face makes him unmistakably Afro-Latino. I was not sure if he was a dwarf or just over the borderline into normalcy, but now I am sure. His voice has the eerie, synthesized tone of a midget or a dwarf (whichever one it is that has conventional proportions but is just tiny).

Unknown voice: "*Ashay.* You're hiding your *ashay.* You need to find it in your daily life, in the lives of those surrounding you.

tape also concluded that Robinson, in his drug-induced state, was most probably the source of the other voice.

* Translations by Ronaldo Pereira of Columbia University and the Universidade de São Paolo. Though Dr. Pereira has stated that the voice spoke impeccable Brazilian Portuguese, while Robinson spoke the language only passably, subconscious expertise in foreign languages is a common and well-documented byproduct of severe cases of MPD (multiple personality disorder).

God chose you and only you to bring the world to the future. It will be a lonely and difficult journey, but you can do it."

"H-hold up. My Portuguese is really rusty and I'm very, very confused right now. What are you, some kind of perverted strip-o-gram? Look, you got the wrong address. It must be one of my neighbors that ordered a naked little South American. But thanks. You can let yourself out."

The little guy's just standing there, staring at me.

"Look, schmuck. You are spoiling my high!"

"Find love, Senhor Ashton."

"Listen, you crazy fucking Brazilian leprechaun, I ain't finding no love with you. Now hop on down the beach before I call the cops. You know, I once held a special two-day seminar for the chief of police himself."

[Sounds of a struggle.]*

"Ah . . . ! Ughhh . . . ! Hey! Stop it! Help . . . !"

[Sounds of struggle end. Then forty-five seconds of panting.]

"I am no leprechaun. I am your friend."

"How the hell'd you get that tiny little foot up to my head?"

"*Capoeira.*† This will be a difficult night for you, but please calm yourself."

"I don't feel so good . . ."

[Sounds of wretching.]

"Hey! Weirdo! Don't dig up that plant! That's a—? Whatever it was, I'm sure it was expensive. Oh!"

[More wretching sounds.]

"Eat these roots. Senhor Ashton. They will help your stomach."

---

* None of the audio experts could agree on the number of persons possibly involved.

† A Brazilian martial art, brought there by African slaves.

Right Here, Right Now

"Forget it! They're pink and they're dirty."

"I could *make* you eat these roots, senhor."

[Short pause. Crunching sound.]

"Tastes like dirt. Is that all you wanted? Little bully. Now, good night. *Boa noite.*"

[Rustling. Then Robinson whispers.]

"Mr. Recorder? I'm gonna try to make it to the French door. If something happens, the assailant was Brazilian, about four feet tall. But hey, you know something, you're not gonna believe this, but my stomach does feel pretty good. More than good. My whole body feels . . . it feels . . . springy."

"*Obrigado.* Thanks and good night."

The little guy's walking on his hands now, better than most people walk upright.

"Let's go inside for the second part."

Shit, he's scampering inside on his hands. Man, can he run!

"Stop!"

Great. Now what do I do? Do I run down the beach, naked, and try to explain this to a neighbor so they'll call the cops? He seems kind of harmless, except for that kick to the head. Wait, I see him, in the living room. What's he doing? Dancing? Great ass. I mean, for a guy midget. Where's this boner coming from? Oh, this is just great, I'm getting turned on not only by a guy, but by a guy circus freak. He looks much taller from behind, though, his legs rising slenderly for miles. I'm closer to the window now and can hear the music. My *Sergio Mendes, Brazil '66.* How'd he find it? I don't even think it was in the right case! And how'd he get the stereo to work so fast? I still screw up and have Spanish talk radio jabbing my eardrums till I remember again which button to push.

The glass of the French door is cool against my cheek. What

a wonderful dancer. I could watch those legs, that butt forever. Oh, I get it. That's why he's so tall now. Black alligator mules with five-inch heels. How'd he know? Uh-oh, he's turning to me now and his breasts are so round and firm, jiggling so very slightly with every dance step. His face is the face of the most beautiful woman I have ever seen, that has ever been. Oh, my God, my heart is . . . not mine anymore. I've got to go inside and dance with her.

"Do you like this better?"

"Oh, shit! It's still you. Your voice. You're still the little guy inside."

Unknown voice #2: Forgive me. I forgot. Is this voice more pleasing?"*

"Yeah. Wow. That's the most lovely voice I've ever heard in all my life."

"Please dance with me."

"You're not gonna kill me, are you? Or am I already dead? Oh, no. I got it. I'm drowning, right, back in the pool, and this is the wonderful fantasy my brain's giving me to ease the pain."

"Please dance with me."

"I'm afraid."

"'Behind each fear is the opportunity of a lifetime.'"

"It sounds better in Portuguese than when I said it."

"I'm gonna kiss you, senhor."

"No. I don't want to die right now."

"But you want to kiss me too."

"More than I want to breathe."

* Though voice-recognition experts were more troubled by the female voice, there is a famous case in England of another male MPD sufferer who could perfectly mimic the voice of ex–prime minister Margaret Thatcher.

"Very well, then . . ."

[Kissing sound. Two minutes, ten seconds of silence.]

"I jus—"

"You are still breathing, true?"

"But I am crying."

"Of course. You were in a coma for five days when you were a tiny boy. Then you almost jumped off Harkness Tower when you were at Yale University."

"Who told you all that?"

"You're hiding your *ashay.* You need to find it in your daily life, in the lives of those surrounding you. God chose you and only you to bring the world to the future. It will be a lonely and difficult journey, but you can do it."

"When I was three, did you visit me in my coma?"

"I knew you would remember."

"Oh, boy. And you're the thing that stopped me from jumping?"

"After you had climbed over the railing you thought, It does not matter that I can never be the smartest here. There is a woman somewhere on the planet who will love me and I will love her too. Start looking."

"It *is* you."

"I have so much to say. But hold me to you. I am so very cold this night."

"Let's snuggle under this blanket."

[Rustling sounds. Tape ends.]

July 5th

The rumbling hum of a slow-moving, prop-driven plane, the heat from the sun on my cheek, the sun's yellow-red brightness on my eyelids are what woke me. Immediately I reached for you, my best friend, but your tape had long since run out. I had no idea where I was and even less who. I was way too scared to think about opening my eyes. All I knew was that I was naked, my neck frozen to the side and my contacts fused to my eyeballs. It wasn't till I realized that the loud whine in my ears was Enrique and his leaf blower that I dared try to pry open my eyelids and peek at to-day's reality.

I was lying on a lounge chair by the pool, the white plastic straps stuck to my body like leeches. Enrique and his son and their leaf blowers were still around the corner of the house. I smiled, thought I'd escaped detection till I struggled up on my elbows and saw the pool cleaner skimming the former contents of my stomach into a bucket. I couldn't see my clothes any-where. The pool cleaner—I keep forgetting his name—was kind enough to pretend he couldn't see me. I'm gonna make him very happy next Christmas. I ran into the house through a

French door. Rosamaria was nowhere to be seen, so I shot for the stairs, my cock flopping till I steadied its upward swing with one cupped hand, while the other grabbed at the banister, pulling me to the second floor faster still.

Rosamaria was changing my sheets.

I'm telling you all this from the car. I'm on my way to the office, then a book signing down the coast. Anyway, back home, Rosamaria dropped the sheets, twisted away, and followed close to the walls till she found the door behind me and slipped out.

"Rosamaria! Wait . . . !"

I hid my body behind the door as I called after her.

"Did you see a woman here when you arrived?"

She was almost sunk out of sight, down the stairs.

"No, sir."

"How about a midget?"

Her eyes and mouth simultaneously widened; she slowly and deliberately shook her head as left and as right as could be. I yanked my robe off the hook on the door and skittered back down the stairs trying to gather the robe around me against the apparent wind of my running. Rosamaria squeezed the railing as I blew past her.

I was instantly in my office fingering through the reference books for my Portuguese dictionary. *Ascua,* ember. *Asfaltar,* asphalt. But no *ashay.*

I jogged to the little living room and stared at the entertainment console. I found the remote, pressed several buttons, and finally the CD player woke up and its thin tray opened up to me in a magical way. The only disk in the player was *Sergio Mendes, Brazil '66.* The down pillows of the slipcover couch were still dented. She told me I was not dreaming, but how can that be? If only I'd installed those videocameras the security guy tried to sell me on. I could roll the tape of myself, naked, roaming the house, talking to, then kissing, figments of my own imagination. I mean, just because I have a bruise on the side of my temple doesn't mean a Brazilian leprechaun kicked me in the head. I could have fallen, hit my head *first*, then dreamed up the story later.

When I get back home I've got to try to find that brand of cough syrup. Too bad the label had long since gone brittle and broken off, just a hard slug of yellowed glue left on the glass.

After I turned off the CD player I fired up my Wizard and saw I had a book signing in Carmel in two hours. I wanted to stop by PES first, so I raced to the shower, brushed my teeth, gargled well (but my voice is still irritated from the puke), and here I am, here it is, coming up fast on the right.

It is almost more satisfying than driving up to my house. Right after you curve around the Herbalife towers, PES appears, and at this time of day, at this time of year, sun blasts loudly from its array of golden mirrored panels, like something that should be generating power on the moon. Several small computer companies and an MRI laboratory are our office-park neighbors. The PES, Inc., building used to belong to a hot software publisher. While he was going belly-up he came to one of my seminars. I'm leasing it for a song.

The entire valley was artichoke and garlic farmland ten years ago. My new TV studio, weeks behind schedule because they can't figure out how to keep the central air-conditioning from rattling so loudly it wrecks the sound recording, squats right behind the office park. When it's finished and when we're not in there taping ourselves, we're going to lease it out to everyone from the AbBlaster® folks to Philip Michael Thomas's Psychic Friends. Geoffrey says it'll pay for itself in thirteen months.

I love this smell. A steamroller is pressing a new layer of this

special asphalt onto the new parking lot because artichoke this-
tles kept bursting through. I love their tenacity and kind of hope
some of them still manage to surface.

I've got to just forget about last night and just get on with my
life.

I'm pulling the Jag up to the low, white-washed cement
block with *RESERVED A.R.* stenciled in black on its face, like a
cheap tombstone sinking. Jill's BMW is next to me, and next
to her the slot for the employee of the month. This month I
picked Juanita Rivera in shipping because she caught a typo on
the box of the latest batch of cassettes. "Let Ashton Robinson
help you challenge all your preconceived notions and ass umptions."

I fired the copy editor and put every single fucking other
staffer on probation.

Gotta sign off now. I'll fill you in on the drive down to
Carmel.

■ ■ ■

As I came though the front door I felt the tension of the place
rise. Like the Heisenberg Uncertainty Principle, a boss changes a
situation merely by observing it.

"Good morning, Ashton."

"Ashton! Hello!"

"Hi, uh, Ashton."

My first name was shot at me from every open door with this
false casualness that I kind of like. I remember working for Dale
and the terror that surrounded him like a smell. I remember trying to look as if I were reading harder whenever he passed. Jill
and the rest of the pretty women on his staff would instinctively

tug down their skirts, double-check the buttons on their blouses with their fingers.

I'm not that type of boss. I'm the surfer boss, but I still never let them forget I'm first among equals. Hey, maybe I can use that *ashay* from my dream in the next infomercial? A lot of folks really dig crazy shit like that. Besides, I have to try *something* new one of these days. I mean, how many new ways can I keep dreaming up to say, "Go for it," before they stop forking over three easy payments of $39.95?

Note to self: Have whoever transcribes this sign an ironclad nondisclosure form. Taken out of context, I could really get burned.

Anyway, I entered my office and my assistant, Lawrence, snapped to attention.

"Good morning, Ashton. The new mock-up of the boxes for the cassettes is on your desk."

"I hope they did not make any more unfortunate ass umptions."

Lawrence froze, studied my eyes to see if he should laugh. Finally he did, yet tepidly.

"I can always tell by the sudden change in this dump that you've decided to make an appearance." Jill filled the doorway to my office, all folded arms and girlish smirk.

"Like a predator entering a happy woods."

"You said it, Boss, I didn't. But listen, those obnoxious officiators in Chicago want to know if you want to stay at the Ambassador East again. The good news is that with just a few newspaper ads and two spots on cable TV, they say your show's already sold out. I still don't know why you just want to hit Chicago and not Detroit, Milwaukee, and Minneapolis as long as you're up there."

"I'm tired. I'm just not up to another big tour right now."

"Isn't Miss Pretty from St. Barths from Chicago?"

"You booked this show before I even met her. Should I take a peek inside the studio, or will I get so upset I might kill somebody?"

"If I were you I'd drive down to Carmel and have a good time with your adoring public. The president of the company himself is flying in tonight to fix the air-conditioning once and for all. Seems he got into heating and air-conditioning because of a Tony Robbins seminar, but now he says he likes you better."

"Well, tell him I'm going to put him in my next infomercial as an example how *not* to run a company if it's not up and running in a week. The bank isn't deferring the interest on our loans just because we had to cancel the first month's studio bookings."

"The CardioRider people and the Miracle Hair folks promise to reschedule, but we lost *The Psychic Showcase*. Their psychics are the worst in the bunch anyway."

"Jill, don't tell me you've called?"

"As a joke! Just once or twice. But one of Dionne Warwick's did tell me where to find a pearl earring I'd been looking for for weeks."

"My God, I thought I knew you."

"It's good to keep you guessing, Boss."

On tiptoes she kisses my cheek.

"You know, the entire staff is pressed to the windows, watching us, Jill."

"It's good to keep them guessing too."

Now let me concentrate on this stretch of PCH. I bought the Jag for these very curves.

Later July 5th

Now, in the center of Carmel, cars settle into a tight pack as gaggles of tourists first lean their heads into the streets on straining necks, then jump off the curb right in front of my bumper and scissor quickly across. As I finally near Bodhisattva Books, more and more of the tourists seem like fans, openly pointing now at my car. A wave of nervousness constricts my heart; the convertible is so exposed, it creates empty space around me that only highlights me even more than if I were walking among them. Thoughts of assassination—and I'm not talking about King's, X's, or the Kennedys'—always come to me at times like this.

Slowly passing the bookstore, I see it is mobbed, notice my old head shot, black-and-white, blown up as large as the top of a kitchen table, mounted on foam core and hovering in the middle of the storefront, twisting slightly, magically. I assume it is attached to the ceiling with fishing line, its movement from the air conditioner's breeze, yet it looks like magic from here. For all I know my Brazilians are behind this too.

Right Here, Right Now

I am readjusting my car in a reserved space behind the bookstore, the gravel popping under my wheels with a sound that I like, like the muffled clatter of underwater stones readjusting as the surf recedes. The man rushing toward me is Birkenstocked, bearded, and name-tagged.

See you later. I'll have to buy some new tapes somewhere for the drive back.

■ ■ ■

OK, here goes. So the guy in the Jesus sandals comes running out . . .

"Oh, goodness, Mr. Ashton Robinson, we saw you drive by and you should have seen how excited all the people inside the store got! They've been lining up for simply hours. Oh, before I forget, could you sign this copy for me?"

He was handing me the book as he trotted ahead of me to yank the steel handle of the glass door, then leaned way out of the way to hold the door open.

"Thank you."

As I entered I immediately noticed the eyes, then their grins, all aimed my way. For my first book, in some cities, I'd be lucky to sign maybe seven copies. Most of my officiators are from those original small batches.

"Hello, everybody! Thanks for coming out. Just let me get a drink of water and I'll be right back to sign all the books you can carry. Did I mention they make a great gift?"

They laughed. They always do. The bearded guy then introduced me to his staff in the back of the store. All were shy and most held their forearms pinned behind their backs. One of them rushed to me with a glass and a bottle of San Pellegrino. He tried to open it but couldn't, cursed himself, and tried again. Everyone else seemed to think this was some sort of disaster. I reached for the bottle and he relinquished it reluctantly. I pulled a shirttail out of my pants, covered the cap with the cloth, and turned. I didn't really need the shirttail but I didn't want the poor guy to feel like a wimp.

"That's for my next book. *Ashton's Household Hints.*"

They all laughed again, then in the silence immediately afterward, the bearded man, the manager, got their eyes and willed them back out on the floor before all the Moosewood vegetarian cookbooks, tales of Shirley MacLaine's past lives, and *How to Convert a Common Sauna into a Sioux Sweat Lodge* were swiped. I usually beg off doing signings at these New Age bookstores, but they do move a helluva lot of product.

Here are some highlights of the people I met.

A sweet, Jewish-looking retired lady: "First, I just wanted to say, I've thoroughly enjoyed all your books. They've really had a great impact on my life."

"Thank you, ma'am. Thank you very much."

The retired lady again: "Could you sign this one for me, Leslie? L-E-S-L-I-E. And this one is for my nephew. He's having the hardest time in school. His name is Sherman. S-H-E-R-M-A-N."

"There you go."

A skinny white woman with bony cheeks and frightened eyes: "Hi. Wow. I'm so nervous. Let me catch my breath. I wanted you to sign this and I wanted to ask you a quick question. I have all your audiocassettes and, of course, your books, and I am from Omaha, Nebraska. We are just here on vacation and saw the sign in the window and said, '*Gosh!*' This is my husband, Elroy. Well, you are always talking about '*Carpe diem*' and whatnot, so I was wondering if you need any help in Omaha, where we're from—oh, I just said that. We drove all the way to Denver to see you last time, but there are a lot of us Nebraskans who just couldn't make the trip."

"If you just contact PES, the number is in the back of the book. Ask for Officiator Relations. And thank you, thank you very much."

A *handsome Korean upper-middle-class woman:* "Oh, hi. You know, you are even better looking in real life. Could my sister over there take a quick picture of us?"

She stole a kiss off my cheek and didn't even buy a book.

Then a white, forty-something middle manager stepped to the plate. Like a lot of the guys who come up to me, he looked around the rest of the line, caught my eye, and smirked as if saying, "What a bunch of kooks! You and me, we're the only normal guys in the room." Then he said, "Hello, Ashton. Can I call you that? You know, I've tried the no-money-down real estate, the self-hypnosis, the nine-hundred-numbers brokering, you name it, but I've got to say PES is the only thing that really works. It's just common sense and all, but you put it all together in a way that really helps. I ain't a millionaire or nothing, probably never will be, but I don't know, maybe now I sometimes try a little harder, thanks to you."

"Why thank you, sir. That means a lot to me, it really does."

Then there was this whisper: "You think you're such hot shit. My wife thinks you're such hot shit, but you ain't such hot shit. Can't even comb your goddamn monkey woolen hair."

The man was stepping back through the crowd before I'd really understood what he was saying. For the first two sentences I was just nodding and smiling, just half listening for the pause where I would say, "Thank you. Thank you very much." Ask his name, sign, smile, and draw the next one forward with my eyes. I don't think I've ever had that happen to me before. And why today of all days?

White male retiree: "Poopsie."

"Excuse me?"

"Could you sign this one to Poopsie?"

Then the really wild part happened:

"Wow, uh, Ashton, we haven't had crowds this big since Dr. Deepak Chopra came to town."

The manager drew the small bush of keys from his pocket and slipped one into the front door's lock. The rest of his staff was huddled around the card table I had signed on, now overturned and looking helpless on its back on the floor. None of them seemed to be able to figure out how to collapse the legs.

"In appreciation for coming down I'd like you to pick out any book you'd like. Anything at all, except the big picture books."

"Thank you, but I . . ."

The only books I can stand in these stores are the ones on exotic sex, but the illustrations are always sensitive pencil drawings of balding, pudgy, middle-aged couples. Then there are the crystalology sections, the birth and rebirth aisles, veganism, tarot, cabalism, yoga, healing, parapsychology . . .

I was just formulating my excuse for not taking a book when my eyes somehow locked onto *The Meaning of Visions,* by V. C. L. Swiney, D.Sc.I. One copy, yellowed and fuzzed with dust, lying flat on the top of an aisle. Only someone my height could ever have noticed it. Only someone my height who the night before maybe made out with a Brazilian shape shifter.

The book was heavier than it looked, and as I pulled it down, floating gray milkweeds of dust gravitated to my dreads. As my thumb cascaded the pages, the smell of rotting cloves seeped deep into my nose. What? A chill suddenly tickled me. I could've sworn I'd just flipped past a photo of my Brazilian! I flipped back, then forth, then paged through one by one, licking my fingers and pinching each page hard to make sure, but it's an old book, and anyway the photo I was sure I'd seen was in color. It seemed to be the only used book in the store.

"Did you find anything?"

"Just this old one."

"Old? We don't have any old boo—Oh! Old Doc Swiney! He left us crates of his works. That was his last one, but I think his peyote book is his masterpiece. Are you sure that's all you want? Why don't you take this *Tantric Sex and the Two Hour Orgasm?* It's one of our best-sellers. My brother and sister-in-law posed for it."

"Uh, no thanks."

"What the hey. Take both."

I thanked the manager with the sex book pinched under my arm at the same time I was trying to read this Swiney guy. The manager was unlocking the back door.

"Are you sure I can't tempt you with dinner? There is an Italian place down the street with fabulous gnocchi."

"I'd love to, but I'm afraid I really have to get back to Santa Cruz."

On each turn of PCH, the tires shriek. I can't wait to get home and see what ol' Swiney has to say. If I drove an automatic, I'd almost try to read him in the car.

■ ■ ■

It seems Mr. Swiney has written about a dozen other books prior, all for this Burning Eye Press. The other titles seem standard

Trey Ellis

New Age fare: *The Egyptian Mystery Schools, The Everyday Trance, The Peyote Cults of Chiapas and Oaxaca.* And this dense book full of charts and footnotes would seem more mysterious if it were at least seventy years old; however, the copyright is just . . . wait a minute, I just saw it . . . 1962.

I was born in 1962.

Swiney was a soi-disant doctor of scientific inquisition (D.Sc.I.), an obscure medical international brotherhood he himself revived that is dedicated to unlocking the so-called seventy-eight mysteries of the mind. *The Meaning of Visions* was supposed to be only the first volume of a series, but it turned out to be his last. Here's what he says in his introduction:

> Visions and Visitations are brought on by drugs, dementia, sleep deprivation, or starvation, yet these preconditions in no way negate the "validity," the "reality," if you will, of the images viewed. Just because the poet Samuel Taylor Coleridge was "high as a kite" on the opiate laudanum, does that annul the beauty—and the truth—of his masterpiece "Kublai Khan"?
>
> I myself have experienced the glory of "Visions" and "Visitations" under various combinations of the above preconditions. My research persuades me, and I trust that it will persuade you too, gentle reader, that "The Vision" and "The Visitation" are some of the only ways we have of linking our consciousness with that of the "Higher" one, the Divine Puppetmaster, if you will.

I don't know what the hell I was expecting. Perhaps a pat on the back and someone saying, "There, there, you're not going crazy. Just next time go a little easier on the expired cough syrup and catch a mellower buzz." It's funny. I would like to toss the book but can't. I feel a sudden, silly hint of fear in my chest, like the hint of sickness you feel the day before a fever. If you run away, it never goes away, I used to say in my very first lectures at the coffeehouse. Sure, it's a platitude, but it's true.

I'm an atheist, pretty much, so what am I afraid of? Of becoming born again, that's what. Of sincerely grabbing the arms of strangers, staring zombielike into their eyes, and breathily whispering, "Have you welcomed him yet into your heart?"

I mean, I guess I do believe there is something more to the soul than the brain, something more to the world than dirt, trees, glass, and steel. I just don't think the answers reside in any book, crystal, or deck of cards. I'll read some more Swiney tonight, but I can't stay up too late. My flight to Chicago leaves San Jose at eight. God knows what might come to me tonight in my dreams.

July 6

"You've been with us before, why, haven't you, Mr. Robinson?"

I held out my jacket—my absolutely favorite Romeo Gigli—and the stewardess plucked it from me carefully and slipped a wooden hanger inside its shoulders.

"Yes, but I haven't flown to Chicago in a few months."

"But I remember."

Chiding, her skinny, white, and French-tipped finger metronomed at me. She flirted like the perky young drill team leader I bet she used to be.

"Did you really advise Chairman Dan, talk him into letting us wear sneakers on the job?"

"Oh, he gives me more credit than I deserve, but I have been working with him for several years now."

"Well, next time you see him, tell him Darlena out of Chicago deserves a raise."

I drew my notepad out of my back pocket and started writing.

"What are you writing?"

"That Darlena out of Chicago deserves a raise."

Right Here, Right Now

"No!"

"Take a look."

I twisted my wrist so she could see the inside of the pad.

"I was just kidding."

"So, you don't want a raise?"

I started to line out the message.

"No! Gosh, darlin', don't do that. That's not what I meant at all. I want a raise. We all do. Had the same contract for three years now."

"I'll put in a good word."

She squeezed my shoulder in exactly the place where it was tight, and my head involuntarily leaned and rubbed against her wrist like a cat arching against an ankle. Her hand involuntarily started petting my dreads.

"Oh! My Gosh! Sorry . . ."

She swayed away quickly, reaching forward to seat back after seat back to steady herself. I'm pretty sure she wasn't rubbing them for luck.

It's fun broadcasting to you like this, live from thirty thousand feet. I was going to hold off till I got to the hotel, but two CFO types here in first with me are mumbling into their own micro-recorders, so what the hell? I'm now under the blanket and re-clined into a zigzag. I'm almost done with Swiney—what a book! I just crammed it into the kangaroo pouch on the seat back in front of me, pushed off my shoes, and rolled an ear over the tiny pillow, ready to nap.

I can't believe I remembered about that coma thing when I was a kid. Mama hates to talk about it. I wonder if anything weird happened to me back then. Only one way to find out.

[Fumbling, then dialing sounds.]

"Mama. It's me."

"Baby? What's the matter? Why you sound so strange?"

"I'm just in a plane, Mama. On my way to Chicago."

"This must be costing you a king's ransom. Call back later from a regular telephone."

"It's all right, Mama. I just wanted to ask you about the time I was in a coma. I was three, right?"

"Oh, why you want and drag up that mess?"

"How long was I out?"

"The worst four days of my entire life. What's wrong, baby? You feel all right?"

"And they never knew what was wrong with me?"

"It just happened, then it stopped. Most things God does we don't rightly understand. Now hang up and call me from a normal phone."

■ ■ ■

Airplane pilot: "Uh, ladies and gentlemen, good morning, this is your captain speaking. I've turned on the seat-belt sign as we begin our final descent into Chicago O'Hare . . ."

My eyes just opened right as the images of some dream broke apart and melted instantly, like water flicked onto a hot griddle. I concentrated, trying to remember *anything*, but this only seemed to drive the images into even darker corners.

■ ■ ■

I was yawning as Susan and Len Dawbridge, the Chicago officiators, rushed me, took my bag, and worked my hand.

Right Here, Right Now

"Good news! Ticketron says you've sold out the Days Inn's Majestic Windy City Room but the hotel's opening up their Regal DuSable Room next door so the spillovers can watch you on TV monitors!"

Everything is exclamation points with these two. Luckily, my hearing was still buried from the flight, so I could barely understand a word they said. Something about how so many regulars would love to meet me for dinner or coffee or something, how it's a shame I'm here only two nights, and something about how the Chicago Bears are sending their offensive line to tonight's seminar.

The driver took my garment bag from Len and laid it in the trunk. Len and Susan stood smiling at me identically as I ducked inside the car. I told them thanks, told them I'd see them tonight. They pursued the driver to the front of the limo, speaking at him slowly, overmouthing the words: "He, needs, to, be, at, the, Days Inn, Hyde Park, by, the, university, by, seven-forty-five, no later. The seminar begins at eight o'clock, understand?"

"They friends of yours, or what?"

The limo driver talked into his rearview mirror as if it were a microphone.

"They, um, work with me."

"So what is it you do, if you don't mind me asking?"

"I'm a motivational speaker."

"Like that freaky-looking asshole Tony Robbins? Or, or that black guy with the hai—Hey, that's you!"

"Yea, that's me. The freaky-looking black asshole."

"I wasn't talking about you. I was talking about him. What the fuck's up with that chin? He looks like that goddamn Lurch, you know, from the James Bond movies."

113

I told him he meant Lurch from *The Addams Family*, who went on to play the character Jaws in a few James Bond films and who, like Tony Robbins, appears to have suffered from the pituitary disorder acromegaly as a child. My head against the cool, dark window, I looked out at a car next to us. Their lane was not moving either. The two men, commuters in dress shirts and ties, their jackets hanging from the hooks over the backseats, were staring at the densely smoked glass of my window. I thought I was safely invisible till I realized I was so close to the glass that they could see me clearly. I quickly withdrew to the middle of the backseat and the dopes kept looking where I used to be. I gave them both the finger and cackled like a kid.

"I don't mean no harm, and I gotta admit I ain't seen much of your program, but you live in this humongous house, right, right on the water, all because you tell people how to do better. Well, my high school football coach did the same thing. We were southern Illinois champs and lost all-state by a fucking field goal. Well, Coach Peel was this amazing man on the field and off. Two of the guys on our team went pro, a couple are doctors now, lawyers, one's an anchorman in Los Angeles. Anyway, the point is, Coach Peel did what you do, only, last year he had to sell his house and me and the other guys had to chip in just so he could keep up his note on this used Winnebago he moved into full-time. Sure, he drinks a bit—now—but can you blame him?"

"I couldn't agree with you more. A lot of what I do I learned from Doc Kirschwasser, my old high school wrestling coach."

"Exactly my poin—"

I closed my eyes and rotated myself onto my back to cut him off. I needed to be alone for a little while. I watched the clouds pass, and then the skinny chrome smokestack of a truck. Out of its round metal lid, hinged in the back, it spoke in smoke. Sometime later I fell asleep.

The limo stopped, almost rolling me off the seat. The heavy door opened and all was instantly bright. The bellman at the Ambassador East stood at attention, waiting for me to right myself. My brain had to catch up to the sudden skip in time. I'm safe in my suite now and I'm gonna take a real nap. Over and out.

■ ■ ■

It's almost three and I'm still wiped out. The towels here are so thick they make you smile every time you dry off. Oh, look, on the TV is Johnetta Sparks. I met her when she was doing sports in Tallahassee, but always knew she'd end up in a larger market. I think she might've even been an officiator for a little while. We had a little thing going on whenever I was in the Panhandle.

That was then and this is now. I'm dialing Nikki Kennedy at work. I have a late lunch with Jenny Jones, at Oprah's restaurant, Eccentric, of all places. But I would love to take Nikki out to dinn—

"Hello. Could you connect me with Nikki Kennedy, please . . . ? Yes, this is Ashton."

Her company's hold music is a local radio station, and the DJ is hawking Club Soirée.

"Gentlemen, no jeans or athletic insignias, please. Ladies, dress to impress." Here, you listen.

[DJ returns, then a song by Boyz II Men.]
Nikki Kennedy: "This is Nikki."

"And this is Ashton."

"It is you."

"I told the receptionist."

"I know. I just thought you might've been my girlfriend, playing games."

"Afraid not."

"I was hoping you'd call."

"Have dinner with me tonight."

"Wow. Sure. I just have to make a phone call. Where do you want to go?"

"It's your town. Where have you always wanted to go?"

"I read about this new Brazilian—"

"Of course. Are you coming to hear me tonight?"

"Yeah."

"We will need to eat early. Pick me up at six. I'm at the—"

"Ambassador East. I know."

"Oh. Well, see you tonight."

"See you tonight."

I can't believe the hotel gave out my information. Jill keeps telling me to check in under an alias, but I would feel silly. I was crazy to have called her. Did you hear how excited she was on the phone? Johnetta would have been easier. "Johnetta, I just got into town, turned on the TV, and there you were . . . ! Yes, I know it's been years. I know, I know, I'm terrible." She already knows the drill and could probably have slipped out to see me right after the traffic update. With Nikki, I will patiently explain the impossibility of a future commitment and she will nod and say, "Of course! Me neither!" Yet the next thing you know she'll end up like that German game-show host—Ute?—quitting her job and materializing on my doorstep. What a mess. I should call back and cancel. Right after I finish this nap . . .

■ ■ ■

Right Here, Right Now

I am still so damn tired! That's probably why I had the hallucination. Swiney says they almost always accompany mental exhaustion. Of course, he also writes that the supreme creative force in the universe, known to Christians as the Holy Spirit, manifests these visions to the chosen few he is calling upon to steer the world down a given path to the supreme goal he will reveal only when the time is right. But besides that, the book is not as kooky as you might think. His actual accounts of visions and visitations throughout history are fairly interesting. For example, I had no idea that George Washington claimed he was visited by the ghost of Ramses II on the eve of the battle of Yorktown and it was the pharaoh's advice that propelled him to victory against Cornwallis.

Oops. My phone is chirping like a robotic bird, the little red light is fluttering. It must be her.

"Yes . . . ? Thank you. Tell her I'll be right down."

Room key, wallet, index cards, mints. It's show time, folks.

Later July 6th

Jesus Christ, let me fill you in quick before I forget anything. Jesus Christ! I'm whispering here in a stall in the restaurant's bathroom. No, I'm not crazy. Believe me. Just listen.

Back at my hotel, I opened my door and there was Nikki hurriedly tugging down her dress. It was a nice kiss, warmed me like a drink. I'd forgotten how sweetly she blushes. I called the concierge and had her dismiss the driver because I thought it'd be more fun to drive with Nikki.

Anyway, we finally got to the restaurant. The valet elegantly drew her out of the driver's seat, handed her a stub, and dove into the car. We entered behind three gay men, identically balding, and two were shirtless but wearing vests. The noise of talking and forks hitting plates and of a beautiful samba was so sharp and so sudden it felt like important steps were skipped between the quiet of the parking lot and this place.

What a place! Palm trees rise from the floor and on toward the glass panes of the high skylights. Immense painted billboards, one of Carmen Miranda and one for the movie *Orfeu Negro* (Black Orpheus), cover the rear walls.

Right Here, Right Now

So, as soon as we sat a ponytailed waiter asked us what we wanted to drink. I ordered *caipirinhas* in Portuguese and he ignited with joy. He asked me how I learned Portuguese, said I looked like I could be Brazilian. Then he looked at Nikki and yammered at her in Portuguese, said she looked exactly like his cousin Ymelda.

As they were talking something caught my eye far across the expanse of restaurant. A midget! Swear to God! But white, clambering up on a chair with, no shit, Claudia Schiffer and David Copperfield!! I almost shat myself.

You hallucinate about a Brazilian midget and a few days later end up in a trendy Brazilian restaurant in Chicago with a midget, an overrated German supermodel, and her gold-chained magician fiancé with skin the color and consistency of a sun-dried lizard! Of course, Swiney says coincidences are just worldly manifestations of the unseen. [Cough.] Damnit! Not that again. Not now!

So, I couldn't let the moment pass, I had to try something. I closed my eyes, reared back my head, and faked a loud sneeze.

"Aaaaaaa-shay!"

The waiter looked at me strangely, then hurried to the bar for our drinks. The busboy arrived with water and bread, and again I faked a sneeze.

"Aaaaaaa-shay!"

The line of water falling from the pitcher missed my glass, shattered off my plate like noise off a drum, and wet us all. He repeated apologies while quickly lifting away the plate and the puddle it held. He retreated to the waiter station and I could see him excitedly chattering with the others, who were all now nodding and pointing my way. All the while Nikki had set her head strangely and was watching me.

"That's a strange way of sneezing," she said.

"It, uh . . . protects the glands from strain without, um, spitting all over yourself."

"Really?"

"They've been doing it for years in Europe."

"Ashay! Like that?"

She said it, and just then a neighboring busboy, older than the rest, perked up his ears too. The waiter returned with our *caipirinhas*.

"On the house," he said. I asked him why and he grabbed my menu and turned it over. At first I thought the page was empty, and just as I was about to ask the waiter to explain, I noticed one word printed in a corner, in typeface as tiny as a photo credit's. *Axe!* That's when I understood! The X in Portuguese is pronounced *sh*, and every vowel is voiced. So *axe* is not English for a long-handled hatchet but . . . *aaaa-shay!* That's why I couldn't find it in the dictionary.

Then the waiter asked me if I wanted to know about *axe**
and I nodded like mad. He called over the old busboy, but shyly—the old guy must be in his fifties—and whispered to him. The busboy then ordered something called *moqueca de peixe* from the waiter for all three of us and he pulled up a chair. He doesn't look like my midget, not really, but he is short, not more than five-four, and dark, dark black, and has short, straight black hair like an Indian's. The waiter left and the busboy quickly hopped back up himself. He said either, "I have to punch out,

---

* A Brazilian Portuguese term imported from Africa that roughly translates as "spirit" or "power." It is a central concept to the Afro-Brazilian religion of Candomblé, their version of voodoo.

wait a minute," or—get this—"I have to punch out, *I've been expecting you.*" He was speaking so damn fast, and *esperar* in Portuguese can mean both. As soon as he left I ran in here to catch you up and collect my thoughts. Nikki must be freaking out. I'll put you right in my breast pocket. I don't want you to miss a word!

[One minute, forty-six seconds of rustling, restaurant chatter.]

Nikki Kennedy: "[Unintelligible] . . . all right? I was [unintelligible] worried. Don't you have to be at the Days Inn soon?"

"Yeah, I know. Sorry about all this. I've just always been curious about this *axe* thing and maybe I can incorporate it into my wor— Wait. I don't feel so goo—"

[Nikki Kennedy screams. Loud thump.]

Nikki Kennedy: "Oh, my God! Ashton?! Ashton?! Wake up! Somebody call a doctor! You! Please get some help!"

[Forty-five seconds of shuffling and confusion.]

Unknown physican: "I'm a doctor. Goddamnit! Give us some room . . . What's this in his pocket?"

[Rustling. Then tape is clicked off.]*

---

* Nikki Kennedy could shed much more light on this episode but she has repeatedly refused all requests to be interviewed. In fact, her attorneys vigorously attempted to block the publication of these transcripts and her Chicago-based, Robinson-inspired "Now House" is the largest in the U.S.

More July 6th

I hide you in the cup of my hand, my lips right against you so I can whisper as Nikki and I ride up the hotel elevator to the ballroom. She keeps staring worriedly, and each time I tell her everything's fine and smile, she just looks even more petrified. I'll try one more time.

"It's fine, Nikki. Really. It's more than fine. It's marvelous! I'm just dictating a few notes to myself so I don't forget. Don't worry, I'm almost done."

Nikki Kennedy: "[Unintelligible] . . . hospital?"

"I told you, I have absolutely never felt better in my whole cotton-picking life! C'mon, we're late!"

OK, so now the elevator doors are opening. Wow. I feel the air of discontent before I see the seminarians all leaning against the walls, mumbling. I'm rushing through them now and they stand quickly, track me with their eyes, hurriedly screw out their cigarettes, and are swept inside behind me as if I were wearing a long robe and they were all standing on my train.

Len and Susan Dawbridge are pinned in a corner by an angry mob of what looks like realtors—a disturbingly large percentage of my audiences. My body is homing for the podium without any help from my brain. I'm feeling more than hearing the murmuring throng subside. OK, OK, now Len and Susan see me and here they go, here they go; they gasp, then look behind me for a culprit, find Nikki, and beam at her their hate. I'm now stepping in front of their eye line and stare at them . . . *There.* They've turned away. I hear a rush for seats behind me as I step onto the riser and—oh, shit—I left my index cards in the breast pocket of my jacket, which right this minute lies neatly on the floor of Nikki's trunk. Oh, I get it. Elvis Costello was wrong when he sang, "Accidents will happen. It's only hit and run." There is no such thing. I turn around and see eyes everywhere fixed on my face. Let me lay you next to the mike. I'm gonna wing it and blow their fucking minds. Look at them all staring at me. They have no idea.

—Am I late . . . ? [Pause. Audience mumbles.] I said, am I late? [Pause.] Some of you are shaking your heads no! Of course I am late! Let me check my watch. Damn! Almost an hour late! You've paid ninety of your hard-earned dollars and you should all be pissed that now you'll not finish till midnight and probably not get home till one! And there's that presentation for the boss at eight-thirty tomorrow morning, that breakfast with your best client. You know what I say to all of that? I . . . don't . . . care. I don't care because this is more important. Tonight, ladies and germs, I am going to change your life.

—I know, I know, for years I have said just the opposite: I'm not here to change your life, just to guide it, reshape it, I used to say. Bullshit. Your lives need changing, not reshaping. All ours do. Mine more than anyone else's in this tacky room. And by the end of this night my life will have changed more than anyone else's—if I have anything to do with it. And I do. And I do not . . .

Trey Ellis

—You see, over the past few days I have had some amazing revelations, and you Chicagoans are the very first to hear this startling news: everything I have taught all these years, everything in the books, the audiotapes, the TV shows, and in lectures like these has been dead wrong . . .

[Crowd murmurs.]

—I'm not being overdramatic for effect. I'm going to tell you things tonight that will shock you. Many—perhaps *most*—of you will not believe me, will leave grumbling for a refund that I will not provide. The French experimental novelist Alain Robbe-Grillet wrote this: "The stammering new-born work will always be regarded as a monster even by those who find the experiment fascinating." The same can be said for new philosophies. For years I have talked about stating an objective and realizing it, about the analytical assessment of risk so the unknown will not remain mythically unassailable. But when have you ever heard me speak about the soul? When have you ever heard me speak of the human spirit and what lies *beyond* the human spirit. What I am talking about, boys and girls, is *axe*.

[Twenty-five seconds of silence.]

—Where was I? Forgive me, I was just in a coma for the second time in thirty years, so this whole consciousness thing is still a little new to me . . . Oh, yeah. The reason I did not speak of the soul until now is because until now I didn't believe in it. I was the secular humanist of secular humanists. God wasn't just dead for me, he never existed. Human potential was all. *"I am the captain of my ship, the master of my soul."* I actually used to quote that drivel! Then the night before last a sexy Brazilian midget showed me that all this surrounding us is as illusory as the set of a road-company production of *Damn Yankees* . . .

—You in the back. Good-bye, sir, ma'am. You are the first to

124

leave tonight, but I promise you, you will not be the last. Terrifying things are going to be said tonight, ancient things. And all of us have spent our lives being trained in cowardice, being trained so that precisely at the moment the higher truth is revealed to us, we may cowardly rationalize it away, relegate it to a fun fact, a quirk. It was just a dream, we say. I was drunk, I was stoned, the cough syrup had expired . . .

—How arrogant we are to feel we control all we survey. How unimaginative! How sad the world would really be if all miracles were explained away. I remember as a child watching *Hollywood Squares*. Remember how the show specialized in strange-but-true information, how it reveled in bursting your romantic bubble? "True or false?" I remember the host Peter Marshall asking Elke Sommer. "Dogs lick human skin not to show affection but because they need the salt." Ms. Sommer, God bless her, said, "False." An ardent animal lover, she could not bring herself to believe that! Yet the answer, according to science, was true! Are we better, or worse off for knowing that? I say worse off. I say the shining beacon of life dimmed a little after that broadcast . . .

[Scattered laughter from a few in the audience.]

—It is not funny. At all. You see, we laugh off miracles, we laugh off the divine when it presents itself to us, but like a butterfly or hummingbird, if you can't hold its attention, the divine just flits off to a more receptive, a more *flowering* mind . . .

—Something important is going to come out of all this; the world just might get fixed! We know that in times of war, humankind is capable of cooperating and completing seemingly impossible tasks. We know that one-hundred-and-ten-pound mothers are capable of superhuman strength to lift the overturned bus off the pinned legs of their young sons. Yet what is our

response? Oh yeah . . . neat, but hey, I'm late for work. WHAT
MORE PROOF DO YOU WANT . . . !!!? Any questions . . . ?

[Eighteen seconds of silence.]

—Look, everybody, I know this is all brand new. I know it is a
lot to swallow right now, especially since you did not come, did
not *pay* to come hear about the hidden nature of the universe
and how, together, we can untap its mysteries and fulfill our evo-
lutionary destiny as sentient terrestrialists. Yet this information
just crystallized for me tonight at dinner (at this wonderful new
restaurant—try the *moqueca*, it's to die for). Anyway, I could not,
in good conscience, keep it bottled up inside. If you have been to
my lectures before, you know that I am usually extremely precise
and well structured. I have usually already given the same lecture
in dozens of other cities, and the kinks—and the spontaneity, I
am afraid—are all gone. This talk tonight, however, is very much
an improvisation, a work in progress.

—Anyway, the crux of my message tonight is this: all you
have is what you have. I mean, what would you do if you were
already in heaven? What if heaven were this overlit, tackily decorated ballroom in a midpriced hotel! What if you had nothing
more to hope for, ever? What would you do? You couldn't kill
yourself because, hey, you're already in heaven; nothing would
change. You'd be disappointed for a second, sure. I mean, where
the hell are the clouds? Then what would you do? You'd have
only one choice: to keep living. To go back to work, back to your
family, back to the Bahamas for ten days every winter. Eventually you'd start making every moment count because each and
every moment was as good as it could ever get. Right here . . .
right no—

—Oh shit! Now I get it. I get what she was telling me naked

by the pool. "You've been so close to it for so many years," she said. "Without knowing it *you've even been saying the right word to release it*, but never in quite the right way." THANK YOU, BRAZILIAN BEAUTY! I'm so glad you guys are here to witness this.

—All right, all right, let me think for a second . . . [Twenty-two seconds of silence.] OK, I think I hear what she means. Everybody close your eyes. Close them tight. Deep breath. Deep, deep breath. And hold. Now let it out. No, wait. I got it. I remember this from a yoga class I took in college because all the cutest girls were there in leotards. Take a deep breath again, but through your nose. And hold. Then on the exhale, all together, we're going to say the only word that ever really matters . . . "Now." Ready . . . "*Now* . . ." Come on again. That was pathetic. Really make it round and long. Inhale and . . . "*Nooooow* . . ." [Still only a few in the audience chant along.] Better, but still weak. Trust me on this, it's gonna be great. Again . . . "*NOW* . . . !" [Many more people joined in.] Good! Again and again, with me. Fifty times. "*Now* . . ." Inhale. "*Now* . . ." Inhale. "*Now* . . ." [The audience joins in. We also hear people rustling and the doors opening and closing for four minutes, thirty seconds.]

—Wow. Where'd everybody go? I could hear them leaving, but I had no idea they were so many. Hey! You big guys at the door! You must be the Bears. Too bad. I feel this new program will have tremendous applications for professional athletes.

—Anyway, the rest of you, how do you feel? I feel great! "Now." What a lovely word! Hell, what lovely three letters! Backwards you get "won." Sideways you get "own"! Just add a *K* and you get "know," which shares the same pronunciation as the little two-lettered demon of negativity but is actually the *second*-most-important word in the English-speaking universe. Put them together and you get "Know *now* . . ."

—Hello? Yes, come on in, fellas . . . What time is it? Oh, my God, I had no idea. Ladies and gentlemen, the maintenance crew has to do their job. But let me ask you all one thing. Would you like to hear more?

[Only a dozen or so people can be heard cheering.]

—We should move to a lounge and let these men get to work so they can go home.

I'm stepping down from the podium and heading for the front doors. There are about fifty left. Not bad . . . Uh-oh. They're rushing away and muttering. Not all of them, maybe, but the lion's share. Have I made a mistake? Is it too late to go back to my old *"Carpe-diem-and-ask-for-that-raise"* routine? A rumor would circulate that one night in Chicago I went nuts, but in the rest of the country I would be fine. God, I don't want to be poor again, bartending again at Club Med, making Sex on the Beaches for leering divorcees at the pool bar, or making milk scream in the cappuccino machine of some grungy coffeehouse for five bucks an hour. I don't want to start all over again; I just want to tell the world what I've learned.

The small handful that believe me are smiling at the door. There's Nikki, an elderly white man in a suit, another black woman with long braids, a short couple, a few others, and up front, the Dawbridges, still here, staring. But are they really all with me, or just sad that I've lost my mind? I must go slowly, resist the temptation to be *too* enthusiastic, to turn shrill and *truly* crazed. That is the only difference between a homeless lunatic with a Catholic girls' school kilt wrapped around his head muttering loudly to himself about how Charles Nelson Reilly has invaded his brain, and Christ. Christ stayed calm, said his piece, and if you weren't with it, *Pax vobiscum* just the same. Time for the soft sell, time to Barry Whiten my voice.

—Don't mind me and this microcassette recorder. Nikki here can tell you I'm glued to it. At first I thought I was just taking notes for a fluffy book about a year in my life. Little did I know that it was preparation to record something much, much more profound. My staff back home is already used to my little eccentricity.

I push the bar on the steel door and hold it for the others. As they pass me they steal strange glances. Nikki is last and at her I smile, but she only hurries past. What? Did I just cut a fart?

The bartender is gone and the bar is dim. I lead them to a corner where the brown velour couches meet and brown velour hassocks squat like mushrooms before them. I sit in the corner and they're jostling for seats around me.

—Where was I?

His listeners: "The Brazilian supermodel-slash-midget was talking right into your ear." "And you shiver." "Yeah, shivered on one whole side of you." "But didn't really know exactly what he was saying."

—This time I couldn't laugh it off. I didn't awaken on my lounge chair, so there was no way I could confuse this with a dream. You know, friends, I used to believe that I was just like everyone else, only perhaps a little more driven. But after these past few days, I think I am slowly coming to the conclusion that I am not like everyone else at all, but burdened with an awesome responsibility . . .

—How rare are the times that we listen to our hearts, or find ourselves truly in sync with ourselves. Isn't that strange? Shouldn't we *always* listen to our hearts, *always* be in sync with our souls? Or if not quite always, shouldn't the out-of-sync times be no more than two or three days a year—perhaps as often as we have a cold? What I'm saying is almost everyone of us in the planet, at least every one of us in the West, has a chronic cold of the soul, yet we ignore it, let it persistently degrade us, till we forget what it ever meant to be well . . .

I'm trying to swallow, but my tongue is too dry, too large for my throat. Past the maintenance man in his orange jumper, his humming electric buffer hovering over the tiles on the floor; and through the front doors, where *Days Inn* is spelled out on the glass, backwards for me; past all that, I see the black sky warming to a lush blue.

—That is it. I was not sure if I was brave enough to share this with the world. I knew I would lose most, if not all, of the audience. But you brave few, you open-minded few, I am so proud of each of you. I can only hope that tomorrow we do not each return to our separate lives as if this night never happened.

His listeners: "No!" "Of course not!" "Never!"

—I leave today, but if you all give me your telephone numbers, I promise to call tomorrow to tell you what our next move will be. If we know and do nothing, we are vastly inferior to those who live and die in ignorance.

I pass around my notepad and my Mont Blanc (a gift from RJR Nabisco) and they solemnly write their names, then pass it down. It reminds me of the Last Supper, only this is just the beginning. Should I tell them? No. I don't know if *I'm* ready for that comparison yet, so I'd bet they're not.

—Oh, and let me give my home number to each of you.

I write it down seventeen times on seventeen sheets—the *exact* number of pages left in my pad. I snap each page out and hand it to Len Dawbridge, on my left, who passes it down.

Right Here, Right Now

Man's voice: "Any of y'all hungry? The cook should be coming in about now, but if he's late it don't really matter. I can open up the kitchen and whip up some scrambled eggs myself."

Glen, the night manager, just said that. He marched on us several hours ago, with a security guard, to ask us to leave. Though he came in on the story halfway, he now seems as converted as the others.

July 7th

We're just pushing back from the gate. A first-class seat used to feel like my second home, but this odd morning it feels odd to me. Nikki drove me to the airport. What an interesting ride.

"I'm scared, Ashton," she said. "The dinner, the seminar, it's all so much to take. It's all so different from St. Barths."

Though there was little traffic, she drove so slowly, and at such a constant slow speed it was almost as if we were being pulled through a car wash. She strangled the steering wheel and tried to lock her eyes forward, but they kept wandering off toward me.

"I'm scared too. I was very successful in my past life. Giving that all up will be difficult. Believe me, I was pretty happy when I was ignorant and rich."

"It's just that . . . at dinner . . . it was all so scary. Then after you came to and the doctor really wanted you to wait for the ambulance . . . Then when my friends and all the rest of them walked out, I felt like shouting at them, 'Don't you fools understand history is being made!!!'"

"You can lead a horse to church, but you can't make it pray."

"You're an amazing man."

Right Here, Right Now

Before my Awakening I assumed we were going to make love. I meant to scan that sex book they gave me in Carmel for a few pointers and hole up with her in my hotel room till the car came to take me to the airport. Instead, I discovered the meaning of my life.

At the curb, finally, I leaned to kiss her good-bye and she gasped.

"Listen to me carefully, Nikki. Do not be afraid of me. Don't ever be afraid of me. Never will I do anything to hurt you."

I outstretched my hand; my fingers brushed her cheek, then continued back to caress the back of her head as I drew her to me and kissed her again, softly. Suddenly, the roots of my hair crackled, electricity pulsed through me, stole my breath. I opened my eyes and saw tears streaking her cheeks. This is all so much bigger than I am.

I carefully backed out of the car, quietly closed the door. Instantly I was amid the craziness of the airport, the repetitive taped announcements, the endless, overlapping rounds of hellos and good-byes, hugs as far as the eye can see, gangs of stewards and stewardesses towing their little rectangular bags on tiny black wheels. Airports are my second home, but I'm now apart from this one that used to be one of my favorites. I used to love to browse the magazines, the local sports teams' tacky souvenirs piled on tables, the food vendors and their tiny carts with awful names like the Sunny Bunnery, Chocolate Chip Yard, or How's Da Chowda? But suddenly I couldn't stand the bullshit. I wanted to topple their tacky little carts, trample their soft pretzels, explode their Louisiana hot links under the weight of my feet, shouting, "Your sleepwalking desecrates the magic of life!"

I've got to find a way to break the news to Jill and the staff. I've got to immediately pull the infomercials and stop taking any more orders for that bile I was pumping out. I'll try to help the staff find work somewhere else. Man, it would be wonderful if I could convert Jill and a few of my favorites to *axe*. But it's a long shot. Jill flirted with dianetics for a hot second in college, and afterward she was so disgusted with herself, she promised never again to be that weak.

Unless, of course, my conversion wears off by the time I step off the plane. The Chicagoans will call me tomorrow at home and I'll politely put them off, tell them to lie low till the time is right. Then I will stop returning their calls. The amazing experiences of the past few days will recede like memorable dreams, no more powerful than powerful scenes from my favorite movies, and just as removed from myself.

God, I hope not. I hope I can keep finding greatness within myself, push myself to the historic status of . . . First things first. If it were so easy to enlighten the world, you wouldn't be the first person since . . . Enough already!

■　■　■

First class is nearly empty, but I think this guy sleeping, the one with his lips twisted and mashed against the plastic of his oval window, is that guy who directs all those silly, treacly comedies, what's-his-name. John Hughes. I think he was on the plane the last time I flew back from Chicago.

Amazing, this book. Not the Swiney one but *Tantric Sex and the Two Hour Orgasm*. I'm glad the plane isn't very full, otherwise I'd be a little self-conscious about the illustrations. Sure, the models are balding and their bodies average, but some of these positions? Here's my favorite. I didn't know it was called the Piercing Tiger. I only wish it didn't make my leg fall asleep.

Right Here, Right Now

Wait a minute . . . here's something . . . Look at the spiritual-ism the author brings to sex. She might as well be writing about *axe*. Interesting . . . the basic gist is to stay highly aroused without coming, to control the groin-centered sexual feelings and through deep-breathing meditation raise them up through your seven chakras. The bottom one is the groin, the top one is the top of your head. Oh shit, listen to this:

> In the highest orgasmic state informants report a light-like beam blasting from the top of their skull. With prac-tice one can sustain this "blasting" for hours at a time. One informant—an inmate at an Illinois men's correc-tional facility—reported a constant orgasmic explosion for three continuous days and nights of well-lubricated self-pleasuring.

When he gets out he's going to be a big hit at parties. But the turning into a human searchlight part, that is exactly how I felt with the Brazilian shape shifter. To replicate that without pot and expired cough syrup would be a wonderful thing. I could defi-nitely include it in my new teaching. Uh-oh, this part might be a little tricky:

> The male must constantly control the degree of the ex-citement of his *lingam*, and through the following exer-cises this will become progressively simpler. The male learns to withhold orgasm longer and longer, until fi-nally, like a great yogi, the male will only orgasm once per calendar year, and then only on the day after his part-ner's ovulation closest to his date of birth.

Some birthday present, but I know I'd lose my mind after a month. Let me flip ahead to the pictures. What the hel—? It reminds me of the assembly instructions for a power lawn mower my dad once bought at Sears. Then pages and pages of arousal charts and checklists, stage by stage cutaway schematics, the bald-headed man now contorted over the crotch of the woman with nearly every articulable part of his body in service to her yoni, and things to remember like this:

> Once the walls of her *yoni* begin contracting, immediately cease the motion of your tongue and press firmly up on her Inner Lotus Blossom (known in the West as the Grafenberg or G spot) with your middle and index fingers once per second while whispering into the opening, "I celebrate the goddess that is about to make herself known to me." The female's legs will involuntarily stretch apart and rise high above the bed, her toes will claw at the air, and her eyeballs will roll back in her head and flutter. A trained yogi can maintain this state of bliss in his female initiates as long as he maintains eye contact with her *yoni* and does not blink. Swami Boppanannadanna (16th Century) is reported to have trained himself to go forty-eight hours without blinking. Female initiates from as far away as Central Mongolia are said to have made the pilgrimage to his small houseboat in Kashmir and their cries were so persistent that the governor of the prefecture ordered the swami's boat removed to a more secluded part of the lake.

Now, that's a fella who had no trouble atall finding hisself a date.

Right Here, Right Now

"Excuse me?"

Stewardess: "I'm sorry, darling, I saw that picture, thought it was my first ex for a second, and just had to come sneak a peak. Hot towel?"

"Uh, thanks, no."

She's back in the galley. She's a dead ringer for my old den mother.

But seriously, this book is exactly one of the tools I'll need. I must create a structure for this spiritualism, just as I did for my motivational theories. Without steps to take, levels to attain, without ritual, humans get lost, soon lose their initial enthusiasm. Let me call the restaurant, find out more about the Brazilian spiritual structures from the busboy.

I just push the blue phone symbol and the thin, rectangular phone cleverly tucked into the arm of my seat rises out of the armrest slowly but relentlessly, like a card out of a deck after the magician sprinkles his fingers over it. I'm racing my credit card through the slot, try it again, then flip the card over to try the other side, but I'm positive I did it right the first time. This way doesn't work either. I flip it over once more, drag it through the slot again, and finally the readout on the phone ticker-tapes, *W-e-l-c-o-m-e.*

I get the number from the matchbook still in my pocket and dial.

What the hell was his name, anyway? Shit. He never told me. I'll hold you right next to the receiver.

Man on phone: "Yeah?"

This person is not Brazilian, for sure. He sounds more like a Cub fan.

—Uh, is this Axe Restaurant?"

"Not anymore, it ain't."

"What do you mean? I was just there yesterday."

"You and the Immigration and Naturalization Service. Didn't you read the paper today, fella? Not a one of them guys was legal. They sent them packing back to Argentina."

"Brazil!"

"Whatever."

"Look, I need to get in touch with one of them."

"There I can't help you. I'm just the contractor on the remodel. We're turning this cave into a Souplantation. They want it up and running in eight weeks. I shouldn't even've answered the phone but I thought you was the goddamn architect."

I don't know what to say. I don't know what he's saying anymore. I just find *Clear/End* on the phone, press it down, and shove the phone back in its tomb. I'm shaking. Stop it! But it's impossible that I just *happened* to visit the restaurant the day before it closed, just *happened* to see the old Swiney book at the bookstore. Can I really be so important that they create a restaurant in Chicago, remodel and staff it, get it great reviews in the local press, just to lure me there one night?

Yet if this is true, then my destiny lies beyond anything I had ever imagined, even at my most arrogant and egotistical. Ahhh! A streaming current just passed through me so intense I had to cross my legs quickly to quash it. But shit, that was wrong. I just read in the tantra book that this ecstatic static, as it is called, is the basis for the infinite, full-body orgasm; but you, me, a Westerner though of African descent, crossed your legs to turn off the receptors, slam the door in the face of all that is wondrous, and say, No thanks, I prefer to remain on the ground. I'm afraid of flying.

I can smell the chocolate chip cookies baking. We must be close to landing.

July 8th

I'm on my way into the office feeling a nervousness I haven't felt since I began lecturing about nervousness, timidity, and cowardice.

Hey, I just realized, I'm not tired anymore. Weird. The Spice Channel and I were trying out tantric sex exercises till five-thirty in the morning. No epiphanies as with the Brazilian, but I see that if you do it right, wow, you could pleasantly lose your mind, quit your job, lose weight.

"Behind each fear is the opportunity of a lifetime." The Herbalife towers have just come into view. PES, Inc. (should I keep the name?) is less than a minute away. A ghost in the engine of the Jaguar pings twice then disappears. Milky fog curls up from the cliffs and streams slowly just above the fields. Time to put on my game face.

A new car is in the employee-of-the-month space. I have no idea to whom it belongs.

Wish me luck. Over and out.

More July 8th

O.K., hold on now. Let me collect my thoughts and get this down right. But most of all I have to keep my eyes on the road back home. I'm really in no condition to drive. I passed through the doors, waved my way down the halls right past my own office to Jill's, shushed her assistant, Lynn, and entered so quickly I was already inside and hadn't yet finished turning the knob. Jill jumped and banged something under the table and winced.

"Damn!"

"Sorry, Jill. I just wanted to surprise you."

"I already got surprised this morning. From Chicago. What happened, Boss?"

"That is why I am here, babe. Who called? Some disgruntled ad exec from McCann Erikson?"

"Len Dawbridge."

That surprised me, so I dropped myself onto her black leather couch and it sighed.

"He said he'd never seen you like that. He said people started streaming out of their seats; he said that he wanted to too, but he stayed for some reason and stayed with you till dawn. I couldn't really get the gist of what he said you were talking about, but for a day it really changed his life. He almost quit his job, but this morning he woke up and—"

"Had snapped out of it. Damn him. That's too bad."

"Snapped out of what? What's going on?"

"This is bullshit."

"What?"

"*This*. What we do. What I have been saying. I realized that a few days ago."

"Thanks to some sexy Portuguese pygmy?"

"Brazilian. Listen, Jill. My friend. Sit down. Do you believe in God?"

"Yeah. Sure. I was raised Presbyterian. But Ash—"

"Wait. This is going to take a while."

I jumped to the door and hung on the knob so I could swing my head around to face her assistant outside.

"Lynn, can you bring us some bagels and two large Pellegrinos?"

I turned back to Jill and threw myself back onto her couch.

"Look at me, Jill. Do I look as if I have lost my mind? No, this is just the new evolution of everything we have been working on. I mean, how long can we go on telling people to *be all they can be*" and expect to get paid for it? From the beginning, from the days backstage working together on Dale's show or slamming back lattes in the Novel, I have been saying there is more to life than *visualizing* a raise, than getting a pretty girl's phone number in six minutes. Yet what have I ever done to dig deeper? How fucking lazy I've been."

Then I heard Lynn at the door.

"Come in!"

She hovered the heavy tray over the cocktail table in front of the couch until I could push magazines and Jill's windup toys away from the landing site. The large bottles wobbled threateningly.

"Thanks, Lynn."

She didn't look at either of us, just hurried out as if invisibly prodded. Maybe she was.

"Come sit over here . . ."

She did, casually.

"Listen, Jill, you know I know that we have worked too hard all these years to throw it all away. You have seen how they look at me at the seminars. What if we could harness that devotion and use it to propel us all to a higher level?"

"*Devotion?*"

"Whatever. But look, I asked you before if you believed in God and you said yeah, sure. Now, in general do you believe there is more to life than what we see?"

"Yeah, I guess so, but Ash—"

"So you are not entirely rational. You leave room for a little bit of mysticism in your blueprint of the universe?"

"Yes, all right."

"Good. Me too. Most people, I'd wager. Now, stay with me. Whether they call it God or crystals, tea leaves, UFOs, astrology, or sheep turds, most of us believe there is more to life than meets the eye. Well, what have you done this week to investigate this other world?"

Jill just shook her head. She was a stone. My chest shrank.

"O-or last week, last month, last year? Most of us know, at least we *feel*, there is the possibility of magic surrounding us, yet we ignore it and keep worrying about breast size, male pattern baldness, and market share! We say to ourselves, Oh, yeah, hypnotism, dreams, we know about them, of course, and luck, ghosts, angels, extraterrestrialists, nirvana, but I'm late for the auto detailer!"

She laughed. Great, I thought. Then she recrossed her legs.

"Those mules are beautiful."

"You like them?"

"Very much. Where was I?"

"You were talking about getting your car detailed."

"I tell the jokes in this outfit."

"Aye aye."

"So, listen, we agree that spiritualism exists. Do we also agree that throughout time some people have been more tapped into this spiritualism than others?"

She nodded, but reluctantly. She also winced and retreated. I talked faster.

"Do we agree that these people can have a profound effect on the history of the planet?"

Again she nodded. But I could see by the quiver in her throat that her heart was suddenly crazed. I had to be so careful now reeling her in.

"Do you think we are long overdue for such a person?"

"Oh no, Ashton . . . no . . ."

Damn! She started to rise away but I snatched her bare knee and held her to the couch. I used hardly any pressure, yet my palm throbbed with *axe*. Jill looked at me and her eyes had never been bigger.

"Do you feel that?"

"My God, you're burning up!"

"Or am I really cold?"

She started to speak, but stopped herself.

"Something is happening to me, Jill, and I think it's something good."

Then I began by telling her about the Fourth of July with my family so she would see how normally the day began. I reminded her about the cough, how I'd had it even in St. Barths but now I'm cured. I admitted to the pot, admitted I didn't know the expiration date of the cough syrup, and she rolled her eyes and smiled. "So *that's* what this is all about," she said. I shook my head, described for her the midget, described for her his change, described the love that filled me, the sudden ballooning of my groin, and it responded again, just then, ploughed down my pants leg as it inflated, obviously. I told her about the reading in Carmel and Dr. Swiney and how even then I was still a skeptic. Then I told her about Chicago, from the limo driver to the flight back and the Brazilians in between. She stared at me with pity. With tears.

"Oh, Ash, you should've gone to the hospital."

"When I came to, I'd never felt better in all my life! Then an hour later I changed several peoples' lives with my words."

"Yeah, but fifteen hundred others walked out, and two of the converts snapped out of it a few hours later."

"Fuck the Dawbridges! You always hated them! Let's call up Nikki Kennedy. See what she thinks of the new message."

"Who? The conquest?"

Anger involuntarily inflated my chest, but I struggled to stuff it back inside like a sleeping bag much too big for its sack. I made myself measure my words in my brain, then distribute each of them, deliberately, into the air, like cards from a deck.

"She . . . and . . . several . . . others are . . . on board, including the Days Inn night manager . . . who came over to evict us . . . but ended up staying all night."

"A Days Inn night manager. I see . . ."

"I already have more people than I had for the first six

months at the Novel. And all of that, all of *this*, began with just one person who believed in me and let me help them. Her girlfriend had just dumped her for a bull dyke with a haircut only Billy Ray Cyrus could envy. She was back on men and threw herself at the first one she saw—who, unfortunately for her, turned out to be her boss, whose attention to women spanned no longer than the six minutes he claimed it took to get their phone numbers."

"Shut up! I got over him and then I went back to Alan!"

"I'm just saying that you were the first to believe in me, believe that I had some wisdom that was worth sharing . . ."

I found myself holding her hand before I remembered doing it.

Her fingers were long and tan, the nails conservatively squared and tipped in white. My fingers were longer and brown around hers, and I concentrated my *axe* into them, which made them pulse. I needed my friend to stay with me. Someone who knew me before I fell off the donkey on the road to Damascus. I'll never forget the first thing she said to me my first day on Dale's set: "Well, that's just *marvelous*. Didn't anybody tell you Dale only drinks caffeine-free Dr Pepper? Jesus Christ! Thanks! He's gonna make everybody's life around here a living hell!"

And now I wanted her to believe that I had been personally anointed by God—or whomever.

So I did a great Jill impersonation, packed the words with her Valley girl singsong, *"Didn't anybody tell you Dale only drinks caffeine-free Dr Pepper?!"*

Jill smiled. That became our first running joke. After we became friends she confessed that that was the day her girlfriend had moved out.

"Ash, is it cold in here to you?"

"Did you just get a chill that electrified your silhouette?"

"What? Are you saying it's your fault I just shivered?"

"And your nipples will soon be stiffening, stretching the skin of their areolas, like two ghosts had just sucked them into their mouths."

She rolled her eyes, crossed her arms, but her nipples *did* push at her blouse. I had no idea it would really work. We both looked. I tried not to smile—it would ruin the effect—but couldn't help a little smirk.

"Nice party trick. But *Ash*, things are going so well right now."

Oh, wait a minute. I'm home. Let me park and put in a new tape.

■ ■ ■

So there I was with Jill. I was too busy trying to remember what it said in the book. I clenched my pubococcygeus muscles, the ones between the balls and the butt, as I drew in breath and rolled my eyes toward the sky, drawing the sexual energy up from my lingam, through all my chakras, and projecting it out of the lips that I was then pressing against hers. I pumped the muscle and my lips throbbed in harmony till the tingling spilled over to the areas of my nose and my chin. When I finally pulled away I was so dizzy I had to hold the couch. But Jill? It was as if I had stolen all the air that had ever been in her lungs, for her whole body undulated as she breathed in, then reversed the undulation as she breathed out. If I'd only known this trick back in high school . . . Jill still had her eyes closed as she raised her fingertips to her mouth like a blind person trying to read her own face.

"Very . . . fucking . . . nice . . . party trick . . ."

God knows I have made love to many women, for the first several years not so well at all, but with practice I thought I had become a fairly conscientious lover (though admittedly a lousy boyfriend). I have made love to women who had been just friends before, even married friends, and the taboo had always heightened the pleasure. And I'd even made love to *Jill* before, one drunken night six years ago in Maui. Yet sex with her this time was already more than I'd ever even imagined. More colors. And she had done nothing to me yet. I stroked the tenderness of her inner and outer Fragrant Petals with my left hand while concentrating my life force into the tip of my tongue, which I then jiggled against all the wet contours of her Tiny Dragon. In the book this force is called *pranha*, also known as *chi* by the Taoists. But *axe* by any other name would smell as sweet.

The unlocked door also added to this wonderful morning. Jill lay on her back on her desk, biting into the pillow her mother-in-law had cross-stitched for her last Christmas: two children bundled in jackets, ice-skating around a frozen pond. Her moan was more a hum, like an electrical transformer, and the little skaters muffled most of it. Following the recipe in the book, I brought her to the edge of orgasm six times for the six-armed incarnation of the goddess Shakti. But each time, just as I felt her about to crest, I lightened the pressure till she calmed a bit, and leveled her back to cruising altitude.

Then the seventh time was coming. Seven for the seven-eyed head of the goddess, and I was scared a little but inserted my right hand's middle and index fingers inside her yoni just as the opening started to contract like the shutter of a camera and suddenly I forgot everything! Damn! I remember thinking. Why'd I leave the book at home! Then it came to me. I pulsed against her In-ner Lotus Blossom (G spot), now swollen and pebbly just as the book said. I pulsed against it rhythmically and firmly. More and more of her sounds spilled from the pillow.

So I concentrated and finally remembered exactly what it was I was supposed to chant. I leaned over the desk to talk right into her. For some reason I crossed myself Catholic style for luck.

"I celebrate the goddess that is about to make herself known to me."

And like a gypsy at a seance she was instantly possessed. Her back arched on the desk, spilling more papers to the floor, and her legs rose up and out with the slow constancy of a levitating magician's assistant. Something scarily Spielbergian was being unleashed within her, an energy not in her but just above her, between her yoni and her navel, an almost visible swirling ball, no, not a ball, a cloud, crackling sexily of static electricity, pure potentiality, a storm cloud invisibly blackening by the second right above her to ZZZAP into her like man-made lightning at the museum of science, and finally she roared, like this, all caps:

"BaaAAAHHHHHHHHHHHHHHHHHHHHHHHHHHHH . . ."

Her noises changed now to something truly otherworldly, sa-tanically low out of her light, tan body of muscles and curves. Her yoni seemed to be trying to swallow my hand, possessed by a rhythm I know she never had. This was unmistakably a religious possession, a *channel* to some other world. That must be what or-gasms are, glimpses into the divine, but we get scared, the feel-ings too vibrant for our bodies, so instead we end them with a traumatic shock, crash ourselves back down to the material world, so afraid that if we didn't we might fly off and never come back.

Finally, she leveled out to a high whine of continuous contractions, her eyes untwisted open and focused on me, eventually, and she smiled that she was OK, don't worry, she was safe on the other side and the water's warm. I started to move my hand away but she shook her head no, wouldn't let me, so I reached my own belt with just one hand, twisted and shook off my pants, stretched my underwear till it finally came off. My erection almost made me faint. I actually pleated at the knees but caught myself like a limbo dancer and kneed up on the desk and fell on her and entered her instantly. At least I think I was in her; it was hard to tell because our entire lower bodies seemed to have instantly fused into one glowing pump. But then I was sure I was in her and out of her and in her again. Our eyes locked and swam together. She looked a bit panicked. I think she thought I knew where all this was going till she saw whatever that look was on my face. And then came an orgasm rumbling within me menacingly, as if I were standing on a train track in front of a curving tunnel as dark as anything can be dark and I heard from the black opening a rumbling, low but constant, exponentially building toward me in a rush but thus far of sound only, and so a little surreal. My brain kept skipping a few frames, couldn't help jumping ahead to the moment when the train would appear out of the tunnel, thundering much faster than my ability to react, and I would be hit so quickly and with such force that not a trace of me would remain. I was there, I was, just one more stroke away from the violent electrocution of orgasm, when this simple thought appeared in my brain whole: *If I come, all this will end.*

Why didn't they ever teach that in camp? Instantly I leveled off, cruised high in the sexual stratosphere. There was something I was supposed to chant now but I completely forgot. Next time I'll have the tantric book on tape and headphones so I can listen simultaneously. In that zone I was in, each stroke was the equivalent of one of my old orgasms, but I kept willing the ejaculation away. I clenched my groin like a fist, closed up everything tight, breathed the energy from my lower half up through the core of my body, like raising mercury in a thermometer, and my heart tingled, then my forehead, then the top of my head. Last night, alone, it was bliss, but not half of what it was with a partner. *If I come, all this will end.* But it was getting more and more difficult. And Jill was no longer rigid but absolutely placid, opened up to me like a flower, her calves pinned high over her head by my shoulders and those amazing patent-leather mules clapping against the soles of her pretty feet with each stroke, and CLENCH! I told myself, CLENCH! Not coming is like climbing a sheer rock face. Not so bad if you concentrate, but lose yourself for an instant, get lost in her calves, in her tightness, in the sounds we made, in the taboo of sex in the office, and an ejaculation would have come and destroyed me.

The woman can scream and orgasm as many times as the spirit moves her, but the male must at all costs conserve his energy; at least that is what it says in the book. Think about it: inside a tiny nut hides a hundred-foot tree. Every time you ejaculate there are as many sperm cells as people in Manhattan. It's a crime to let them out, to waste that energy, until you are ready to create a replacement for yourself, then wither and die.

You should've seen Jill. Her eyes were rolled up in her head like those of a snake handler I once saw late one night in a documentary on PBS, eyes rolled inward to see into the self. We stayed in that place for ninety minutes, slow movements so we wouldn't chafe, yet enough to perpetuate her continuous orgasm and the continuous glowing energy that started behind my balls and that I kept drawing up through all my chakras and that was perpetually consuming me like a cool fire.

July 9th

Today's was the best swell we'd seen all spring. Near double head-high, clean shoulders. I was out in the water by six-thirty, so the lane wasn't jammed yet. By nine, I heard, the water was a parking lot of surfers, and by ten four fights had broken out because somebody got dropped in on, got snaked, or maybe their fin sawed a line through the other guy's board.

But this dawn it was a high school reunion as I paddled out to the lineup. Two guys I didn't know whispered and pointed, but the rest of them just caught my eyes and jutted their chins once. To each I did the same.

"Hey, Owen, Pablo. Hey, Todd, when'd you get that mushroom-cloud tattoo? Cool."

"Dude, I got it a while ago. I wanted to balance out my fucking arms. You know . . . ?"

He showed me his other shoulder and a tattoo of a dove.

"You still got Africa on your arm, Ash?"

"Till the day I die, bra'."

"Fun day at the office yesterday, Ashy? That blonde Betty of yours is bitchin'."

Pablo said this. His sister works for me in shipping. She was last month's employee of the month. "Betty" or "Lisa" was surfer-ese slang for a cute girl when we were in high school. Betty for Betty Rubble of *The Flintstones*, and Lisa, I guess, because 90 percent of the white girls in California were called that. Anyway, when Jill and I finally left her office, the staff did not even try and scatter, to feign nonchalance. We nodded at them and marched straight to our cars.

Pablo was too busy grinning at me to notice the first wave of the set. It rose over his head like a phantom. I fell onto my belly and paddled hard till I felt the wave start to rise under me, and snapped to standing. He got tumbled in the washing machine of the breaking wave, but I was high on the shoulder, snapped, and dipped deep into the bowl of the wave, bottom-turned, and drove for the shoulder again, rode and rode, dragged my finger through the flesh of the wave, then stomped on the tail and slowed till the water mountain caught up and swallowed me, and I crouched and the lip curled right over my head, and there I was, in the green room, the tube. I left the world, as I did yesterday, only by myself this time, and in that quiet, time didn't so much stand still as *stretch*, and I realized, as the sun made the meaty, miraculous curving cave of water surrounding me glow green like green glass, that like the orgasm and like dreaming, the tube ride is another hint of the Other Side that has always surrounded me and that I have always ignored.

I ignored them because they were soon over as this tube was soon over, screwing closed quickly, so I leaned forward to accelerate out of it just in time, and the sound and the wind of the real world rushed back and instantly pushed the experience deep into memory, which is right next to fantasy, which is nowhere at all. I kicked out of the weak white froth, all that was left of the wave, fell back on my board, and paddled back out to the lineup.

"That tube was mine, you millionaire motherfucker."

I paddled up to Pablo as he pulled himself back on his board, snorting water out of his nose.

"I'll let you have the next one."

"The next one I'm gonna motherfucking *take*, bra'."

He paddled hard to pull ahead. He kicked my ass in the eleventh grade for making out with his girlfriend, Maria Lopes. It was after a football game; we were drunk on rum and Tab (her favorite) and didn't mean anything by it.

"Send my best to Maria."

Without turning back he raised a fist in the air and unlatched his middle finger. Maria's his wife.

With my index finger as a hook I stretched the black collar of my wet suit away from my neck, pressed my chest into the board, and sped forward. Already, a new set of hills of water was steaming this way from the horizon. Buried inside one of them, just for me, was another quiet tube.

More July 9th

I'm by the pool now. It's been quite a day and the freakiest parts haven't even yet begun.

First I called Nikki. I was as nervous as if I were asking her out on a first date.

"Nikki Kennedy, please."

"Hello?"

"It's me. Why don't you come to Santa Cruz? There's a business class ticket waiting for you at O'Hare."

"Uh . . ."

"Or did you lose your resolve, like the Dawbridges?"

"They didn't!"

"They ratted on me. Called Jill. Told her I was nuts."

"A-a-are you?"

"Yes. Now come to Santa Cruz so we can evolve to the next level."

"I'll be right in. One second . . . The Lean Cuisine file should be on Sherry's desk . . ."

For a moment I thought she was speaking to me in code, not

to some colleague. Then her voice was right into the receiver again, but whispered.

"Should I just quit? Right now?"

"Only if you want to grow."

I let the silence work, measured it like a musician before I dropped back in with:

"American Airlines, flight six-two-five to San Francisco, eight-twelve P.M. The ticket will be at the gate. And don't forget to give them your frequent flyer number."

Then I called Susan at her home. I figured Len was probably at work.

"Dawbridge residence."

"I thought you believed in me. I thought you believed in yourself."

Again, I worked the silence, imagined her panicked eyeballs searching her tacky TV room of game-show-like furniture for what next to say.

"We worried about you, Ashton. Thought Jill should know."

"She does know. And she's come aboard."

"Oh, God, it's just all so . . . You know, that midget from Brazil, that restaurant they just closed down. You're a very persuasive person, but the next day, Len and I were talking, and it's just so much to take!"

"I'll send you a postcard from the Other Side."

■ ■ ■

"Days Inn, Hyde Park. May I help you?"

"Yes, could I leave a message for Glen, the night manager?"

"He's right here, sir."

I heard whispering, then:

"Hello?"

"Glen? This is Ashton Robinson..." Then silence. "Glen...?"

"I-I'm here. I've been hanging around since you left, sleeping at the hotel. Waiting."

"There is a ticket to San Francisco for you at O'Hare. Eight-twelve P.M. I'll have a limo pick you all up."

"Ashton?"

"Yes?"

"I knew that was you before Clifton—he's the day manager—before he answered the phone."

"See you tonight, Glen."

He might give me trouble later on. Len and Susan, though they betrayed me, have a skepticism that is natural; that I myself had until Chicago. Glen, on the other hand, was convinced after about thirty-five minutes. What also worries me is that he looks exactly like my crazy cousin Kevin. Shapelessly large, a bloodlessly light tan color, eyeballs so heavy they seem to strain the pockets of his lids; just a few stringy black hairs tangle on his head and just the cap of his chin.

■ ■ ■

Next I had to ready the house. First I called World of Beds. They had seven bunk beds in stock, so I said I'd take them all if they could deliver them and assemble them in the hour. They're right down the street and got here in twenty minutes.

"That's OK, Rosamaria, I'll show them the way. You just go to the Price Club and load up on food. Take the Land Cruiser; you remember how to push down the backseats? Hey, guys, be careful of the walls! And Rosamaria, don't forget I want canned goods, and that milk that lasts for months. I want the freezers full!"

"I'll pay you guys to disassemble the queen-sized beds and take them away."

"Don't look like they've ever been slept on, man."

"And now they never will, unless you want them yourselves. Come on now, we've got six other bedrooms to do."

I ordered the sheets and extra pillows right after I got off the phone with the last of the Chicagoans. Damn. Bed, Bath and Beyond still hasn't shown up. Everything's got to come together, for in just five hours this pharaonic mausoleum will turn into Enlightenment Ground Zero.

"Anybody home?"

The manager of the bookstore down in Carmel stood in my doorway, limboing a bit under the weight of the cardboard box of books in his arms. In the doorway he had to turn quickly sideways, out of the way of the bed deliverymen, who marched back in with more bed rails under their arms like battering rams. I rushed to the book guy and took the box.

"That was quick, thank you."

"Oh, it's just my pleasure, Mr. Robinson. I'm happy to have your business. I just hope I got what you wanted. You kinda left it up in the air a bit."

"What I think I said was, give me the best book on every discipline you stock."

"Well, we had a lot of arguments on that in the store, let me tell you. But believe me, you've got enough reading material for a few months!"

"I have until this afternoon."

He laughed. I smiled, just my cheeks, then strained my lids

away from my eyeballs for a second in an eerie, crazed hypnotist way I've been practicing in the mirror these past few days. It worked. He instantly shut down, folded his shoulders in on himself, and looked down. People are going to have to start listening to me if they want to transcend.

"How much do I owe you?"

"Oh! Uh, I don't know. Can I mail you the bill? I know you're good for it."

And he was gone.

I swung the books high, balanced on the palm of my hand and leaning against my shoulder, and the motion turned on a memory long buried: of carrying trays of pastel blended drinks to the upper-middle-class French, German, and American guests of Club Med Bora-Bora. Two days later I confessed to my boss that I was the American brother of Yannick Noah, was immediately promoted to tennis pro, and my salary tripled. A month and a half later Yannick Noah and his Victoria's Secret model girlfriend showed up, and I had to slip out on a cargo ship with just my long board and a gym bag of dirty clothes.

Here by the pool now I arranged the books in small piles like cairns marking a trail. *Hypnotism and Self-Hypnotism for the Serious Seeker; Dream Telepathy; The Enigma of Out-of-Body Travel. Buddhism for Beginners; Transcendental Meditation;* and *Just Tao It!. The Crystal Realm; Pyramid Power: How to Use It Before It Uses You; The Tarot and Your Vital Organs; A Short History of the Hex Signs of the Pennsylvania Dutch. Dianetics,* the Bible, the Koran, the Book of Mormon. *What Your Dreams Mean, Really!; Sun Signs.* Books by Shirley MacLaine, Shakti Gawain, Deepak Chopra, Gurdjieff, Erhard, Blavatsky, Edgar Cayce, John-Roger . . .

I started with the hypnotism book because it was short. Last year I swapped a set of my audiotapes for a set of speed-reading tapes from this guy who was later indicted for mail fraud. Still, his techniques work. It's been only a few hours but I've already buzzed through about half of the books. The only problem is my left eye won't stop twitching. But I can't slow down now. I have to cram in as much as I can so I'll have something more to teach them tonight—if they come—than just saying *"Now."*

Even More July 9th

"Are they here yet?"

"No, Jill, you are the first. What did you tell Alan?"

"I told him you were having a party. I knew there'd be no way he'd come."

"They are moving in, you know. We will be working on this twenty-four seven. Enlightenment is a full-time job. Buddhist monks, Taoist monks, Catholic monks all realize this."

"I know, I just . . ."

"You're afraid. And you're married."

"But I'm here right now, aren't I?"

"How much of you?"

I stared at her. Not as crazily as at the bookstore guy, yet longer than a normal man would. They used to say that Gurdjieff could make his followers' legs go numb with just his eyes; that Madame Blavatsky's glare could extinguish candles; that a mean look from an Indian fakir could impregnate a woman who had offended him with a hyperactive child.

I walked her to the living room, where I'd moved the two

long leather couches from the wall to the center of the room in a chevron facing the antique club chair my designer bought from the estate of Don Ameche. A minefield of pillows filled the space between. Rosamaria loaded the bowls with more corn nuts (my weakness) and loaded the refrigerator hidden in the bookshelf with miscellaneous Snapples.

"Can you tell me a little about this new system? How exactly are you going to teach us what you do?"

I shook my head at her.

"I would rather wait till the others arrive. If you do not mind, I'd also like to collect my thoughts for a while. You could watch a movie off the satellite?"

The truth, of course, was that I was not at all sure what I would tell them. I knew what happened to me, but had no idea how or if it was translatable. After the Buddha's enlightenment he taught a handful of students who in turn taught handfuls themselves. Buddhism took hundreds of years to establish itself as a major religion. Not that I expect any sort of similar success. But it would be nice if "Axeism" would one day be as big as, I don't know, maybe the Mormons. By 1846, just nineteen years after Joseph Smith had that first vision and just two years after his death at the hands of a rabid mob, the Church of Jesus Christ of the Latter Day Saints numbered in the thousands and began their trek for Utah. What did he or his successor Brigham Young tell his flock every day? Why did they give up their Presbyterianism, Methodism, Catholicism, Baptistism to follow him across America? How courageous they were! It's easy to be a Mormon now. They have a *state*, for God's sake.

Yet in the beginning, you have only your word.

I went back up to my room and had the hardest time trying to decide what to wear. Robes, a dashiki, something vaguely Brazilian? None of that is me. I even thought about cranking up the heat and us all lolling about naked. Maybe later.

My closet is its own boutique. I have so many clothes, and the armies of hangers stretch double-decker behind so many sliding mirrored panels that many of the pieces—shirts especially—feel as foreign to me as if I were looking at other people's clothes on a motorized rack behind the counter at some dry cleaner's. Years ago, traveling, it used to be so different. I used to live in an old *Sex Wax* T-shirt. Every other day I'd rinse it out and stretch it across my board. It thinned and thinned and would dry as brittle as parchment until the words *Dr. Zog's* and the *arm Water Sur* of *Warm Water Surf Wax* had evaporated into the sun. I know I didn't throw it away—I would never do that—but I have no idea where it could be now.

I heard the footsteps before the knock.

"Mr. Robinson? Your company."

Rosamaria announced them through the closed door. Instantly my heartbeat accelerated, made me force my lungs full of air. I suddenly didn't have time to change. All I could think about was how many of them really had the guts to get on that plane.

I remember, as I raced downstairs, the hard drumroll of my feet hard-slapping the edge of each stair. Jill was smiling at the stair's bottom. I glimpsed Rosamaria just before she closed herself into her room. I inhaled strongly, then opened the front door. The tires of the two limousines were crackling the gravel as they climbed the drive. I stabbed two switches by the front door and the fountain lit up, dramatically from below, and water spurted, then flowed more naturally out of the angry mouths of my four stone lions.

The limo doors opened before the drivers could hustle

around to open them, and the students looked around open-mouthed. Suddenly I was Willy Wonka and they had come to visit my chocolate factory.

"Howdy, folks! Glad you could make it."

They jumped. Nikki was in the first car along with a short, elderly Italian couple, the Landis; Yvonda, a dark brown black woman with long braids; the Sandillas; Lanie something; and Nicholas Harris. Out of the second car wandered Glen; Brian V. Hillsing, the old guy, wearing the same suit he wore in Chicago; and the Tewkses, as well as—get this—their two little girls. I still have no idea what to do with them.

"If everyone will take their bags and come on in, I'll show you to your rooms. You all will remember Jill here from my infomercials."

"Hi!" they all said in a friendly, Midwestern way. I held one door for them, Jill the other, and though the doorway is eight feet tall, many of them ducked a bit, almost genuflected, as they entered. I quickly tallied their heads as they passed . . . nine, ten . . . eleven. Eleven out of seventeen who would quit their jobs and move in with a stranger. Not too bad.

Nikki was the last inside.

"How was the flight?"

"Oh! Wonderful. I've never flown business class before; my boss never ever let me."

"Yeah, Mr. Robinson, for years I been smelling them chocolate chip cookies they make, but this is the first I actually got to, you know, eat one."

"I am only going to say this once. Call me Ashton, everybody, especially you, Glen."

His high yellow blushed pink, but the strange scar on his neck turned red like that big red spot on Jupiter. I like him.

"Now down that hall is the kitchen. It's full of every type of food imaginable. Tomorrow we'll devise a schedule of cooking and cleaning. Up this way to the bedrooms . . ."

I felt exhilarated, yet curiously I also felt like the last lord of a medieval manor reduced to giving tours of his ancestral home. (*"On your right, a portrait of the sixteenth earl of Wickhamberry and his faithful foxhound Cicero."*) The couples whispered to each other as they stepped up the stairs slowly.

"The four bedrooms on the right will be for the women and the little girls, and the three on the left for the men."

The two younger couples, the Sandillas and the Tewkses, frowned at me and stopped. My first test. I closed my eyes, concentrated my *axe* into the palms of my hands till they tingled, and reached for the two closest, Mr. Sandilla and Mrs. Tewks. Each petrified under my touch in an awkward pose. I stretched my eyelids back a bit, swept my glare across all four of them as I spoke.

"For us to get to the Other Side together, conventional, societal bounds such as father, son, sister, mother, husband, wife, must be obliterated. Not overnight, of course, but that must be our eventual goal. Of course there will be quiet time for just you and your mates or you and these lovely children here, yet our goal is a personal relationship with the divine, ultimate, and true fabric of life that is so much beyond all that! Yet if it is already too difficult for you four, of course I will understand . . ."

And I stepped away, opened my arms and my chest to the stairs and the door. The husbands and wives quickly conferred with just their eyes. Mr. Tewks might not last too long, but his wife nodded yes quickly and got him to nod yes too, for now.

Their little girls, maybe about six and nine, but I'm terrible with children's ages, could tell their parents were no longer in control and started to panic. They both seemed just a sudden noise away from uncontrollable tears. So I squatted down to their level and rolled my eyes crazily for them, something that always used to work on my niece and nephews. The littlest Tewks giggled and let me stroke her hair, but the older one just twisted herself behind her mother's waist.

The Sandillas were easier. They're having marital problems anyway. Most of my seminarians are. And the Landis just smiled at each other, like wise old wizards, already convinced.

"All right then, stow your gear and we'll meet downstairs in fifteen minutes."

I bounded back down the stairs three at a time while Jill raced after me stair by stair but fast as a blur. I could hear the *F*s and *S*s of them all upstairs, whispering.

"Kind of an odd group you've got there, Ash."

"Are you including yourself?"

"Of course."

"So, how long are you going to be my only day student?"

"I guess until you can convince Alan to move in too."

"Bring him to dinner tomorrow night."

"Seriously?"

"Even when I'm joking."

"Rosamaria's gonna have her hands full, don't you think?"

"That reminds me! Tomorrow I'm letting her go. I am going to have a house full of people with nothing to do all day but contemplate the divine and housework. But have Geoffrey pay her for the rest of the year. No. Pay her for two years. I've always liked her and what she really wants to do is start up a Salvadoran restaurant in town."

I fell onto my club chair sideways, legs crooked over the chair's arm, in feigned nonchalance. What if they don't stay? I mean, who wouldn't accept a free plane ticket? Live in a mansion for a few days, take some pictures with that black guy on TV with the funny hair (even though it was after he went nuts)? Christ didn't fly in the apostles, especially not business class. I closed my eyes and remembered the midget, remembered puking in the pool, remembered the love I felt for him when he became that Sonia Braga–looking babe. That was all prelude. The real show was about to begin. I panicked, forgot everything I was planning to say. Then I moved my leg and got stabbed through my jeans pocket by the edges of the six index cards I had stuffed there. Suddenly, I didn't need to pull them out. I just closed my eyes and visualized what each of them said.

After I don't know how long, I heard more than just Jill in the room and opened my eyes. They were all there, staring. Nikki was up front with Jill. She wants a special place in all of this, I can tell.

I rotated my ass, bucketed in the chair, to sit normally.

"I'm so proud of all of you for coming. I realize that this must be one of the scariest moments of your lives . . . Mine too. So let us start with the easy stuff. Tell everyone your name and why you came. Nikki?"

She straightened her spine quickly, and quickly she cleared her throat.

"Uh, Nikki Kennedy. I first met Ashton in person in St. Barths, then he came to Chicago, and, um, I believe in him."

She slouched back against the couch to signal she was done. Jill was next and I could see her trembling. In the long silence I had to catch her eyes and nod before she finally sat up and talked.

"Jill Lowry. I've known Ashton for going on seven years now. I'd heard about what happened in Chicago and was convinced he'd lost his mind . . . Then on Friday I confronted him about it and he revealed his *axe* to me, and, well, you all know that it is too powerful to ignore. This is, um, difficult for me because I knew him . . . before, but believe me, I am with you."

What a pal. I fortified her with a long look, then a nod and a smile.

"My name is Lydia Sandilla and my husband, Henry, and me have been looking for the kind of experience Ashton talked about with the short Brazilian and in that restaurant for years and just hope that he can—you can—maybe teach us how to get there ourselves?"

I was wrong. Until she introduced herself I thought the Sandillas were the Tewkses and the Tewkses the Sandillas, because Mrs. Sandilla is blonde. Then the elderly white man in the suit pushed himself off the couch to stand. He seemed like one of those cranks in talk-show audiences who take the mike from the host and give it back only under duress.

"My name is Brian V. Hillsing and I am eighty-three-years young today . . ."

Everyone clapped. This really *was* turning into a bad rerun of *Oprah*. But for real he didn't look a day over sixty. I remember pretty much everything he had to say, but tomorrow I'm going to pick up a good mike, run it through the stereo, and maybe even set up a videocamera. Three hundred years from now these archives might be a national treasure.

"I knew Mr. L. Ron Hubbard personally, he having served on the same destroyer as myself in the Pacific Theater during the war. I was one of the first subjects to be analyzed by his patented E-meter and I can tell you for twenty-four years I benefited a heckuva lot from his teachings. But when I heard this young man on the TV, I said to myself, Don't worry about his hair, he's got something new to say to you, Brian V., so listen up, write away for that system he's talking about. And so I did. Then I heard him live back in Chicago and, man! L. Ron never had so much fire! When you called I said, 'Hell, yes, I'm coming!' I've done all I can with the material world, made and lost fortunes, wives, children, low-to-middle-income subdivisions, and now I'm ready for what's been behind it all, all these years."

He's gonna be trouble. *L. Ron Hubbard?* Is that really where all this is heading? I was thinking much more along the lines of Mary Baker Eddy, Martin Luther, or Siddhartha.

As the rest stood and testified, one after the other, relating their past experimentations with crystals, sweat lodges, peyote cults, Gurumayi, even the cabala, my *axe* drained from me till it puddled sadly in my shoes. Are they all just weak-willed New Age freaks ready to follow the first multimillionaire to come their way with dope and a dextromethoraphan-induced vision of a better world . . . ?

Or maybe I'm too hard on them. Perhaps they were just more evolved than I was, had already started investigating the Other Side while I was still coaching Jiffy Pop account associates how to ask for a raise.

Lanie and Nicholas Harris testified, the forgettable Professor and Mary Anne of our little menagerie. She told us he took her to see me for their first date! Then Glen talked last.

"Glen Bullock. I've been the night manager at the hotel for, like, the past eighteen months. I worked at the airport before that, while still finishing up at Apex Tech in hotel and restaurant management. My mama, my uncles, everyone in the family worked at the airport. Food service, terminal maintenance, skycapping — the Bullocks are famous at O'Hare! I was a baggage handler for Delta, so I could, like, fly anywhere in the world for just, you know, the tax on the ticket. But I got lonely. Nobody else ever wanted to go with me. Forget about girls. Why'd I come? I wasn't raised any religion at all, never tried any, you know, New Age neither, but after a while you start to miss something in your life. I just felt I was sitting there in that Days Inn reading my Stephen King till the sun rose again and the day manager showed up, just waiting to die. I don't wanna ever wait to die no more."

Everyone smiled at him kindly. Me too.

"Thank you. Thank you, everyone. I think what we have all been saying is that we sensed something wondrous yet hidden in the boring everyday of our lives and have all gathered here to pan for it. My hat is off to all of you, for it seems that you had begun your investigations well before I had. While I was coaching Jiffy Pop account associates on the best ways to ask for a raise, you were trying every door you could to find the Other Side. However, I hope you will all agree that those other doors were just closets, most just shallow broom closets, but some, sumptuous walk-in closets, to be sure. Yet in every case you had to leave the same way you came.

"*Axe*, on the other hand, is not a closet but a passageway. It is not made out of wood and there is no knob. You have walked past it, near it, *through* it every waking day of your life! Yet it is the *way* that we will all learn to walk through that will forever alter our psychic geography. There are pads and pencils by the bowl of corn nuts if anyone would care to take notes . . ."

Yvonda, the brown woman with the long braids and an ex–Seventh Day Adventist, was nearest them and passed them around. Maybe I'll give quizzes once in a while.

"So, our task, twenty-four hours a day—and I mean twenty-four-hours a day—is to prepare our inner selves for this invisible corridor so one day we will pass through and never return. One day, no time soon, probably, but one day, I promise you, I will be walking through this very room and I will Disappear. If you were watching very carefully, and practice very hard in the days immediately afterward, you will all Disappear too . . ."

Don't ask me where that came from! It just leapt right from my *Axe!*

"That's right," I continued. *"Dis-ap-pear!* We will leave this world and leave our bodies, our personal histories, and join the truth of the Other Side as the pure essence that all humans understand to be their true nature when they are honest enough to see through their socioreligious acculturation! So. How will we prepare ourselves for our transformation? Like monks we will all dress similarly. But no, no brown robes or ugly burlap tunics. What we're trying to do is strip away materialism, not act like sophomores at a frat party . . . !"

They laughed. I smiled.

"So I've decided we will all shop from the same store. I'm talking about a place where they now sell everything from shoes to underwear to jackets and belts. A place that obliterates class distinctions yet provides enough diversity that we won't look like a Southern pep squad on a bus tour of the Californian coast. Of course, I'm talking about the Gap."

Just then one of the children, from their room upstairs, was screaming between hyperventilated sobs. Mr. and Mrs. Tewks instantly straightened on their pillows on the floor and seemed to be telepathically wrestling. The scream then rose many octaves past any singer's natural range and was rapidly approaching the level of feedback at a rock concert. Mr. Tewks hurried to his feet and tried to quickly pick his way through the others folded on the floor, who quickly cocked their shoulders out of his way as he passed. Mrs. Tewks begged me not to be angry with her gray eyes, surprisingly pretty on her plain face.

"I guess someone's not too fond of Gap Kids."

As the others laughed I smiled at Mrs. Tewks, and her stiff shoulders sagged as she sighed.

"So, will dressing ourselves in all-cotton khakis probably made in China by imprisoned political dissidents change our relationship with the universe? Of course not. But it will help build us as a family. We'll eat our meals together at scheduled times; our food will also help us eventually combine our *axes*, interlock them, to raise us all to the next level. Have any of you ever surfed . . . ?"

Nobody.

"Well, hear those waves out there? On a good south-southwest swell with a moderate offshore breeze, you have some of the cleanest head-high sets on the planet. I will teach you how, and in a few years you might find yourself in the green room, the barrel, the tube, of a thundering wave, and maybe, if you're lucky and we've prepared you well, you'll never come out. I can't think of a better place from which to Disappear. How about skydiving? Early next week I think we'll all do an accelerated free fall from five thousand feet. Does anyone have any experience?"

Mr. Sandilla's hand rises slowly.

"Henry?"

"I was a captain in the U.S. Rangers for ten years before I retired and joined the Drug Enforcement Agency."

Uh-oh.

"You're D.E.A.? Henry, that's great."

Shit. I was thinking of scoring some 'shrooms for us for lunch tomorrow from this Deadhead at the surf shop.

"I'm on leave now, of course."

"Excellent. By the way, what have the rest of you told your employers?"

"I'm retired."

"I quit."

"I ain't tell him nothing."

"I-I had some vacation saved up. Then I-I-I'll tell them the truth."

"They sacked me two months ago; that's why I went to see you in the first place."

"Excellent. And as the first brave class, of course your food and lodging will be entirely covered. But listen to me well: this is not a month- or two-month-long miracle course. None of us can expect enlightenment instantaneously. The very nature of enlightenment is that it sneaks up on us when we least expect it. The Buddhists have a wonderful koan. The disciple had been studying with his *sensei*, his teacher, for twenty-five years, and neither of them had yet attained satori, enlightenment. One day, completely fed up, the disciple stormed up to his *sensei* and said, 'Master, I can't take it anymore! Tell me now once and for all how to find *satori*! The master had been sitting *zazen*, Zen sitting meditation, for eight hours straight. He looked at his crazed disciple, grabbed the meat cleaver his wife was using to fix his lunch with his right hand, and whacked off the tip of his left index finger. Instantly, the *sensei*'s eyes rolled up into his head and a peculiar bliss seized his face. Finally, after all these years sitting on a pillow, he was enlightened! The disciple, envious, snatched the same meat cleaver and whacked off his own finger. 'Owww!' he shouted. 'Shit! I'm bleeding! MY HAND!' See, it didn't work for him. Buddhist literature is full of these kinds of stories. The moral for us Axeists is this: the road to eternal bliss is indefinite, and all of our paths are different yet convergent . . ."

This they wrote down slowly. Good.

"In honor of Mudamenta, the Brazilian midget/beautiful woman who started this all, and as part of our spiritual development, I will give a group lesson in Brazilian Portuguese every afternoon from four to six. I call him/her Mudamenta because in Portuguese it means 'change.' The rest of our spiritual practice is going to be rigorous but wonderful! Besides our 'Now' mantraing, we're going to explore everything from the Jewish cabala to Tibetan visualizations to Candomblé. The latter is the animist religion of Brazil, brought there by West African slaves. *Axe*, in fact, is a Yoruba West African word, and is central to the Yoruba religion and all its New World offspring: Candomblé, Santeria in Cuba and Puerto Rico, Voodun in Haiti, and hoodoo in our own American South. Ricky Ricardo's popular song "Babalu" is an appeal to the fierce Santeria god of the same name. It will be our reveille and our taps. In fact, it's late, I'll play it now, off one of my favorite CDs, a reissue called *Ricky Ricardo Swings Mambo!* I have set the autotimer on the CD player so when next we all hear it, it will be five-thirty in the morning, time for tomorrow's first session of meditation. So, to all of you brave explorers, I say, welcome and good night."

" *Ba-ba-luu . . . ba-ba-lu-u-u . . . ba-ba-lu-WYAYYY!*"

When I was little I remember singing along with Ricky and little Ricky on reruns after school. I used to try to play along on a little plastic bongo my uncle Bosco (now Woleyima) brought back from Senegal. This afternoon, while I was buzzing through *Cuba and Its Saints*, I came across the reference to Ricky Ricardo's god and finally realized why I had been obsessed with that song all these years. This last week has taught me that coincidences aren't, and that information arrives when you need it.

I stood up, and this released them. They slow marched upstairs, except Nikki, who pretended to be studying a lithograph in the living room and Jill, who swayed from foot to foot and kept looking away. As I neared her, Jill ducked a shoulder under the strap of her handbag. She tilted her wrist to check her watch.

"Five-thirty, huh?"

"Five-thirty, sharp. Can you see yourself out?"

Jill's eyes shot to Nikki before snapping back to me.

"I know the way."

I am interested in how this static between them will be resolved.

"Ashton, wh-where do I, you know, my room is the first one, but—"

I sat Nikki down on the arm of the couch and squatted beside her.

"Nikki, you know you are a very special person to me; you are one of fifteen souls selected to share my journey. Before finding *axe*, I was an extremely solitary man. My *parents* have never even spent the night here. Yet just because we knew each other before, just because we have tenderly made love, does not automatically grant you the position of first among equals. But know this: before July Fourth ever happened, I wanted you to be my lover. Yet it did happen, and everything changed, and what we are all in search of now is so much more important."

Her face was stiff and made ugly as she nodded quickly like the works of a clock, and her eyes stayed wide and round.

"What about her?"

Nikki tugged her head twice at the front door just as it closed.

Right Here, Right Now

"Babalu" was ending and Ricky headed right into my second-favorite song, "Cuban Pete."

"Jill has been with me from the beginning. That is why I am allowing her a little time to decide between the outside world and our work in here. Other than that, I promise you she is no more equal than the rest of you. Now, why don't you go on up to bed? I'll turn off the lights."

"*My name is Cuban Pete, I'm the king of the rhumba beat. When I play all the girls go boom-chicky-boom, boom-chicky-chicky-boom . . .*"

July 10th

Today was a good day, all things considered. I'd never used the stereo's autotimer, so I screwed it up and didn't get up till I heard Jill ringing the bell. I went downstairs and turned "Babalu" loose on all forty-six speakers hidden in the walls throughout every room in the house and terrace. Not loudly, of course, but loud enough to wake them.

We "Now"-ed aloud, cross-legged on the carpet, for twenty minutes, then stretched and shook out our legs and sat right back down to try Hindu meditation. I tore a mandala out of a book and placed it in the middle of the rug. We all encircled the perfectly symmetrical, ornate drawing of Shiva and Parvati ecstatically entwined, twelve arms between the two of them, heads nested together but mouths open in orgasm. Like all good mandalas, there was no right side up or upside down; the gods' position and the lotus blossoms and the shouting tigers surrounding them all seemed balanced from every angle. Even the Tewkses' little girls joined in, though Mr. Tewks didn't seem to want them staring at two Indian gods eternally fucking. Mrs. Tewks just made sure their little backs were straight as they easily locked their legs into full lotuses. With my long legs I can't do better than the half lotus for now, and even then, at the end of the twenty minutes, everything from my right knee on down to my toes had fallen asleep.

By sunrise we were in the kitchen and breakfast nook, and I ripped the shrink-wrapping off a white board and Magic Marker set I'd had lying around but never opened, and hung it on the wall next to the Basquiat I paid too much for. I divided everyone into four work teams, splitting up the couples. Today, Team Siddhartha cooked dinner, Team Nazarene set the table and cleaned the kitchen, and Team Mahomet helped Rosamaria clean the rest of the house. Team Chango had the day off.

After breakfast I cornered Rosamaria in the pantry and asked her to stay on another few days to teach the teams the ins and outs of the house. I have no idea where the plunger is, for example. When I told her how much her severance pay would be, she had me repeat it three times.

Around eleven, Santa Cruz Jeep/Chrysler/Plymouth delivered the minivans, green with yellow pinstriping like the colors of Brazil's flag, and we struck out for the mall. We invaded the Gap, and the teenage salesgirls, when they realized we were all together and all shopping for every possible item of clothing, suddenly got very skittish and panicky. Eight thousand, six hundred and fifty-six of my dollars later, even before the last of us had filed over to the food court for burritos on brown plastic trays, the Gap girls had already rushed into a huddle of whispers.

The only thing the Gap doesn't sell is shoes, so after lunch we went over to the Wild Pair. Amazingly, they had high-heeled mules in stock in all the women's sizes. Mrs. Landi giggled and said she wore a pair just like them when she sang with the USO

in Korea. I and all the rest of the men are wearing white Jack
Purcel tennis shoes. I let Mrs. Tewks buy little Sally and Cindy
anything they wanted. (That reminds me, I have to have my office call the school board and see what California state law has to
say about home schooling.)

We came back to *chi gong* meditation. It was going pretty
well until I forgot the last hand position and had to go find the
book. At least I thought it went pretty well. It's so hard to tell if
your positions are right from the blurry black-and-white pictures
of this skinny, bearded old Chinese man going through the mo-
tions. It's like learning to tango from drawings of black footprints
on a page, fat heels for the man, dot heels for the woman, and all
those numbers, arrows, and dotted lines. Perhaps I should bring
in guest lecturers. Yet only as a last resort. It is vital that my au-
thority never be questioned. Anyway, I didn't feel much power
from it, not nearly as much as staring at the mandala this morning. It was more like an aerobics class in slow motion, all of us ex-
panding across the patio, our arms floating outward like cranes,
then contracting with our breaths as we drew inward, curled
over, and raised a leg like a mantis. But I'll give it a couple more
tries.

Oh, at the mall I also bought all the body boards and body-
board flippers they had, to start teaching them wave dynamics. In
front of the house I paddled out on my long board and taught
them all how to catch a wave and steer the body board into the
curl. Brian V. was a natural, said he was stationed in Hawaii during the war and dimly remembered trying to surf once with a
buddy of his. Lydia Sandilla whispered to me that she wanted to
bake him her famous icebox cake for his birthday. I had planned
on outlawing all birthdays and holidays except the Fourth of July
as just more conventional, debilitating ties to this (illusory) mate-

rial world, but, oh, what the heck. Sure the old guy's nuts, but nice enough, and the little party should help gel our sense of family.

After the beach there was a run on the bathrooms. I've tried to plan for everything, but the whole shower/hot water thing has yet to be worked out. I could let some of them use mine, but it might wreak havoc on the power dynamic.

That night after surfing I popped the cardboard label off my Gap jeans and searched my bathroom for the nail clippers to snip the four tiny weaves of white thread that had bolted the cardboard to the pocket. I pulled on a new Gap polo shirt and the rough cotton felt like a hair shirt compared to my favorite old Ralph Lauren. I guess that's the point. And all those pretty loafers? When will I ever wear them again?

Halfway down the stairs I smelled the chocolate of the cake baking, a roast simmering in some rich red wine. My mom cooked Thanksgiving here last year, and that might be the last time anyone has used anything but the microwave in that vast kitchen. Mrs. Landi and Lydia Sandilla and the forgettable Professor (Nicholas Harris) and Glen milled in the kitchen. Lydia was their crew chief. Most of the eight burners of the commercial stove rumbled with flame. Mrs. Landi opened one of the commercial ovens and a powerful scent clouded the room. The men were at the island washing vegetables in the sink just for that purpose, which I have never once used.

"It smells like heaven in here. I almost Disappeared!"

Everyone chuckled at my very little joke, except Glen suddenly got very worried.

"This is the most amazing kitchen!" said Lydia. "You know, I dreamed about having an island one day, but the kitchen in our apartment is just so small!"

"I hope you like sauerbraten. When we were stationed in Germany, the local liaison's wife showed me how to make it."

"It smells like a holiday."

I heard Team Nazarene float into the dining room, the plates, glasses, and silverware clacking sharply, heard them dragging all the extra chairs from the walls to a table so long it had never once been totally covered in plates. I entered the room and they smiled at me. Out in the den the other two teams were gathered around the remotes, turning on and off everything but the TV that they stared at. When they saw me some jumped, as if I were a dentist catching them playing with the knobs on the dental chair.

"Relax, everybody. Make yourselves at home. This *is* your home now. Here, this remote turns on the amp, preamp, and home-theater receiver. Then this one is for the satellite dish. That telephone-book-looking thing is the satellite TV guide. And that little remote is for the TV."

Yvonda gave it a try and eventually got a picture on the screen, then a picture within a picture that even I have a little trouble getting rid of. It was time for the Simpsons, so I ratcheted to them past the other channels.

"Hey!"

Everyone was excited. It was my own infomercial. I thought they had all already been pulled. But I guess I remember Jill saying some of the stations wouldn't kill the spots and refund our money unless they could find another buyer for the airtime.

So on the fucking TV I saw my old self in St. Barths. On the screen Nikki was staring at me, and the other students patted her on the back, shouted, and whistled, and she blushed, tried to hide her head on her lovely shoulder. Sixty diagonal inches of me yammered about being right there, right then, and how fear inhibited action. Everybody was frozen where they stood. The real me pushed past their shoulders to squash the remote. Line dancing on the Nashville Network, loud and absurd, replaced me on the screen. Eventually I found the *mute* button and the room instantly quieted.

"No watching bullshit. Got it? No watching bullshit! Especially *my* old bullshit. Don't you all understand it poisons the brain, takes you ten steps back for the half a step forward we have made today! Don't you see this is not a joke? Not a vacation in a big house by the sea! I have repudiated my past, and so must you all! Television is the most effective and surreptitious programmer of mediocrity in the history of this tiny planet! I mean, think about it. What's worth watching? *The Simpsons*, *The Larry Sanders Show*, Bravo, the Independent Film Channel, and maybe CNN's *Style with Elsa Klench*. That's it! In fact, that is all we will watch. No Australian-rules football when we should be sitting *zazen*, no MTV's *The Real World* when we should be making an offering to the *orishas*!!"

It was only afterward that I realized my chest was heaving and I must have been squeezing the life out of the remote in my hand because the hatch for the batteries had opened up and the batteries rested in my palm like robotic turds. No one could look me in the eyes. Not Nikki, not Jill. I must have been channeling Genghis Khan or somebody. I never yell.

The two little Tewks girls were breathing more quickly than I was, so I dropped onto the couch and pulled them up, one on each knee. They hid in the crooks of my arms. Mrs. Tewks petted the littler one's red hair, then eased her own face up to mine.

"No *Seinfeld*?"

Many of the others grumbled, pawed the carpet with their feet. I shrugged. I made my voice soft and deeply fatherly.

"I don't get what the big fuss is, but all right, at least for a little while. And the girls can watch whatever you feel won't poison them too much."

"How 'bout *Home Improvement?*"

I chopped Mr. Landi a look that made the poor little old guy almost gulp it back before it was all the way out of his mouth. I took him aside later and apologized, but right then I wanted to make sure that lesson wasn't lost on any of them. I switched to *The Simpsons* and it seemed like they were all starting to relax again.

Suddenly, I wanted to eat. I suddenly wanted us all to eat together, right then. I wondered if I could will Mrs. Sandilla to step on it, or will the burners to burn a little hotter. Maybe I could repeat the thought in my head till it blurred into a chant, concentrate on my third eye till it tingled, and beam the thought out of my third eye into the kitchen like a live satellite feed.

Mrs. Sandilla, hurry up, I am hungry. I want us all to enjoy our first full meal together. The burritos in the mall did not count.

I repeated. And repeated. And repeated . . .

■ ■ ■

"Dinner's ready, everybody."

Mrs. Sandilla found an apron somewhere and held a gravy-wet spoon in her hand. On TV, simultaneously, a similar housewife with a wet spoon was calling her family in to eat Stove Top stuffing.

The more I learn about the magic of this world, the less I understand.

Everybody pushed themselves out of the deep couches and the chairs and rushed toward the aromas.

Right Here, Right Now

■ ■ ■

"Calling the all-powerful forces of the universe, we beseech ye to guide us on our never-ending search for the invisibility of enlightenment. We vow to be indefatigable and ever-vigilant, for though we know the road is most difficult, no destination in the universe is more worthwhile."

We held hands around the table, the Mary Anne character (Lanie something) on my left, and Brian V. on my right. Brian V.'s old, spongy hands were much softer.

"Dig in, everybody. Team Siddhartha worked too hard on all this to let it get cold."

I reached for Lanie's plate and added some meat and passed it to Brian V., who shook onto it a cloud of mashed potatoes from a wooden spoon. I encouraged him to pass the plate down, and eventually everyone got the hint, and soon all the plates were floating an oval around the rectangular table past every station of food. I made sure everyone got a little of everything that first time around. They could be more specific for seconds. Mrs. Sandilla had asked me if I wanted us all to fix our own plates in the kitchen, and though more efficient and fine for breakfast and lunch, that method degrades the communal excitement of shared big meals.

The first loaded plate came back around to me, but I landed it before Lanie.

"Wow! Thanks!"

I lifted a merlot I'd been saving and started to tilt it toward her glass.

"Uh, is there any white?"

I shook my head at her sternly.

"A, with the roast, white wine would taste like dishwater, but

B, and this is important, everybody, so listen up. Aren't we studying *all* the diverse paths to the divine? Well, what about ancient paths? The Greek followers of Bacchus used wine—red wine—to bring them closer to the gods. And of course I needn't remind anyone that at that Last Supper Jesus sure as hell wasn't serving any plucky little chardonnay."

So I filled her big glass full, filled my own, and passed the bottle along.

"Drink a lot, loved ones, and after dinner we shall dance."

I pulled the house remote out of my pocket, aimed it at the red plastic eye next to the dining room light switch, and soon music—Joni Mitchel's *Court and Spark*—seeped out of the wall speakers. The music injected more energy into all of us; we talked louder, ate faster. The Professor/Nicholas and Mary Anne/Lanie eyed each other across the green beans. Mr. Tewks cut the meat smaller for the girls. Nikki and Jill looked like a pop duo in their sundresses, indentically sized, styled, and flowered, but differently colored. Yet though they sat next to each other, I don't think I heard them exchange a word.

■ ■ ■

Later, Team Nazarene was cleaning the kitchen while the rest of us were in the main living room drinking more wine, lifting the furniture, and shuffling it to the walls. I'd loaded the CD player with James Brown, Lakeside, Parliament/Funkadelic, the Ohio Players, and Prince, and set it to shuffle and turned it up very loud.

As soon as Team Nazarene entered, I began the lesson. I had

Right Here, Right Now

Mr. Sandilla set up the videocamera in the corner.* Imagine if the Last Supper had been televised? Or if before the Buddha sat down at the base of the *bodhi* tree he had a bunch of surveillance cameras set up to record the look on his face at the precise moment of satori? So I nodded to Mr. Sandilla to roll tape. I'll give you the gist of what I said here because I'm afraid the music was up too loud. I should start wearing a body mike.

"My talk will be brief, so we can all stand up for it. In fact, we *have* to be standing. Everyone, feel the floor with your toes. Feel the texture of the carpet on the balls of your feet, on the pads of your heels. Ritual movement, otherwise known as dance, is one of man's first methods of seeking the divine. Of course, it is most famous in sub-Saharan Africa, but what about North Africa's whirling dervishes? Dizziness is their way of altering their state, and tonight we will explore that as well . . ."

I rolled out the cocktail cart with several bottles of generic cough syrup. With PES dissolved we're going to have to economize, and I figure we're going to be going through a lot of this stuff, so I had Rosamaria pick up a case at the Price Club.

"I don't know if this syrup will be as strong as the labelless, expired bottle that started me on my journey, nor are we going to add marijuana, so Mr. Sandilla here of the D.E.A. can rest a little easier. Besides, none of you are ready for that cocktail yet. The girls are so young they won't need anything to help tap into their true selves. Their imaginations have not yet calcified, and we will

*This tape, along with the others that were recently leaked to *A Current Affair*, then recklessly broadcast, uncensored, on pay-per-view, was recovered from Robinson's home safe by the house's new owners. His recounting of this first session is largely corroborated by the tape.

all dedicate ourselves to keeping them so free . . ."

I unscrewed the metal cap of a bottle and passed it to Glen, unscrewed another bottle and filled Jill's empty wineglass with the thick, cherry-flavored liquid.

"Finish your wine, then add the cough syrup. Sounds like it will make you puke, right? It's supposed to. Peyote, yage, hallucinogenic mushrooms all have a similar effect. There are two bathrooms on this floor, but I recommend just heading out the French doors for the terrace and leaning over the balcony. Let the ocean clean up after you. Jill, could you get several face towels from the linen closet and a bottle of mouthwash from a bathroom, to leave on the terrace? Thank you . . ."

They were all staring into their glasses and I could see each of them breathing.

"I see many of you are scared. You should be."

I stared at the syrup in my own glass, its viscosity, the way the lights in the room reflected from it dully. My legs suddenly lost themselves under me for just a moment, reminding me that I was already very drunk. Then suddenly, interestingly, the memories of Jim Jones and the Guyana massacre and Marshall Applewhite bloomed in my brain. What did they serve their followers? Kool-Aid and cyanide? Vodka and Nembutal? Every eye in the house, including my own, was on my glass.

"Don't worry, folks. It won't kill ya."

And I tilted it down, sucking the syrup out of the cup. The extra alcohol clear-cut my insides and I felt lighter immediately. Then a shiver started at my knees, wiggled through my hips, and blasted through the top of my skull. I closed my eyes to elongate the feeling.

Eventually I reopened my eyes and looked to the first one I saw—Glen—and nodded. He drank, and then Jill and Brian V.

and Nikki. I nodded at the Tewkses and the Landis and Yvonda and the Sandillas, and they drank too. Lanie and Nicholas Harris were close together, whispering and holding hands. I stared till they saw me; still they hesitated; then finally they also drank up. The shiver passed through all of them like a wave. Then smiles and some giggles of released nervousness from all parts of the room.

"Did you all feel that shiver? Shivers are *axe*, little bits of it, slipped into the everyday. But what do we do when a shiver seizes us? We hold on, can't wait for it to end, maybe even rub the part of us still tingling to return ourselves that more quickly to our everyday mud. You probably just felt it begin at your knees and rise through your body to the top of your head, right . . . ?"

Smiles and open-mouthed nods from them.

"That was *axe* passing up through your chakras to the crown of your head, your lighthouse to the cosmos. Enlightenment is a constant shiver, perpetual orgasm, never-ending tickle. No wonder we Disappear! The physical body thinks it can barely handle even just a few seconds of pure ecstasy, thinks it will rattle itself into spare parts! But it's so much more durable. So, the next time a shiver possesses you, don't close yourself up! Open up to it! Concentrate on how to keep it going! The next time you are dizzy, first guide yourself to someplace soft, then *indulge* the dizziness! Wight now fow exampu . . . I . . . feel . . . di . . ."

■ ■ ■

The next thing I remember was a pillow pressing at the skin of my face in a weird way. Weird because at first I could have sworn I was still standing. I touched my chin, the rest of the skin around my mouth for wet signs of puke, but I was dry except for a line of drool. I made my eyes open and saw all of them huddled around me like a stand of redwoods. No, not all of them, for I heard someone wretching outside; it sounded like a woman, a little higher pitched than a man's puking sound, then the cough, then a deeply guttural rasp. I blinked quickly to try to jar myself back. I needed to reassure these people. I forced my eyeballs to calm down, to focus on something, and stop orbiting my face . . .

"Almost, ladies and germs! I almost did it . . . !"

As I sat up their hands warmed my back, helping me up. They all felt so friendly.

"I just got a tiny glimpse of what Disappearing will be like. Man, are we in for a treat! Dance! Why isn't anyone dancing!"

Eventually I struggled the remote out of my pocket and turned the stereo way up. Prince's "Little Red Corvette." I danced alone but kept my head low like a bug till my blood pressure recharged enough so that I wouldn't pass out again. I saw feet with painted toenails, dancing near me; they could have been Jill's, but Nikki is so light skinned they could have been hers as well. Then big, milky tan feet that could only have belonged to Glen, and an old white man's knobby, hairy feet. Either good ol' Brian V.'s or quiet Mr. Landi's.

I made myself stand tall and sway like a Deadhead twirl dancer and noticed they were all following my lead.

"No! No! Don't follow my steps! Remember, the paths are many but convergent! *Feel* the music and express *yourselves!*"

I cabbage patched and running maned, smurfed, snaked, and washing machined. Yvonda and Nikki, obviously enough, were great dancers, but Mrs. Tewks surprised me with a few of her moves. Brian V. hunched over to hold hands with Cindy, the youngest Tewks girl, as she pogoed high, tethered by his hairy arms, her blond ponytail lagging just behind her head's ups and downs.

Right Here, Right Now

I found myself laughing. We all were, I think, but I have no idea how long it had been going on. I danced out the French doors to the terrace, where Glen was now puking over the balcony. They all bunny-hopped behind me. I had to shout over the music, loud even outside.

"So, right out here, after I'd vomited in the pool, right out here is where my destiny was first revealed to me. Then back in these doors to the couch by the stereo. That was just last week; before that I'd never heard of *axe*! But Mudamenta told me I had to find the *axe* within myself, and I had to bring it out in others. And here y'all are! So dance! Dance hard! We'll all concentrate on freeing our spirits, our fucking spirits! And maybe, just maybe, the little Brazilian midget will come out again!"

Oohs and aaahs from the students. He/she might come, with more instructions; that would be wonderful. All the spiritual techniques we are studying, they seem a little scattershot. Maybe he/she'll come back and give me another hint?

Nikki spun and stopped, but her little Gap sundress kept spinning, screwed itself high up her thighs, and the entire half of my body flushed. Our lovemaking was already spectacular, but that was before I learned the tantra. I remember thinking that last night, with her, would have been one for the history books.

"I have an idea, everybody. Dervish time! Come on!"

They danced near me and I encouraged Sally, the older Tewks girl, to come in the center of us and spin and spin and spin in a circle.

"Ahhhhhhh!"

Her crying instantly stopped us all. She shoved through the wall of adult bodies with her hands high and butted into my stomach with the top of her head as she fled inside and up the stairs. Mr. Tewks started after her when my arm automatically sprung out and stopped him.

"See? She's already lost some of her childish openness to *axe*. Don't worry; we'll work with her tomorrow."

Her little sister, Cindy, however, jumped to the center without prodding and started spinning herself. Giggles of pure joy sounded from her little throat. James Brown's "Papa Don't Take No Mess" was now the loudness, and her face was soon a blur and she collapsed, but we were all around her and all caught her and lifted her high, and her eyes orbited her head and her cheeks were slack and she couldn't stop her hyperventilated giggling, and we laid her down on a lounge chair and the Tewkses stroked her cheeks with the back of their hands till her breaths were more normally spaced and less audible.

"Again, Daddy! *Please!*"

We all laughed. But I looked at the Tewkses, then moved my eyes toward the French doors. Mrs. Tewks got the hint, lifted her little girl, and carried her to bed.

"That is how it's done, ladies and gentlemen! Give in to the moment, explore the stratospheres of emotion!"

I called them all to me with my outstretched hands and pulled Jill into the center, and we spun her and she spun herself, her arms out and head back, around and around till her legs failed and she fell into Glen and Mr. Sandilla. We all crowded under her to lift her to our shoulders, and we spun her even faster, and she wheezed in such a high pitch it sounded more like a whistle, and we lowered her gently to another chair, and when her eyes started to slow down they found mine and widened and she ground her thighs together and ground her teeth.

I found myself feeling exactly what she was feeling, what we felt together in the office. A sexual chill raced up the silhouette of my shoulders and I closed my eyes to revel in its charge.

When I opened my eyes Glen was spinning himself and the others surrounded him. He's gotta weigh fifty pounds more than I do and there's no way they could raise *my* 210 pounds. But he spun anyway, and when he started to fall I caught him mostly myself and eased him right to the tiles of the terrace.

"Tickle therapy, people!"

And our hundred or so fingers reached for him like he was the keyboard of an organ, and we were all Jimmy Smiths playing fast and possessed, and big Glen arched and twisted and curled.

"I see her! I see her!"

Glen's eyes were shut, but the eyeballs were moving so much you could see their trace inside their lids.

"Who?" I asked him.

"Mudamenta. But now she's gone! *He's* gone!"

"He'll be back, Glen. He knows where to find us."

"Uhhh-nnnh!"

That deep sound, from a female, made me turn. Lanie was twisting on the tiles while Nicholas Harris knelt over her, tickling her stomach, then up and under her arms. Theirs is the longest first date in history. I crawled over to help him, careful of my bad knees on the hard tiles, and the others came crawling too. Lanie was soon smearing her thighs together as Nikki was, but her sounds were even more explicitly orgasmic. Her face is so aggressively plain in its natural state that the shift—so gorgeous when aroused—surprised me completely. She just might be the closest to getting there of all of them.

"Ahhhh! Ahhhh! Ahhhh!"

"Listen up. We've made some wonderful strides today. I'm so

very proud of all of you. We have already explored deeper than most seekers do in a lifetime. We all deserve a round of applause . . ."

We all clapped and Mr. Sandilla, who I don't think said a word all night, hooted and whistled through his fingers. I'll have to ask him to teach me how. It always seemed like something I should be able to do.

"Yet there is an entire realm of human interaction that we have completely ignored thus far . . ."

Between the wine and the syrup, my own voice to my own ears sounded amplified by a bullhorn, but a hundred yards away. My tongue was two sizes too big for my mouth.

"I am speaking of sexuality, of course. I have been studying some esoteric sexual meditative methods, and Jill can attest to their efficacy . . ."

I looked for Jill, and others did too. I finally saw her inside on the portable phone. She said she was going to spend a few days with us; tell Alan she had to go down to L.A. to sign up more clients for our new studio. Mrs. Tewks skipped past her, hurrying to join us again outside. I turned back and saw Nikki's amazing black eyes on me, on fire.

"Women, in general, are so much more advanced than men, so much closer to the reality of the divine. Think about it. We see it clearly in their orgasms. Women orgasm and transform themselves, at least for a little while. Men orgasm and simply release. A friend of mine at Yale likened the male orgasm to *a really good pee*! What woman would describe her full-body, reality-shattering convulsions like that? So—and I know this is unusual, but we few gathered here are unusual, special people—I will initiate the women into the practices of the perpetual cosmic orgasm first, and after they have mastered the techniques, hopefully in just a few months, they will be able to in turn teach the men . . ."

That sure as hell got their attention! Mr. Tewks and Mr. Sandilla squinted at me as if that would've helped them understand.

"We have to remember that the conventional bourgeois limits on human behavior have done nothing but imprison us in these tattered shells of meat and blood we call bodies! Mrs. Tewks, could you come here please?"

I pulled myself up to a deck chair; the others were stretched out on the terrace or sitting at my feet. She and her husband intently confered, whispering, eyeing each other so deeply, examining the other for the slightest sign of a nod yes or a shake no. I noticed how their bodies swayed slightly, floating with a gentle current like kelp underwater. I thought it was just the Tewkses, then I noticed we all were. We shared a rhythm even though we could barely hear the music. The cough syrup must have been in just the middle of its run.

"Mrs. Tewks, you do not have to—this is an exercise you do not have to engage in right now. Yvond—"

"No."

Mrs. Tewks's voice was the clearest sound I had heard all day. She looked to her husband once more and smiled. She listed as she walked to me.

"Don't be afraid. Just a simple demonstration."

I moved my hands off my lap so she knew where to sit.

"I will concentrate my *axe* into my lips and let you sample a bit of it."

I drew my lids down over my eyes as I inhaled and summoned the sum of my essence into my lips. When their vibration seemed to be at a maximum, I peeked just enough to know where to aim, and tilted my head till my lips touched hers. I felt dizzy and displaced, and projected that energy through my lips and into her soul. When I finally pulled away and opened my eyes, I saw hers were still closed and her face and shoulders slack.

"Keep your eyes closed, please, so you can concentrate. Now, think carefully. How do you feel?"

"Very . . . fine . . ."

"Could you feel my *axe*?"

"Yeah . . ."

"Tell us, Mrs. Tewks, if I kissed your yoni, your sex, with that same power, how would you feel?"

She nodded quickly and a buried hum vibrated her throat. I looked past her to Mr. Tewks. His eyes tried to meet mine but kept retreating.

"Mr. Tewks, does she suddenly love you any less? Is she suddenly a worse mother? Of course not. But she carries the divine within her, and as a woman she is simply closer to touching hers than you are to yours. I will merely teach her some meditative techniques that you two will be able to practice on your own for the rest of your time together on earth. And to those of you without mates, when you are ready, I will assign you each a lab partner."

Mrs. Tewks's thumbs pushed several of the small buttons back out of the buttonholes of her cotton blouse. I shook my head.

"Not here. My room is more comfortable. And Lanie, you two're on the same team, so I'd like you to join us. At your levels right now, my *axe*, fully unleashed, would be too much for one person. Last week, with Jill for example, there were times when I was a little afraid for her heart."

Right Here, Right Now

Lanie's swaying neck suddenly stiffened. She sat up at attention. Nicholas Harris spilled across her legs, unconscious.

Then Jill returned outside.

"Whaa-a-at? Did you call me . . . ?"

Her face was so slack she had to tilt her head back to see through the narrow line between her eyelids.

"What did you tell the husband?"

"I told him where I was, really."

She forced her eyes round again, at least for a moment, to underline the moment. But they were soon too heavy and her eyes again narrowed. Her information seeped into me slowly, and in slow motion I smiled.

"Excellent. Now could you and Mr. Sandilla get the video-camera from my office and set it up in my bedroom? The women of Team Nazarene and myself are about to practice the tantra."

"Oh."

I looked over to poor Nikki and she seemed to be thinking so hard her lips were moving. I'll certainly make love with her soon, but it was important that my first not be with the sexiest, the most available. I've got to explain that to her today.

"Sweet dreams, everyone. I'm so proud of all of you. We're making much faster progress than I could ever have imagined."

I shooed them all inside but Mr. Tewks.

"Could you help me with Nicholas Harris?"

I took his hands, Mr. Tewks squatted and grabbed his shoes, and we shuffled him inside. I thought about leaving him on a couch but changed my mind and steered his weight to the mouth of the curving staircase and tugged him up, stair by stair by stair. I was on the downside of the buzz by then, which was good for this heavy lifting and for screwing two new women all night long. We were halfway between floors.

"Jim," I said. I don't know why, it just came out.

Step.

"Gerry," he said.

Step.

"Gerry. Sorry. But I cannot tell you how brave you are . . . How quickly you have shed this bullshit we have been steeped in since the day we were born . . . ! That is why I chose you and your wife for this first, crucial experiment . . . ! Mr. and Mrs. Sandilla of the D.E.A.? Forget about it . . . ! No, I have been watching you both. Even back in Chicago, you two caught my eye . . . As I said before, most people might take a few months to master the tantra . . . but I bet your wife will get it in just a few weeks . . . and then she'll be able to teach you, and wow . . . ! Believe me, you're gonna thank me . . ."

He still was silent as we crested the stairs, breathed and rested, then started up again and wobbled down the hall. Thank God Nicholas was in a bottom bunk. We swung him a few times till his butt rose enough to clear the bed and swung him in. Though Gerry has the upper bunk, I tilted my head at the door to ask him to follow me back outside. Some of the others trafficked the hall, brushing their teeth, carrying towels into the bathrooms. They tried not to look at us, which only increased the tension. I pulled him to the darkness at the end of the hall.

"Look, Ger, let's not talk teacher to student but man to man. She's not going to be whispering sweet nothings in my ear, I assure you . . . Look, I've got an idea. Why don't you listen by the door? In cases like this your imagination can be your worst enemy. If you listen by the door you'll hear that I am merely giving them chills and tickles and perhaps a sense of disembodied dizziness—just centered on particularly sensitive and culturally taboo areas of their bodies.

"I . . . I still don't, um, know . . ."

"C'mon, just pull up a chair. In fact, I insist. What have we been talking about ever since Chicago? *Extremes of emotion.* You're afraid of listening in because you're afraid of the extreme emotions you think you will feel. Well, if you feel those emotions, great! Cry, wail, scream! Explore them and see if they bring you closer to that place we're all trying to head for. Remember, many roads, one goal . . ."

I squeezed both of his brittle shoulders and widened my eyes, kept staring at him until he could find enough man in himself to stare back.

"But I do not believe that you will cry, or wail, or scream. You love your wife and she loves you, and you will be joyous knowing that she is experiencing the most prolonged period of ecstasy she has ever known. Who knows? You might even find yourself aroused? A large black man with your small, white wife."

"No! God! I—!"

"It is quite all right! It is not you but our society that has invested the image of black men with hypersexuality. I'm sure you've read *Penthouse Forum* at least once. Over ten percent of the letters describe this very fantasy. You'd be abnormal *not* to have these feelings! Instead of running from them, where they will nip at your heels for the rest of your days, turn and face them! Wallow in whatever you are experiencing and I guarantee you, you will rise to the next level . . ."

He was suddenly quaking. I think I hit the nail on the head. Jill and Mr. Sandilla stepped out of my room with the empty videocamera case.

"Uh, Jill, you can bunk with Nikki and Mrs. Landi."

She looked to us both quickly, then disappeared.

"Ger, just pull up a chair. Oh, and there are some paper towels under the sink in the bathroom."

Though I could see he still hadn't made up his mind, I smiled with pride as if he already had, shook his hand, and slipped inside my bedroom. He badly wanted to watch. It was obvious, but he'd never allow himself to admit it.

They were sitting on opposite sides of the bed, their backs as straight as chairs. Lanie kept fingering a pearl in her necklace. I noticed her thighs inside her nightgown, puckered and puddling. Mrs. Tewks's nightgown was floor length and flannel. I didn't know she wore contacts, but there she was in red plastic glasses, oversized and a decade out of style like Sally Jesse Raphael's.

"Hello Lanie, Mrs. Tewks."

"Call me Janice, please!"

"Janice, of course."

PART THREE

Santa Cruz and Boron, California

December 1st

I'm still thinking about last night's chicken. It was the most amazing thing I've ever tasted. The Chinese butcher brought them over in small boxes made of brittle wooden slats. They smelled and complained. Sally and Cindy were trying to reach through the cage and touch the wattle of the white rooster when I saw them, leapt, and saved their fingers.

Glen, Mr. Tewks, Mr. Landi, and Mr. Sandilla were on congos, bongo, and talking drum on the terrace when the women paraded out in long white Gap cotton dresses, the girls last. The jingles of the bells encircling all their ankles at first reminded me more of Christmas than of an ancient animist ritual. The women danced a slow shuffle just as they'd seen in the show *Ritual Dances of Santeria* that I'd taped off the Discovery Channel. They snaked their line into a circle and started clapping.

I bought the knife last week from a dealer in African art up in San Francisco. I'd never killed anything bigger than a large beetle before. When I was traveling through Africa I remember stepping off the barge I was taking down the Zaire (Congo) River into the tiny town of Bumba at dawn. Herdsmen were walking their skinny cattle into the fields, lazily swatting their bony cow asses with long sticks. After they passed I noticed a thin man kneeling over the neck of a bleating goat. The goat stared emptily in my direction, whining like a human child in a language I faulted myself for not understanding. All the while the man sawed at its throat with what looked like an old butter knife. I knew he'd never break the skin, so I relaxed. Yet suddenly, *"Bloo-bloo-bloo,"* the whining stopped and this sound came from someplace lower on the goat's neck. From its neck a shadow spread across the brown ground as its blood seeped into the dust.

I had been sharpening my knife several times throughout the day. I circled the wooden cage three times clockwise, then seven times counterclockwise. I invoked Eshu-Elegbara, the trickster deity, took a deep breath, then unlatched the gate and quickly reached in and snatched the smelly white rooster by its neck. Its feet paddled crazily in the air; a talon got hooked on my white pants and ripped them and scratched my thigh. The word "infection" immediately bloomed in my skull.

On cue, as I pressed the rooster's neck against a large flat black stone, the beats from the drums rose and swallowed my thoughts. The women twirled circles in their bare feet, their bells crazed now, rhythmless. I wanted to look away from the rooster's pure black dot of an eye but made myself stare as I cut his head from his body. My hands, his white feathers, instantly were speckled red as I quickly held his open neck over the brass bowl and the rooster's body pumped its blood into it in waves, nearly overflowing it.

Later, after it was plucked and the feathers saved in a leather pouch I'd hung over the fireplace, I'd thought about having Team Nazarene make *moqueca* or some other traditional Brazilian recipe. But I had a jones for fried chicken and if I've learned anything in these past five months, it's never ignore craving or intuition. Mrs. Tewks used corn flakes and a lot a pepper in the batter. Anyway, they're wrong when they say roosters are too tough to eat. It was the best fried chicken any of us had ever tasted.

[Sound of door opening.]

Jill Lowry: "Oh, there you are. Excuse me, Ash."

"Oh, hey, Jill. One second."

Jill just found me. I've been in the garage, supposedly stripping the wax off my board, but as you know, I've mainly been talking to you. I love having a house full of friends, but once in a while it's nice to be alone again.

Jill Lowry: "We're ready with the video when you are."

"I'll meet you in there."

A big swell from Baja is supposed to be hitting early tomorrow morning, so I want to get the new wax on tonight.

Jill Lowry: "Uh, Ashton? Can I get you anything?"

"No thanks, I'll be right there."

"Any, um, any ideas about tonight? Would you maybe like to, um . . . ?"

"Sure, Jill, that'd be great. I'll be right in."

[Sound of door closing.]

She just left. The whole Nikki/Jill thing is still unresolved. I don't even try to pretend anymore that I don't feel anything more for them than I do for the other women. More than half of the tantra sessions involve either the one or the other. (Never together. Not yet anyway.) Yet between the two I feel different yet powerful emotions. My relationship to Nikki is certainly closer to a Western concept of wife (except for the fact that I am hardly monogamous and we barely ever get any time alone). Jill is more of a confidant. Perhaps Nikki is my queen, Jill my prime minister.

I'd better get inside. Tonight's video is of last night with Yvonda and Mrs. Landi. I'll never forget that first night with Mrs. L. I can't believe she's just ten years younger than my grandma! I had already practiced the tantra with all the rest of them and I could sense her disappointment each night when I didn't choose her. So one night I took an extra hit of the syrup and brought her in with Nikki. Wow. All night she surprised us with these amazing tricks and nibbles she says she learned from her days in the USO. Now I know why Mr. Landi's so quiet. If I were a normal man she might've knocked me into a coma months ago.

Yvonda's no slouch herself, and last night, when they both decided to bear down on me, I tried chanting, I tried jamming my tongue hard against the roof of my mouth, and I even tried my old high school trick of conjuring the image of Abe Vigoda, the old guy from *Barney Miller*, and still I just *barely* managed not to ejaculate. Yet I'm proud to say I haven't slipped in the five months since we began. And the books are absolutely right: I *do* have much more energy and mental acuity.

December 11th

"I'm sorry, Ashton, but you can only count them as dependents if they're blood relatives under the age of twenty-one or full-time students."

"Damn! But I've been paying for their *everything* for almost half a year! What if I adopt them and have them all change their names to Robinson?"

"I . . . wouldn't risk it. Especially not with that old guy in his eighties. You're kind of an audit magnet as it is."

Geoffrey, my business manager, and I sat close by my desk, leaning over the various islands of receipts. My personal corporation's fiscal year ends December 15, and this year's been so crazy, what with shutting down PES, founding a new religion, and all. It was especially chaotic today because the workers were finally getting around to installing that crane for the bungee-cord jump over the driveway. The jackhammering this morning was driving me nuts.

"Why am I an audit magnet? Just because I'm trying to help people? Wonderful things are happening here, Geoff. Just come to dinner with us this week and you'll see."

Little Cindy rushed into the office without knocking, rooted around between our legs, and came out with her Power Ranger doll. Mrs. Tewks was right behind her but reared up at the doorway and knocked delicately.

"Cindy! Leave them alone now. I told you I'd get the Pink Ranger later. Your sister's waiting for you in the kitchen and you're gonna be late for school . . . ! Sorry, Ashton."

"It's all right, Janice."

"Would you and your guest like a chocolate chip scone? Team Chango is just pulling a batch out of the oven."

"Geoffrey?"

"They're not laced with some kind of crazy—"

I stopped him with my eyes.

"All natural, Geoff."

"Then, sure."

Mrs. Tewks reached down, and Cindy raised her arm and let herself be led away like a little red wagon drawn by its handle.

"One of yours?"

"That little white child?"

"I've heard stories."

"Like what?"

"*Stories.*"

"From whom?"

"Everybody."

"Geoffrey, we go back to high school. We were the only black guys in our senior class. And I'm your biggest client. Tell me."

"Biggest client by far. And your friend. That's why I'm telling you. People are starting to ask around."

"Who?"

"I don't know. They won't say. But Jill's ex is one of the ones talking."

Right Here, Right Now

"Pencil-dicked piece of shit! I'll—!"

Geoffrey was staring at my right hand. I must have been waving it to summon all of my *axe* into the eye of my palm. It started throbbing, almost visibly. If that fucker had been right there, right then, I'd have unleashed it on him and stopped his fucking heart. They can't stop us now, not when we're so close! But Geoffrey wasn't ready for any of that. I calmed myself.

"Look, we are just a bunch of like-minded people come together in an experiment in alternative lifestyles. Why does that so threaten people?"

"You fired all of PES. Sure, you paid them three times more severance than the law required, but they're all still out of a job. I'm sure some of them are talking. And they say you've had some vacancies . . ."

"It is intense in here! And I would be the first to admit that it's not for everyone. This boring guy left after two days. Reminded me of the Professor on *Gilligan's Island.* And last month this nice old man, Brian V. Hillsing, the guy in his eighties you were talking about, he didn't want to go but got declared incompetent and dragged out of here kicking and screaming by his asshole of a grandson, some hotshot New York litigator, and two federal marshals."

"And now you've lobbied the city council for your own bungee-cord-jumping thing?"

How much did he really need to know?

"Look. Tony Robbins and this hypnotist guy Marshall Sylver started off teaching people to walk on hot coals and broken glass. You know, conquer your specific fears so you can conquer the world. I myself was saying the same thing for years. Well, this is . . . sort of . . . like that."

"At one hundred and six thousand dollars in liability insurance a year with a fifty-thousand-dollar deductible!"

"I don't know how much those guys paid to insure the hot coals, but it couldn't've been cheap . . ."

Just then a large fly slid into the room and nervously traced a complicated geometry. I summoned my *axe* into my right hand till it throbbed again.

"Geoff, let me show you something. See that fly . . ."

I pointed over him, and his head rotated through every possible position till he spotted it.

"Yeah . . . ?"

"The Taoists call it *chi,* the religions of the African diaspora call it *axe,* but infinitely more important than its name is its meaning, *the breath of life.* All our schooling and the values thrust upon us by this material world bind up our *axe* till we hardly have any life force left in us at all. That fly, on the other hand, is pure *axe,* unthinking, just one hundred percent being."

"That's great, Ash, but I have to get into the office—"

"I will manipulate that fly's *axe* and drive it out of the room."

Geoffrey was already collecting his papers as I waved my hand over my head. I felt that my arm, from my elbow to my palm, was glowing. As the fly floated by the bookcase I inhaled deeply and . . . tak! I shot out my hand, aiming the eye of my palm right at it.

"*Now!*" I said on the exhale.

The fly kept flying.

Geoffrey's eyes were so full of pity. That fucking "Babalu" song was forever in my brain. That's why I couldn't fully concentrate.

There was the fly, rattling around in a corner. I could have struck then but it was by the laser printer, and God knows what full-strength *axe* might've done to its electronics. So I waited . . .

Right Here, Right Now

There . . . careful . . . more to the right . . . that's better . . . *"Now!"* I caught it right in my beam and drew my hand to the open door. The fly was swept to the window, where I closed my fist, extinguished the beam, and the bug suddenly rose up and away on its own and none the worse. I looked to Geoffrey and his eyes believed for a moment, then he shook his head and soon made himself forget what he just saw. That's all right, he doesn't need to be there now; it's enough that he's starting along our path.

"I . . . I don't know, Ashton."

"Suit yourself. After all, that was just a small party trick. The point is, we are onto something here and I don't want to go broke before we finish."

"You shoulda thought of that before you pulled your in-fomercials. Before you closed down PES without first renting out the building. Before you built a TV studio that still doesn't work. Money was coming in faster than my people could add it up! You were going to expand to England, Canada, Germany, remember? You could use some of those deutsche marks round about now. I mean, I don't see why you can't put this new stuff on a set of audiotapes the folks could order out of the back of an in-flight magazine."

"They promise the sound problem will be fixed in the TV studio in a week, then we can start renting it out. And I've told you dozens of times, my new system isn't meant for everybody, at least not yet. So much of what we do here is one-on-one."

"That's what I heard."

"Look, maybe I can find a way to introduce people to this new system without scaring most of them away. I'm just afraid that it will be like Chicago, where I came on too strong and only retained these dozen or so out of several hundred. I'll work on it and maybe bring Rom and his video crew over to shoot some test segments."

"That's music to my ears, but unfortunately we're still talking three or four months until you're back making anything close to the money you used to. This is what I've been trying to tell you since October; you need cash *now*. A lot of it. Now, if you'll just let me sell off those Gap shares . . . ?"

"No."

"You must know something nobody else in the world does, because it hasn't moved in months! Your tax bill is more than whole townships! We dump Gap now, take the capital loss, and you get to keep this little cottage of yours."

I shrugged as I stood up to end the meeting. He's been on me about those Gap shares ever since I bought them. Besides, it's time for *chi gong*.

"If you ever want to come bungee-jump, just give a call."

December 13th

"Mmmm! Team Chango has done it again. Yvonda, what do you call this again?"

"Chili con noodles. You know, instead of con meat."

"Well, I for one just love it . . ."

Mmmm-mmmms ricocheted around the table.

"Not only is it delicious but extremely economical, I'll bet. Which, ah, brings me around to tonight's dinner table topic . . ."

They looked at me expectantly, as they always do. My heart beat like an angry creditor knocking on the door. I was so fucking embarrassed! What if I have to send them home? What if this is all over and we have to turn back, when we're so very, very close!! I *know* that just over the next hill lies Disappearance.

Or what if they just drifted away as the money ran out? It would kill me. The day before they came for the house I'd fake my own death and disappear (the regular kind, lowercase).* I'm too old and now too famous to go back to Club Med as a GO (gentil organisateur). I'd be bartending on Columbus Isle and

---

* Enough said.

some bald man with an oiled, taut and huge potbelly would be pulling his daiquiri off the bar when he'd snap his fingers a few times before saying, "*Now* I know where I know you from . . . !"

"Changes might be coming, people. I mean, I know they are coming; they are necessary. From tonight on, only three hours of sleep. We need to meditate more. 'Babalu' will blast at five, then sitting meditation till sunrise, then right to the bungee jump to make us present minded, then *chi gong*, yoga, and chanting. I don't know how much more time we will have together, so let us make the best of it . . ."

They looked confused.

"No, I am not planning on Disappearing anytime soon. I hope so, of course, but nothing in my dreams has tipped me off since that dream last month about the dove that landed on my shoulder and shat a substance that turned my arm into shiny steel. And speaking of dreams, I haven't asked you to turn in your dream journals in weeks, so let's do it tonight. I hope they are more legible this time, otherwise, what's the point? But I digress, I guess because the subject at hand is so unpleasant . . ."

That got their attention.

"Well, we are an extremely rich family. We live in a mansion by the sea. Yet our research will continue only another month or so, unless we find a way to generate a significant income . . . It's a shame. I feel we are so damn close, don't you?"

"Yeah!"

Nikki and Mrs. Tewks shouted the loudest, but no one was quiet. If I do have to work at a Club Med, I'd love to have Nikki working there with me.

"Thanks, you are all the most wonderful people on the planet. But friends, what if we have to stop and turn back, only to find out, perhaps after our deaths, that we were just one hill crest away from Disappearing? What if a year from now we're all back at our jobs gazing out the window of our narrow workstations, flimsy pens of green burlaped movable walls; back on the mental chain gangs that will imprison us for the rest of our days . . . ? I don't know. Perhaps we could find jobs around here somewhere, but the monthly nut on this joint is twenty-eight grand."

Arcing whistles, then they all shrank into their chairs.

Mr. Sandilla raised his hand before he spoke.

"Ashton, excuse me, but Lydia and I have been talking about this for weeks, and . . . Well, you helped us sell our place back in Chicago last month, and . . . Well, I wasn't raised to get something for nothing, and . . . we'd like to throw the proceeds from the house into the kitty."

"Henry! Lydia! Your home! No . . . Wow . . . I . . ."

I can't remember the last time I cried. I don't really know if I ever have. But thick tears were painting my cheeks. A hundred and sixty-five thousand smackers. It won't cover the entire tax bill, but it's the most wonderful gift I've ever gotten. My cousin Mtume is a realtor in Chicago. He sold it for them last month. My Adam's apple was stabbing my throat. That's when I noticed they were all crying too, even Mr. Landi, who hardly ever even speaks. I love these people. I really do.

"Damn, Yvonda, this chili must be awful spicy; everybody's eyes are watering."

They laughed, but the laughter just squirted everybody's tears out faster.

"I'm in."

"I am in."

"Me too."

"We're in."

"I love you all. I do. This will all help. Thank you!!! Spartacus couldn't have been any happier when his men leaped up and pretended to be him to try to save his life from the Romans! We'll still need to do this other thing to save us, but what a wonderful gift you all gave me today!"

This confused them. I didn't want to mention my new plan just yet, but now that they're pitching in their money too, I couldn't keep them in the dark.

"Look, I have told you from the beginning that you all are the chosen few, that no one can come in from the outside and take your places. But perhaps there is something in what we are doing here that can help others perhaps one day ascend to our level. It will by no means be the home version of our work—that would trivialize your courage and sacrifice in coming here. But we need to start thinking about the next level, about communicating a little of what we have learned to the vast unwashed, those poor souls living every moment of their lives in the dark. Yet we will have to be careful. Too much too quick, and the weak might get scared off. All of you but Jill were there in Chicago, so you know what—"

The phone chirped just then, and we were all instantly alert. The phone never rings anymore. I pushed quickly to the kitchen and picked up a phone.

"Hello?"

"Uh, yeah. Glen? Glen Bullock. I need to speak to him."

"How did you get this number? It's not listed."

"Glen Bullock. I'm warning you, mister."

"Tell me who gave you this number."

"Wouldn't you like to know? See, the motherfucker's kidnaped him or killed him, won't let him talk to his own damn family."

This last part was not said into the telephone.

"He is here, sir. I will put him right on, sir. But I would simply like to know how you got my unlisted phone number."

"We want to talk to Glen or I tell them everything."

"Tell who . . . ?"

Silence, but an echoey one. As if other extensions, other phones even, patched in from far away, were also listening in.

"Who shall I say is calling?"

"His brother-in-law, with the Illinois State Police, and his mother and sisters."

"Gle-en! Te-le-phone . . ."

Nothing. Then he arrived, always bigger than you last remembered him, half in the doorway, apologetically.

"For me?"

"Your brother-in-law, the Illinois state trooper."

"He ain't a trooper, he's a clerk."

I extended the phone to him, relieved only a little. He was afraid, but I aimed the receiver at him till he took it.

"Uh, hello, Antoine, wh-what's up?"

I should have left, but I did not. Nikki's mother kept leaving messages with the PES answering service until she finally called her back and told her she was fine; told her what I told them all our covers would be: she was working for me now and couldn't get her own phone because of bad credit. The old lady wanted to come visit at Christmas. Nikki told her it was a bad idea, but she's got this frequent flyer ticket that's about to expire. Alan, Jill's husband, called once on this phone; he must've gotten the number ransacking one of her old purses.

On the phone Glen crumpled and looked down in a guilty way, automatically in the attitude of the scolded. He just grunted indistinct responses, but Antoine, or perhaps his mother now, must have been shouting. I heard the noises from the phone from where I was standing, barely incoherent, tantalizingly so. I retreated around the corner.

"I told you. I'm *fine*, all right? He's a wonderful man. I . . . I'm just working for him . . . What . . . ? Odds and ends . . . Dammit, Mommy, I told you I haven't needed those pills for years."

Pills?

Christmas Eve

Today I was crucified by my own fucking sister. Aw, that's not what I mean. It sounds worse than it was. In fact, I'm actually glad it's out. My Secret. I was going to tell them soon, just maybe not on Christmas Eve.

I saw Papa's headlights from my office window. The gate's been acting up, so I've been leaving it open. Even if Papa does the electrical, they say it'll cost ten thousand bucks just to replace the motor, and right now I have much better things to do with what's left of my money. Besides, what kind of religion hides behind an automatic gate?

Team Nazarene, of course, orchestrated our Christmas celebrations. Mrs. Tewks hasn't stopped working all week. Chocolate chip, peanut butter, and Mexican wedding cookies have been baking in the ovens nearly round the clock. She even made an amazing-looking wreath out of seaweed and driftwood, modified, she said, from a Martha Stewart design.

Everyone got new clothes from the Gap. One of my credit cards is still good, so what the hell. Then last night, after making love, Mrs. Sandilla went back to her room while Nikki stayed and we watched *Willard* off the satellite dish till dawn. It was a beautiful night. Both of us still naked, Nikki spooned behind me and neatened my dreads. She thought it was just for Christmas, but it was really for opening that front door and greeting my folks.

"Merry Christmas Eve, baby!"

Avon was helping Mommy walk, but she pushed away from him to hug me. Papa just shook his head and spoke first.

"Merry Christmas Eve, boy. What kind of wreath you got? Can't you afford no regular green one?"

Behind me they all excitedly crowded each other like paparazzi. As soon as Mommy let go, she must have seen them all over my shoulder, because I saw how her eyes suddenly dimmed.

"Mommy, Papa, Avon, these are my students. Everybody, my parents and my brother."

"Hi!"

You can't blame them for being excited, finally meeting the parents of their spiritual leader, but I kind of wish they'd turned it down a notch. Jill broke out of the pack to hug Mama.

"Mrs. Robinson! Merry Christmas! You look marvelous! How have you been?"

"Jill. I'm just fine, baby."

And Nikki pushed through too.

"Mrs. Robinson? Mr. Robinson? Avon? I'm Nikki Kennedy."

"From Chicago? Why, I've heard all about you."

With her cane, Mommy levered herself away from Jill, right to Nikki, in movements faster than she'd made in years. Nikki flowered.

"You have?! I mean, I've heard a lot about you too. Can I help you inside?"

Mommy gathered Nikki's arm and squeezed it right underneath her breasts and let her walk her past the others and inside.

Papa walked in behind her and Avon scanned the women. He stopped in front of Yvonda and introduced himself.

The tree is a spectacular, fifteen-foot Douglas fir. I convinced the Boy Scouts to give it to me for the price of trees half its height because they never end up selling all the really tall ones. Everybody had already started hanging seashells and paper ornaments Sally and Cindy had made in school. Mrs. Tewks came out of the kitchen hugging a bowl of eggnog. I hurried to relieve her.

"Smells nice in here, boy. A house smells nice full of baking."

"Mrs. Tewks here has been working those ovens non-stop."

"Pleasure to meet you, Mrs. Robinson."

The front door chimed and everyone stopped.

"That must be my sister."

Allison barely let me hug her, but Terrel and Jerome were great.

"Hey, Uncle Ashton. What's up?"

"Nothing but your presents under the tree."

And they ran inside.

"You really went and did it this time, didn't you?"

"Your present's under the tree too."

"Some damn Kool-Aid and cyanide?"

"How'd you guess?"

"Mama and Papa don't know what's going on here. But I do. I've heard."

"We're studying together. That's all."

"Listen to me. You sure as hell ain't Christ. And if you pretend you are, he'll punish you."

"Especially around his birthday."

I thought it was kind of funny, but she didn't smile.

Trey Ellis

■ ■ ■

The turkey was stuffed with chestnuts and was the best I'd ever had. The conversations I overheard seemed plain enough, which was good. Mommy wanted to know everything there was to know about Nikki. Even Papa talked basketball a bit with Mr. Sandilla and Mr. Tewks. I didn't need to warn the others not to talk about our studies. I knew they had enough common sense not to scare my folks—even Glen, who turned out to have been a college football star. After Yvonda blew Avon off, he spent the rest of the night commiserating with Glen on how close they'd both come to being drafted by the pros.

As soon as they'd finished dinner, Terrel and Sally chased each other around the house. Allison couldn't keep her eyes off of them, convinced, I am sure, that that little white girl would try to brainwash her child while she wasn't looking. I'm sure that's what pushed her over the edge.

We were all having dessert while we finished trimming the tree. The Motown Christmas album was playing, and Jill, Nikki, and Yvonda were stringing popcorn. Avon snuck up to me with a nudge.

"Mmm. Mmm. Mmm."

"Mmm, mmm, what, Avon?"

"So what're you, doing that African thing? Wife number one, two, and three?"

I shouldn't have, but I was feeling devilish, so I nudged him back and pointed out Mrs. Tewks, Mrs. Sandilla, Lanie, and Mrs. Landi.

"And four, five, six, and seven."

"Damn!"

I held my finger over my lips and walked away.

Right Here, Right Now

"Ashton! Ashton! Here's the star!"

Cindy held the dried starfish high over her head and on tiptoes. Like I always do I pretended I still couldn't reach it, and she
leaped in the air and giggled like a circus animal. Then I took it
and started up the ladder by the tree.

"Here I go, everyone. Henry, get ready to plug in the lights."

Mr. Sandilla stood by the outlet. All eyes were on me.

"Careful you don't get a shock now, baby."

"Mama, he should be used to shocks by now. Didn't they
shock him back at that mental hospital in New Haven?"

"Allison!" Mommy pounded the floor with her cane.

"Lord have mercy, girl!" said my father.

I didn't lose my balance, hang off the tree, and crash it to the
ground. Nothing so dramatic. I just closed my eyes and breathed
a few deep *ujjayi* yogic breaths so I wouldn't leap off that ladder
and rip my sister's weave right out of her head.

"Most hospitals haven't used electroshock therapy in years. I
was just under routine observation for a few nights."

"Routine after you try and kill yourself."

I threaded the point of the tree into the metal coil affixed to
the back of the starfish and slowly stepped down the ladder. The
Jackson 5 were singing "Little Drummer Boy."

All of the disciples seemed on the verge of tears.

"It's true, people. Remember me telling you I had some
problems at Yale and left? You see, though I was perhaps the
smartest kid in Santa Cruz High, when I got to college and got
my first papers back from my professors, I'll admit I was shocked.
A stack of failing grades was a considerable jolt to my considerable ego. Still, I limped along, all the way through half of my junior year . . .

"It was one of the last nights of the semester. I had just gotten

221

back a paper on Coleridge that I thought was good enough to publish in a journal. My professor disagreed and gave me a C minus.

"At the same time I was dealing with Kathryn Moi, a Kenyan I had been in love with since our freshman year. Some of you might have heard me talk about her.

"It must have been one in the morning. She knocked. 'Would you care to go walking with me, Ashton?' Even after three years I never got used to this regal, dark black woman speaking the English of Diana Rigg, you know, from the *The Avengers* . . . Well anyway, to make a long story short: we made love just once, then heartache, bad grades . . . I wasn't the first student to overreact to a string of bad news and climb to the top of Harkness Tower. Is that what you were referring to, Allison?"

But she was already pulling the boys' jackets down their arms, searching for her purse, and heading for the door.

January 15th

"I . . . I don't know about this, Ashton."

"That is exactly why you must."

"What if the band snaps?"

"Mrs. Landi, the army lifts trucks with them. You only weigh one hundred and thirty-eight pounds."

"Oh, Lord. But I'm sixty-nine years old!"

"I knew you would have the most difficulty, that is why I chose you to go first."

I was sitting on a small steel chair bolted to the steel platform. Next to me, under a cockeyed white motorcycle helmet, she stood. I talked into the police walkie-talkie Velcroed to my sweatshirt as I looked across the driveway to Mr. Sandilla in the cab of the crane. Lucky for us he worked all sorts of heavy machinery in the marines.

"Let's take her up, Henry."

"Roger that."

The great diesel motor started loudly; black smoke and smell were in the air at once. I saw Mr. Sandilla flipping and pulling rusty rods on the control panel. We jumped the first bit up and

Mrs. Landi spread and froze like a cat. I held her eyes with mine, wouldn't let her look down. Mrs. Landi gripped the railing as if she were steering a runaway dragster right into a brick wall. Instead, we rose very slowly into the dawn.

"Just keep looking at me, Mrs. L. Keep looking at me."

My voice was the voice of a hypnotist. If I yelled at her, "NOW! NOW! NOW YOU ARE GOING TO DIE!!" she would have.

The steel cable spooled back on the great drum on the body of the crane, and our platform rose toward the peak of the rusty, skeletal geometry (they told me a brand-new crane would have been ten times more expensive). I thought I might have had to pry her fingers off the railing and shove her from the platform. I was a little afraid her fear would have given her supernatural strength. She'd have grabbed me and hurled me over the side with her, yet since her ankles were attached to the bungee cord she'd be fine and just bounce, while I rocketed past her and broke myself all over the fountain in the middle of my circular driveway.

"Oooooh, Gaaaaaawd!"

I looked down and knew exactly what she meant, but made myself smile at her. We were high, hotel rooftop high, heart-filling view of the ocean and the amusement park down on the pier. I saw the mountains, a few miles inland, reddened by the dawn and interlocked and winding like the scales of an amazing lizard. All she could have been thinking about right then was her death. Air clattered in and out of her lungs. If I weren't trying to found a major religion, I'd have let her down. That ride itself was what the lesson was all about anyway, surpassing your own limits.

"AHH!"

Right Here, Right Now

"It's all right! It's fine. There, there. Give me a hug."

The platform had suddenly jerked, stuttered. For the next disciples I reminded Mr. Sandilla to be more gentle when he brought the platform to a halt. I was hugging her up there to make her feel better, but also so I could gauge her heartbeat. It tapped inside her sweatshirt crazily. I stole a look at my watch and counted. A hundred and sixty beats per minute! I held her and smoothed her curved little back. The mike on my chest sat right above the steely bristles of hair on her balding head.

"We're OK, Henry. Just give us a few more minutes."

"Roger that."

"Mrs. Landi, Eleonora, *sta calma, cara mia, sta calma. Tutto andrà per bene, te lo giuro.*"

She peeled just her face from my chest and stared straight up at me, her pupils as big as a doll's.

"Y-you speak Italian? I haven't spoken it since my mama died, in nineteen sixty-nine."

"*Ma certo, cara mia. Io parlo direttamente alla tua anima. Forza. Tu ce la fai. Io lo so.*"

I told her to be calm and to just go for it. Told her she could do it. I am speaking directly into your soul, I said.

Finally, I felt her heart's tapping slow, snuck another peak at my watch, and again counted. A hundred and ten beats-per-minute, still high, but dropping into a healthy range for her age. I peered over her brittle shoulders, down at the bungee cord that hung from her ankles in a huge loop in the air, back up to the underside of our platform, where it was connected to a thick steel ring. The guy who sold me the rig swore the cord would never stretch more than a hundred feet at max load, and the crane is 165 feet high. Yet from up there the long cord sure looked a lot longer than that. If only the city had let me set up on the sand, we could have jumped over the ocean. That way, if we were a little off, the jumper would just get his hair a little wet.

"*Sei pronta?*"

I asked her if she was ready.

"*Pronta*," she told me.

So I carefully stepped away, making sure she was still standing when I stopped holding her. I edged to the metal railing and unlatched the gate. I snuck another look down and my balls glowed. They were all down there looking up, mouths open, like hungry chicks. I retreated past Mrs. Landi to my metal chair, sat, and held myself to it.

"Here's what I want you to do. I want you to remember how we practiced it down below. I want you to walk to the edge like I just did, and don't look down, just out at the pretty view. See the pretty mountains? Good. Good. Then I want you to just step off the edge whenever you are ready. Take your time, sweetie, but remember, you will have taken your biggest step yet toward Disappearing. It will be so wonderful, so sweet to fly; then you'll feel the gentle tug back up.

"Everyone envies you going first. And everyone loves you . . . Whenever you are ready . . ."

She was not shaking, but I wish I could have seen her face. Mr. Tewks videoed from below, but the lens wasn't good enough to zoom in on the look in her eyes.

Old women look ridiculous in sweatpants. Over her tiny white sneakers her white ankles were tattooed with blue veins and clamped by the bungee rig like bondage paraphernalia. For a long while she still did not move. Not even a little.

"*Io ti amo, Signora Landi . . . Ora . . . 'Ora' vuol' dire 'now' . . .*"

'AIIIIIIIEEEEEEE-AAAAAAHHHHHHHH . . . !"

Oh shit! She did it! Scrambling, clawing at the air, running cartoonishly in space as she tipped downward, falling over her ankles, stretching the bungee down and down, her body long and suddenly graceful. The folks below ducked and darted, but here she comes, back up at me, oh no, what if she smacks against the bottom of the platform? But no, she was falling again . . .

"AIIIIIIIEEEE . . . !"

She screamed only on the down strokes. Interesting. But then she was bounding back up again, but slowly, and down once more, and it was over. She hung by her ankles, her thin white hair straight and down, her face a drunken red.

"He-he-he-he-he . . . !"

She giggled maniacally, but that made the others laugh down below. I was laughing too, now that you mention it. I talked again into my chest.

"OK, Henry, bring us down. Slowly."

"Roger that."

And we jolted and descended and the others crowded under her, stretched their hands up to gather her from the sky. They guided her head and shoulders horizontally, hugged her, patted her, laid her on the ground, and worked off her ankle braces.

"Whoopee!"

Mr. Landi shivered as he hugged her, but his wife was suddenly a schoolgirl. They all got larger as I descended upon them like a Greek god in a high school play. They looked up at me, giggling. I hopped off the platform while it was still a few feet in the air and grabbed Mrs. Landi by the shoulders.

"Close your eyes! Quick! What do you see?"

Her head gyroscoped around her neck.

"Oh gosh, I don't know. Static and spinning. No, wait, here

comes something. Bubbles, what I just did, the falling part, the mountains . . ."

"Excellent! Now, remember this feeling, lock it into the front of your brain. You are more alive than any of us right now. Prolong it as long as you can, long after you have opened your eyes . . . Ladies and gentlemen, what we have just done is build a memory for this courageous woman. She was just living in a heightened state and continues in that state even now. Look at her chest swell, the flush of her cheeks. Now, who's next?"

The helicopter must have been thumping over us for a while, but only now was it getting so loud that I felt compelled to look up and twist to spot it. It was one of those little glass bubble ones, an oversized mechanical fly, drifting around the perimeter of my property.

"Actually, people, that's enough excitement for today. Let's head inside. There's a new *siddha* yoga chant I'd like to try out."

I smiled for the helicopter, pretended to laugh, pretended to make a game out of shooing everyone inside and away from their binoculars, telephoto lenses, and Big Ear supermikes.

January 22nd

"So, you've had this bursitis in your shoulder for how long?"

Mr. Landi sat in a kitchen chair before the group, wind-milling his shoulder and wincing.

"Oh, gosh, I don't know there. Long time, though."

"Let's see if this will help."

I opened the sterilizer, and steam from it rose. I withdrew the first acupuncture needle and stared at its thinness, which neared invisibility. Everybody else was staring too, but most of all Mr. Landi. I picked up the manual and tried to look up "bursitis" in the index with my free hand.

"Nikki, could you please come here and hold the book open?"

I raised one of the pink plastic ears I'd picked up in China-town along with the manual and set of needles. The waxy ear was tattooed with little red dots for each of the hundreds of acu-points. Each point was marked in black ink with a name like T1,

SC10, AH3, or L5. I held the needle just next to it.

"So, it says here, for acute bursitis of the left shoulder, simply insert the needle eight millimeters into the T three spot, also known as the Yanho'u Pharynx and Larynx, or the something-or-other in Chinese characters. It says it's located at the inner surface of the tragus opposite the orifice of the external auditory meatus."

I smiled as if I understood a word of what I'd just read.

"Sounds simple enough. And . . . voilà."

I speared the plastic ear right in the T3 dot.

"Are you nervous, Anthony?"

Mr. Landi shook his head no.

"Excellent. I am proud of you."

I held the plastic ear right next to the real one so I'd know just where to poke. T3's deep in the crotch of a high curve; you know, that place in which you swipe your finger from time to time and come out with a gray dollop of crud that you feel compelled to sniff before wiping on your pants? Anyway, old Mr. Landi's entire ear canal is lined with soft white fur, so the exact spot was damn hard to find.

I aimed and as I started to push I saw all the other disciples squinting and reeling backward out of the corner of my eye. I pressed one of the girls' grade school rulers against his ear with one hand and kept pushing till the needle sunk its eight millimeters. When I let go it jutted from him comically, waved in the wind.

"And how do you feel?"

"Fine, sir."

"And the bursitis?"

Again, he windmilled his arm. Paused. Tried it again.

Right Here, Right Now

"It just popped, but I . . . I honestly don't think it hurt like it used to do . . ."

He smiled and sat straighter.

"Goddamn!" he said.

That made everyone smile. Me too.

January 23rd

===============

Beep-beep-beep . . .

Every time the microwave goes off I think it's an electronic detonator about to explode a bomb. Mr. Tewks strode in from the kitchen bearing a large steel mixing bowl of microwaved pop-corn. The rest of us were in the den, crowded into the couches and pillows on the floor.

"Anybody want a Snapple?"

Yvonda's head was in the minibar's refrigerator, and as she pulled out drinks, Lanie took them and passed them around. Mrs. Tewks returned from having put the girls to bed.

"All right, are we ready? Henry, roll tape."

Henry loaded the tape, and the TV screen screamed a blue that exists only electronically, and the word *play* appeared in white. On the tape, Nikki, Jill, and I clinked wineglasses and slid the cough syrup down our throats. I dropped my robe from my shoulders and threw it. It flew heavily to the chair, like a ghost. The women shrugged out of their robes and laid them over mine. They both wobbled a bit in their mules on the deep carpet, so I sat on the bed.

Right Here, Right Now

In real life, I aimed the remote at the stereo, and Fela Kuti's funky Nigerian beat of high, happy guitars added to our sound track.

On the video, I started on Nikki, crawled over the bed, kissing up her body. It was then that I noticed a huge pimple on my ass. I wish someone had told me. As I'm dictating this I'm rubbing Clearasil into it. The good thing about televising yourself naked four times a week is it makes you stay in pretty good shape. My first time with Mrs. Sandilla I remember an accidental close-up of my gut as I walked past the camera. I banned desserts and dairy products for a month and finally got the StairMaster fixed.

Anyway, on the screen we all watched as I stroked Nikki's outer lips with my thumb and forefinger while blowing gently across her yoni. This always drives her crazy. With the other women, the ones I do not celebrate with as often, it is sometimes hard to keep straight all their peculiar preferences. You stroke Mrs. Tewks's belly while she is orgasming and she says the hairs on her head catch fire. Bite Lanie's nipples right after a clitoral orgasm and she swears her body starts to dematerialize like Captain Kirk's when he is beamed down to another planet.

On the screen, Jill lay next to Nikki and was pleasuring herself. After all these months this was the first time I'd had the nerve to put them together in one session. The tension added an extra section of instruments to the symphony.

Behind us, over the headboard, you could just make out the little chalkboard, like one you might find on a loading dock: *196 days without an accident*. That's how many days it'd been since I'd ejaculated.

Nikki can be a little slow to come the first time; that's why I started with her and laid myself in a position that wouldn't permanently damage my neck. But on the screen Jill's pelvis was already tilting and then gyrating, which can only mean that she had already brought herself very, very close. I tried to keep Nikki humming down the right road with my tongue while I quickly reached over and inserted my fingers into Jill, and as soon as the contractions began I pressed up on her G spot, and thar she blew. Everybody clapped, Mr. Landi whistled, somebody stomped their feet. It's silly, I know, but somehow it's become kind of a tradition around here, the same way people applaud whenever a waiter drops a tray of glasses.

Live, Jill rolled her eyes and shook her head, yet on the tape we could make out only the whites of her eyes under her flickering, half-closed lids. She is loud and loose and easily orgasmic, and sometimes this inhibits the other woman.

It was certainly the case last night, because Nikki tapered off considerably. So I had to bear down, concentrate on her clitoris, investigate each millimeter of each fold with the hardened tip of my tongue, hunting for that spot that would coax her out again. Usually at this point on her arousal graph it's between ten and eleven on the clock of her clitoris, but I think I might have burned out that section, because this time it didn't really respond. So my tongue rooted through the other folds, investigated ridges I'd previously ignored, but her arousal kept stepping down and down and down. In desperation I tried the far other side of her clitoris, and as soon as I tapped around three o'clock her hips suddenly danced as if I'd put a quarter in a slot. I swept over her topography with the wet roughness of my tongue and she was soon rushing closer and closer. Cartilage in my neck was beginning to fossilize, but I knew if I repositioned myself even a fraction I'd lose ground and have to fight again to retake her hill.

We watched Jill reaching for the sky with her arms and her

legs, dancing on her back with a ghost. But gradually she subsided, her mind rejoined her body, and she rolled over, catted across Nikki's legs, and nuzzled into my balls. I remember being so intent on delivering Nikki to her orgasm that I'd forgotten my own sex, but Jill instantly reminded me, swept *axe* through my body with a force that seemed to have me floating well above the bed.

Live, Mrs. Landi shifted forward and squinted to study my penis disappearing and reappearing inside Jill's hollowing, then filling, cheeks. She's embarrassed by her partial plate, and confessed to me that Mr. Landi never let her do it to him, in fact, had coitus with her only about four times a year. The first time he saw her fellating me he made this strange, gagging sound and the rest of us locked our eyes forward out of politeness. But I just had to sneak a glance. He was pushed to an edge he didn't know existed within him, and only good things can come of that. Now he applauds louder than the rest when his wife comes, and last week when we were in the sixty-nine position he commented that he finally understood the symbol and the essence of yang and yin: male and female, old and young, black and white.

But on the screen Nikki was right there, right at the door to otherworldly bliss. I knew just the key . . .

"I celebrate the goddess . . ."

I didn't even have to finish. She was already coming, so I reached in and pressed her G spot like a doorbell, and she kept coming. Again, the others applauded.

"Attaway, Nikki, I didn't think you were going to make it this time," said Mr. Landi as he reached forward and squeezed her neck, his white fingers roped with veins and peppered with liver spots.

After a half dozen loud, tortured peaks, I let her down in steps, and when she was ready to understand English again I asked her:

"Would you mind going down and helping Jill?"

The me on the monitor twisted over on his back and spread his legs so there was room for both of them. He then raised his head and stared past the landscape of their backs and legs and right into the lens of the camcorder.

"So, right now . . . a powerful pleasure is welling . . . welling in my lowest chakra. If I didn't do anything about it, I would orgasm and ejaculate both sperm and much of my very soul into . . . into Jill's mouth . . . Wooooo! . . . Nikki's nibbling at my testicles is concentrating even more energy into my . . . lingam, so I must lock, yes, uh, lock my PC muscles, close the lower gate, and breath this tremendous energy up through my body and out into space. They are . . . amaz . . . amazing. The combination is—oh, they just switched and the change . . . boils my brain . . . One second . . ."

And my head gyroscoped, then fell back to the bed while they worked on me diligently, minutely, delicately, like an innovative tag team of surgeons. Somehow I stopped them and scooted my ass out of range. My breathing was audible on the tape. There was a long pause before I spoke again.

"You two don't like each other. You compete over me and my affection. So, I would like you two to kiss."

On the screen they both winced. For all the openness about our sexual exploration here, only Mrs. Landi and Lanie are unabashedly bisexual. With the others it is extremely rare, and I haven't pressed it. Mr. Sandilla and Mr. Tewks suddenly leaned toward the TV to the same severe angle as Mr. Landi.

"Ashton, I don't . . ."

Jill looked away.

"You don't have to. But your mutual animosity is an energy. In your heightened ecstatic states you could perhaps convert that animosity into a level of response that even I have not yet experienced."

On the screen Nikki looked from me to Jill, her eyes twitching with thought. Then she pounced on Jill, kissing her down to the bed, but kissing her angrily, almost like punches.

For five months we've been reviewing tapes, even fast-forwarding through the slow parts, so by now most everyone is beyond the obvious pornography of the sessions. But tonight, watching, I could feel how the entire room was possessed by thoughts of sex.

I stared at Jill on the floor in front of me until she turned from the TV. I smiled. She blushed. But Nikki, though she sat right next to me on the couch, could not move her eyes from the screen. I was worried about her, so I slipped my fingers around hers, and she squeezed them too hard.

On the screen, Jill contorted as Nikki worked her mouth down Jill's torso to her yoni. Jill soon held her knees out and wide and she was yelling and growling. Of course, with Nikki's head down at work, her butt was high and facing me.

I will never forget that moment, feeling as if I had just then invented the hard-on. I remember wanting to say something into the camera but I could not divorce myself from that present reality. I remember two thoughts coming to me: *(a)* I had no choice but to insert myself inside her, and *(b)* if I did, I would ejaculate and I would die. Suddenly I understood the male praying mantis, who knows his head is going to be eaten by his bride the moment after he comes, *and does it anyway*; the worker termite, who knows once in his life he's going to be flown high in the sky by his queen to mate, then dropped to his death on the hood of some distant school bus, *and doesn't care.* If her yoni were a high-voltage electrical outlet, I would have entered her just the same.

In the recap session I watched myself hold Nikki's hips and rock into and out of her. I looked pained and weepy on the screen. Nikki backed her hips against the ends of each of my thrusts, screwing down on my root, spiraling more and more *axe* into my groin till it was all of me, till all of my soul had condensed there, against my own teaching. She then reached through her own legs and her long fingers caged the taut sack of my balls. As Jill started coming again she reached up and clamped my nipples as solidly as jumper cables on a battery terminal.

"Ack! Ahhhhhh . . . UHHHH! Oh! Gaaaaaaaaawd, Gaaaaaaaaaad, nowwwwwwww!!!"

I watched myself collapse over both of them as I twitched spastically, but *really* spastically, as if something were very, very wrong. I collapsed Nikki onto her belly between Jill's long legs, which held the both of us against her like tongs. Our throats were all quiet now, but our bodies still periodically twitched. It didn't look pleasant; it looked the way you would fuck the night before the world ended, or if you'd fallen onto the third rail.

The long silence afterward was terrifying to watch. Until then I had no idea I'd passed out and stopped breathing, still inside Nikki, still between Jill's legs. No one watching clapped. We all saw it. Saw what it meant. My eyes were half open but all dead. On the screen Nikki raised her head as best she could, pressed between my weight and Jill's thighs, and looked up Jill's body to Jill's eyes. The women were equally panic-stricken. There is no way I was still in that body on the screen. That body was empty. Nikki on the screen spoke first:

"Did he . . . ?"

"Oh, my God!"

"Should I shake him?"

"I don't know!"

"Maybe not just yet."

Silence on the screen and there in the room. Mrs. Tewks and Yvonda were sobbing. I counted the seconds in my head as the shell of my body lay vacant on the video.

. . . fifty-three Mississippi, fifty-four Mississippi, fifty-five Mississippi, fifty-six Mississippi, fifty-seven Mississippi . . .

On the screen I finally blinked. All of us watching finally released the breaths we'd been holding, and our hearts skittered to catch up. I blinked again, then my throat made a deep noise as I finally took another breath. Then I rolled off Nikki but lacked the strength to raise my head from the mattress. I closed my eyes and almost immediately could be heard snoring.

The real me jumped to my feet in front of the TV.

"Holy shit, everybody! All day today I thought I'd just come, come hard, come for the first time in months, come truly, as if I'd swallowed an M-eighty that'd liquefied my essence and fired right out of my dick, sorry, my lingam. But I had no idea I'd really done it. I thought I'd know it when I finally Disappeared!"

"Jesus Christ!" said Henry Sandilla.

"Like Lazarus!" said Glen.

"That's why you two have been so quiet all day. Nikki, Jill, why didn't you tell me?"

"We talked about it but we weren't sure."

"We wanted to wait for the video. We were so scared."

"Y-y-you did it, didn't you?!" said Mrs. Tewks.

"What do the rest of you think?"

In different directions they all looked away from me.

"Glen, do you think I Disappeared?"

"Yes sir. I know you did."

"Mr. Landi?"

He nodded quickly, several times. The others mumbled their accord.

"You're right. For fifty-seven seconds I was on the Other Side. Did you notice the difference between Disappearance and sleeping? Henry, go back and replay that part, right before I came."

We watched again, as my eyes bulged like the eyes of a horse in a thunderstorm. I shook and came and went slack over Nikki's beautiful back.

"Did I just pass out? Henry?"

"I've seen guys passed out from the heat in the service. They didn't look like you. No sir. You were gone."

"Nikki, tell us what it felt like."

"I've been trying to describe it to myself all day. I mean, all of my body was filled with you almost as if—as if I'd turned into your, your lingam! The tip of my tongue was the tip of your, you know, on Jill . . ."

"I felt that, Ashton. I-I felt that too."

Jill's voice was so tentative. Nikki, on the other hand, was suddenly eerily serene.

"But when your *axe* was pumping inside of me and kept pumping and I'd already finished orgasming and was just floating, felt like I was floating, I mean, a little bit above the bed. Suddenly I couldn't hear anything but I saw on my eyelids clear as day a flower bed being watered and tulips, all different colors, popping up in fast motion, in—what's it called—time lapse."

"Wow . . ."

"Oh, my God."

"Jesus Christ . . ."

Right Here, Right Now

I don't use condoms because I got us all physicals months ago and planned on never again coming. There in the review session I closed my eyes and saw a little black girl.

"I just closed my eyes and saw a little black girl in a starched dress and tiny high-top sneakers waving at me. You, Nikki, are carrying my child."

March 2nd

I have only poked my head in the new studio once since the ventilation's been fixed. Jake, the fitness guy, was the first to rent it out, so I figured I had to stop by last week and say hello. I knew him from the first and last meeting of the Infomercial Industry Leader Super Summit. Then today, watching our tiny crowd climb the metal stairs noisily, scoot down the rows of plastic chairs, and sit, watching the techies hang heavy lights from pipes on the ceiling, watching the cameramen maneuver their cameras across the floor like fat robotic dance partners, I remembered how much I missed this part of the job. Growing up I used to hurry home from school each day to catch the end of the *Mike Douglas Show*. I'd sometimes make my sister and brother share a couch while I interviewed them from Daddy's La-Z-Boy.

"Are you sure you don't want a little something for your lips?"

Glenda, the makeup lady, grabbed my elbow to spin me around and was already jabbing at an open container of red pebbles with a small brush and aiming for my lips. My head twisted before my whole body stepped back.

"Glenda, no."

"C'mon! You used to, remember? You know it looks better on TV."

"I don't care. I'm different now. All natural."

She sulked till she saw Jill coming, brightened, and pulled some other potion off her utility belt and attacked. Rom Casciato and his stage manager stood on the stage in the spotlight. Behind them large pictures of the Buddha, Christ, Mahomet, Moses, Chango, Shiva, and Zeus hung from the ceiling on invisible wires. On all the TV monitors, the frozen title card said, *PES, Inc., Presents AXE: THE SCIENCE OF RELIGIONS*. I stepped onto the stage with them, conscious of the eyes and the whispering of the audience behind me.

"Hey, Rom, let's get this show on the road."

"Or what? We go into overtime and you pay yourself even more money? You own the fucking studio, for chrissakes."

A rage glowed inside me, the eyes of my palms throbbed. If I really wanted to, I'm sure I could've aimed it at his chest and stopped his heartbeat. But I just pulled back my eyelids and burned him with the whites of my eyes. He stepped back quickly, and he and the stage manager threw looks at each other as they retreated.

"C'mon, ladies, move it! I want us up and taping in two minutes! TWO MINUTES!"

Rom clapped as he talked, and spun, and everywhere he looked, the all-male crew hurried.

I looked to Jill and pulled her over by jerking my head over my shoulder. I sat in my chair and Jill trotted quickly on her heels, sat, and simultaneously crossed her legs and whispered.

"Are you going to talk about the, you know, sexual aspects of the new teaching? I'm still in the middle of the divorce and, you know . . ."

"I told you. I told all of you. This is only going to be a rough overview of what we do at the house. The audiotapes are just transcripts of some of my evening lectures."

"I-I know! But sometimes, you know, you like to improvise . . ."

"Don't worry, I want to run this on Nickelodeon's late-night slot, and I don't think they'd appreciate me airing last night's tape of you, me, and little old Mrs. Landi."

"She's an amazing woman. I'd like to know where she learned that little thing she does with her pinkie and the bump on the bridge of her nose."

"She did that to you too? But how—?"

"IN TEN, LADIES AND GENTLEMEN . . . NINE, EIGHT, SEVEN . . ."

The lights ignited like stars, curtained the audience from us in a sudden white cloud. Camera one pushed in on Jill, and the red light lit. Our cheesy theme song filled the soundstage, and the audience applauded and hooted. Words on the Tele-PrompTer rose and vanished. I've got the transcript right here, so I'll read you what we said:

"Welcome to a very special edition of Personal Empowerment Television. I'm your host, Jill Lowry, and our guest once again is none other than one of the most widely studied and sought after motivational speakers in the country, a man who has advised senators and captains of industry, a man who single-handedly brought himself from rags to riches in little over three years . . . Ladies and gentlemen, I give you Ashton . . . Robinson!"

Camera two's red light lit. It was farther back for a wide shot. I smiled and humbly waved at the sound of the hooting crowd that I could not see.

Right Here, Right Now

"Thanks, Jill. Thanks for having me on your show— Wait a minute. I'm not going to pretend anymore. You work for me. I'm *paying* for this infomercial, so let's get real for a moment . . ."

I peeked at the monitor as camera one pushed in on Jill for her shocked expression. She overdid it a little, but I think I'm the only one who noticed. I stood and paced; my heartbeat was insistent. I found camera three and stared into the darkness of its glass. I didn't use the TelePrompTers. I'd pretty much memorized what I was going to say.

"I am asking you, humbly asking you, for a half hour of your time. I have been away for a few months taking stock of my life, my teachings, and I think I've come up with something that will truly change your life as much as it has changed mine. I've spent years investigating the nature of success and wealth and happiness, but until recently hardly any time at all studying our *spiritual* well-being. I have been wrong. Throw my old tapes into the trash. Burn my books. What I am going to share with you over the next thirty minutes is the real thing. Or at least it has been the real thing for me and my research assistants over the better part of this year . . ."

I paused, and camera three's light went off. I turned to face camera one, and right on cue its light came on.

"Look at my clothes. Remember how I used to dress? Armani, Hugo Boss, and Romeo Gigli. Now look at me, and what do you see? The Gap. All my research assistants and I now wear nothing but Gap socks, Gap underwear, Gap jeans, dresses, and ribbed Ts. We don't waste our brains shopping and gazing at our images in mirrors. We are too busy scientifically exploring the world's various forms of meditation and religious worship, exploring every avenue imaginable toward our personal Enlightenment . . .

"Think about it. What cultures on the planet have the most intimate relationship with the spirit world? Unquestionably the so-called primitive ones. Take the Mandjildjara of Australia and the !Kung of southern Africa's Kalahari Desert. They each spend just about three hours a day hunting game or overturning rocks in search of some juicy grubs. So, what do they do with the rest of their days? They explore the magic of their minds!

"And what about us? What about so-called *modern* man? We only have time to truly activate our brains about six minutes a day—the average amount of time we spend on the toilet . . ."

I heard laughter behind the lights, and that egged me on.

"But don't just take my word for it. Jill, how do you feel you have changed thanks to *axe*?"

The TelePrompTer helped her.

"Well, Ashton, I was in a nowhere relationship of verbal abuse and neglect for seven years—I guess because I felt that was the best I deserved. But your curriculum of studying the science of religions has awakened in me a thirst for the mystical that has truly enriched my life! You talk about the hidden magic of life, how it is there in front of us every day if we would just learn how to look. Almost like those Magic Eye posters they sell in malls. You're teaching me and the rest of your research assistants how to see the spiritual wonder that silently surrounds us, always and everywhere."

The camera swung around to me, and I smiled at her. The TelePrompTer's words disappeared.

"And one more thing . . ."

Uh-oh. We'd barely begun and we were already off script. The camera rushed backward to catch us both. I admit I was worried.

"Ashton, I always knew you were special, but I never knew how special until you brought *axe* into my life. I am so grateful to you. And I have never been happier, or more proud of what I am doing."

That's when she started crying. I stood and drew her out of her chair and held her against my chest. The camera quickly rolled to the foot of the stage and poked right past my elbow. Rom doesn't miss a trick. I slow-danced us around so her pretty face on my chest was in close-up. Then I peeked at one of the monitors and saw another camera was sweeping the crowd. Many of them, and not just my people, were misty eyed too. Jill pushed herself off my chest and pushed the tears off her cheeks.

"I'm sorry. I just . . . This is important to me . . . And it's important to the world. I think we have some other research assistants in the audience . . ."

A production assistant crabbed up to her in a low, squatting waddle to stay off camera, a big black mike high over his head like a torch. She took it and stepped to the bleachers, and the house lights rose. She leaned over the first row of watchers to aim the mike at Mr. Landi.

"What do you have to say about *axe*?"

"Hello. My name is Anthony Landi, and I would just like to say that *axe* is real important to us seniors and señoritas. I have never felt better and more full of energy. I thought I'd seen just about everything, but whoooeee! Some of the stuff that goes on at the mansion . . . !"

Jill took back the mike. I looked up at the control booth and guessed that the largest shadow was Rom. I motioned to him to cut Mr. Landi's last few sentences. I knew he wouldn't stick to the words on the prompter, but a lot of my old PES subscribers were elderly, and Mr. Landi looks like a retired senator. Jill stepped up two aisles and reached for Lanie who stood and smoothed her dress.

"Hello, my name is Lanie Silver, and a new friend had dragged me to see Ashton in Chicago several months ago. I'd never done anything like that before at all! At first I was skeptical. No, I'll be honest, I thought he was off his rocker! But then I listened some more and the truth of what he was saying just hit me, and stayed with me, and I have been a research assistant ever since, and like Jill I just think this new technology could change the way we think about the world."

As she sat the *Applause* boxes flashed over the audience, but they were already clapping. Some were my old office workers, the ones I've brought back to handle the new orders (I hope, I hope), but most were just locals and tourists rounded up at the Santa Cruz pier, folks who had nothing better to do than watch a taping and get free sandwiches and soft drinks. They applauded for Revolutionary Spiritualism just as they would have for the GutBuster®. Suddenly I was disgusted, briefly contemplated throwing a tantrum, driving them all out of my studio with my wrath. But I controlled myself. It was the Tewkses' turn.

"Hi, we're the Tewkses, also from Chicago, Illinois. I'm Janice and this is my husband, Gerry. Ashton's lectures and the books he has us read and the different techniques he has us master are so thrilling, so exciting, we just can't remember what our lives were like before!"

"Ah, yes. Gerry Tewks here. It's unusual and all, and at the highest levels sometimes it is very difficult, but the results are . . . wow! Women seem to respond more quickly than men, but when we men get up to their level . . . *watch out!*"

They turned to each other, kissed, and sat to more applause.

"Anyone else want to say something?" said Jill.

On the far side of the bleachers Nikki stood, and Jill danced past the knees of the people in the top row to join her. I haven't seen Nikki naked in almost a month, but with her clothes on, though she's not yet obviously showing, she is starting to fill in beautifully. However, that famous glow they speak about is nowhere to be seen. I can't remember the last time she smiled.

The camera aimed up at Jill and Nikki from the bottom of the bleachers.

"Yes, thank you. My name is Nikki Kennedy, and I have never, ever felt so open and ready for change. All thanks to that man, his teachings, and his very being. We research assistants are so very lucky because we have such intimate access to him, but I'm sure the taped lectures will quickly put you too on the road to spiritual growth—"

"Enough, Nikki, enough! I'm blushing. And yes, black folks do blush. But thank you, Nikki, Janice and Gerry, Mr. Landi, and the rest of you good people for—"

"Excuse me, Ashton. Can I add something more?"

I didn't have a choice.

"Go ahead, Nikki, of course."

"Like Jill said, I just want you to know that we love you, and can't thank you enough for everything you've done. And . . . oh boy, I'm not going to cry . . . oh . . . when the Brazilian midget comes and takes you away, I just pray that I'm with you when you Disappea—"

"Thank you, Nikki! Thanks again! So kind of you, but let's cut to the chase, shall we? Let's listen to one of my first lectures on the new system so the good folks at home will have some idea what it is they are in for!"

I looked up to the control booth, and the house lights

dimmed, and we heard an excerpt from an early home lecture to the disciples. Nikki knew she was in trouble because she widened her eyes to look at me. I warned them all, no talk of Disappearance, nothing about the midget, cough syrup, dope, tantric sex. We were trying to introduce the world to our world, and our world is so far ahead of theirs they can't help but see ours as a monster.

The recorded me was almost finished. The audience was nodding with my words. The stage manager held his earphone to his ear, nodded, then raised his finger and pointed to me. The video finished and the lights came up.

"These audiotapes are but a fraction of what we are researching here, but they provide a good introduction to our studies. And unlike earlier PES technologies sold for profit, I feel the *axe* system is so vitally important to the planet that I will send you the first tape for *nothing but shipping and handling.* Jill, could you tell them how to order?"

"Sure, Ashton. Just call the eight-hundred number on the bottom of the screen and have your credit card number ready. For just ten ninety-five shipping and handling, we will rush you the first of Ashton's ten-tape *Audio University.* And when you remember that earlier PES systems cost upward of one hundred dollars and were not trying to guide you to the path of total enlightenment, you will realize what an amazing offer this truly is . . ."

Later March 2nd

The ride home in the van reminded me of the bus rides home from away games that we'd won when I was on varsity soccer. Our happiness was collective. Despite the glitches, we all knew that the taping went well and perhaps was the beginning of establishing *axe* as a world religion. Mr. Tewks was talking about the look on the outsider's face next to him when Jill started to cry. Jill said she didn't know what came over her, but once she started she couldn't stop. We all agreed there wasn't an outsider there who wasn't touched by our stories. It's nice to finally be *sure* we're not all nuts.

It was as we passed a Jack in the Box that I remembered I'd been so busy, so worried, I hadn't eaten all day.

"Anybody want drive-through?"

They cheered, Sally and Cindy higher than everyone else, and I found myself smiling at my sudden popularity. I can't wait till my daughter's old enough to glow with happiness just because I offered her fast food.

Mr. Sandilla started his blinker early so Glen, driving the

other van, would know to follow. He turned us into the parking lot and followed the drive-through lane around the back. The line of cars was long. I finally noticed Mr. Sandilla's throat moving, his lips moving. I had no idea what he was trying to say.

"Uh, Ashton?"

"Yes, Henry?"

The folks in the back were loud, but he was quiet.

"Do you think, maybe, I'm ready for some tantra?"

"Do you think you are ready?"

"Yes. I think so."

"I think you are right."

"Really?"

"Definitely. Tonight, in fact."

"Oh my gosh."

"I talked with Mrs. Landi about it last night. I think you two would be good together. She could teach you a lot."

"Excuse me?"

"Mrs. Landi and you, tonight."

"But I-I just assumed—"

"That you and Mrs. Sandilla would sleep together? No. I'm sorry, but not yet. Think about it. Think about how messed up you two were before you began your training. You rarely had sex then and were in and out of counseling. Didn't you say you'd even asked a friend at work about a good divorce lawyer! You two screw now, and wham! You're both back to square one."

"But . . ."

"You resent the fact that I and all the women in the group have made love with your wife."

I aimed my voice just a little past him. The others tried to keep talking, but I knew I'd suddenly kidnapped their attention.

Ever since my brief Disappearance with Nikki and Jill, all of the women have been much freer in their experimentation with bisexuality.

"No! I mean. I'm not perfect. But I'm trying and—"

"You are an excellent student, and we will all examine the videotape of you and Mrs. Landi, and if you do as well as I think you will, your next partner will be your very own wife, if that is what you desire."

"Videotape?"

"Of course. You are not just fucking for your health. It is for the health of the group. You and the rest of the men have been practicing celibacy, a noble and time-honored meditational discipline. The women and myself have been practicing hypersexuality, an equally time-honored technique. We can all of us benefit from examining your transition. My only advice is that you make sure the soles of your feet are well scrubbed. Dirty feet can look really nasty on camera."

"Hello, may I take your order?"

Before I had the chance to poll everyone, a knock on my window made me jump. It was Nikki, looking scared. I powered down my window.

"I'm sorry, Ashton, but could I speak to you?"

"Now?"

I turned behind me and saw she had left the other van's door open. I opened my wallet, drew out a hundred-dollar bill, and handed it to Henry.

"Get me a Jumbo Jack, a medium diet Dr Pepper, and pay for both vans, please."

"S-sure thing, Boss." Henry was still a little off-balance from our talk.

I walked Nikki to the mini plastic playground by the Dumpster and squatted on a tiny red sea horse connected to the earth by a coiling cable of steel. She squatted over a frog.

"What can I do you for, Nikki?"

"I just wanted to say sorry for mentioning Disappearance and everything. I know you said not to, but I got carried away, and when Jill got carried away it seemed all right, and—"

"It is all right. Don't get upset. Remember, Dr. Watson said not to get upset. It taxes the baby's heart. And—"

"I can't watch anymore, darling, I can't. Not when I'm getting fatter and fatter."

"You are not getting fatter. The baby and the placenta are growing. I swear you've never looked more lovely. Mrs. Sandilla and I were talking about it just the other night."

"I get upset. You just said I shouldn't get upset."

"We are a community. Togetherness is part of our therapy."

But she was choking and hiccuping on her tears. I hurried off my sea horse, kneeled on the ground in front of her, and hugged her lap.

"I . . . never . . . liked it. The watching . . . and . . . now . . . it . . . hurts . . ."

She is so kind and so beautiful. If I were a normal man, she would be more than enough for me. I tried to forget the eyes of the others were targeting us from the smoked windows of the vans.

"I'll move the videotape review to eleven-thirty. Your excuse for missing it will be you just don't have the energy."

"Thank you!"

"But why couldn't this have waited till we got home?"

"I told you my mother wasn't feeling very well? Now she wants me to go visit her. Soon."

"Have you told her about the baby?"

She shook her head like a small child.

"What are you going to tell her?"

"You tell me what to tell her."

I went back to my sea horse and rocked. It seemed to help me think.

"Tell her the father works with you at PES. Of course do not mention Disappearing, the midget, or our living arrangements. Tell her you two are planning on marrying as soon as you get back."

She eyed me hard. I fought myself not to look away.

"Ashton, you know I love you."

"I love you too. We will fly you tomorrow. Coach, if you don't mind. We still have to keep the belts tightened until the new orders start coming in."

"No, Ashton, I mean—"

I rose and leaned over her and kissed her and drew her off her sea horse kissing her still.

"I know what you mean and you know what I mean. But let's get back to our junk food—wait a minute, you shouldn't be eating this crap. Maybe just the french fries."

She laughed the tiniest bit, and I felt so wonderful.

"When you get back, after our next visit to Dr. Watson, we'll spend the rest of the day together. Just you and me. It would mean a lot to me."

"It would?"

I closed my eyes to conjure my *axe* into my palms and slipped them under her blouse to lay my hands on her belly like wings.

"O-oh!"

Not just her belly, but her whole being shuddered.

"Shhhh . . . I am telling Yemayá that we love her. Wait a minute . . . now I see her clearly. She's smiling . . ."

April 25th

I can't sleep. You'd think I'd sleep like a baby. Yvonda and Lanie were with me last night and we tried out the new rings I had strapped to the ceiling. For Glen's birthday Mrs. Sandilla boiled lobsters. The girls screamed and wouldn't touch their food. Money troubles are evaporating now that the spots are running. Last week we moved six thousand units. A lot of my old clients, especially the athletes, for some reason, are now begging to come visit. A few have even hinted about wanting to move in. But I kind of like the group the size that it is now, although I have been toying with the idea of setting up some sort of telecommuting thing. Off-campus disciples could maybe buy a custom-programmed satellite dish and we could all videoconference. Still, I've been lying here for hours impatiently waiting for dawn.

I miss Nikki. She's been gone almost two months, and her mother doesn't get out of the hospital until next Friday. She sounds so strange on the phone. Maybe I'll fly out there for a surprise visit. I'd like to wake Mr. Sandilla up and go for a predawn bungee jump, but the neighbors have slapped us with a restraining order: no movement of heavy machinery before eight.

Trey Ellis

Speaking of Mr. Sandilla, after all these months on deck he couldn't get an erection with Mrs. Landi. He tried to turn his back to the camera and spit on his hand, but he forgot about the wall we'd just mirrored to catch my every facial expression if I ever Disappeared again. The reflection of his look of weary humiliation was even more pathetic than if he'd been in close-up. I know he'd like to blame it on her age, on her heavy egg shape, but he's seen the other tapes. In fact, she recently had his wife so hyperventilated I had to drag Mrs. L. off her by the ankles.

The good thing about his failure is that it should keep the other guys at bay for a while. The women and I are so much closer to Disappearance. I don't know if the men will ever get there. I just don't have the heart to break it to them.

Glen's family called again. I'd still like to know how the hell they got my number. Mrs. Tewks's mother wrote her a letter demanding to see her granddaughters. She of course had to mention Koresh and Applewhite. Yet this problem of the relatives is only going to get worse. If the sales projections really are as rosy as Geoffrey says they are, perhaps I will fly them all out for a weekend and lavish them with presents.

"*Ba-ba-luuu! Ba-ba-luuu-uu-uuuu . . . !*"

I poke the remote by my bed and the song stops there. Time to start the day. If that hurricane from Fiji has hit, surfing the next couple of days could be awesome.

Later April 25th

OK, here's what just happened the rest of the day. It was all, oh, so *lovely* I will try to faithfully record even the most minor of details. That way I won't step on the rock 'em, sock 'em punch line.

Naked, I stepped into my black sweatpants puddled on the floor, squatted, and raised them up to my hips. My hands found the arm holes of the black sweatshirt, then I pulled my head through the middle even as I was opening the door to the hallway. Here they all were, all barefoot, all silent, the men in teal Gap sweats, the women in rose. The girls are in yellow till they menstruate. They all parted and I stepped past them and led them down the stairs. In the living room our *zafus*, meditation pillows, were piled in a pyramid. Silently I took the top pillow and the egg timer and opened the doors to the terrace. The red tiles were freezing, as always, and as always gave my feet a nice chill. In the west, the sky was not yet even hinting the vaguest light. In the summer, when we began, the thin flat clouds over the sea were already rusty by the time we had begun this first session.

I set the egg timer for an hour, sat on my *zafu*, and pulled my legs high onto each thigh in full lotus. Our "Now's" this morning were particularly deep and round, somber but throaty and nuanced as the "Owww's" slid down the scale to "Oooooh's" before evaporating. "*Nowwwww . . . oooooohhhhh . . .*" It's so lovely I was about to contact a record label about cutting a CD (just add a cool techno beat and I'm sure we'd go platinum, maybe double). But after what happened later, who the hell knows?

With the chirp of the egg timer I knew it was time to stretch and heard them stretching behind me. The sky before me was now quite red. I massaged my right foot, which had fallen asleep, and twisted eccentrically before I stood.

"Good morning."

"*GOOD MORNING!*"

They answered more or less in unison. I stepped past them again, this time to the inside so I could shower before the rest of them used up all the damn hot water. I put in a new, hospital-sized water heater back in the fall, but somehow they still find a way to use it all up.

Mr. Landi, Glen, and Mrs. Tewks and the girls had beaten me to the kitchen. Mrs. Tewks was making sandwiches for their lunch boxes, and Mr. Landi and Glen were sharing the paper. I was reaching for the handle on the coffee carafe with one hand while the other reached inside the pantry for the Honey-Nut Cheerios. Like most of the food in the house, this box was car-toonishly large. You should see us when we go to the Price Club. We bring both minivans, and whatever team is shopping returns drowning in their seats in a lumpy sea of paper towels and toilet paper, cases of frozen ground chuck, and the huge pump bottles of ketchup and mustard you see lined up on the counters of hamburger stands.

"If you want to ask him something, just ask him."

"I'm scared, Mommy."

"Don't be scared. You know he won't bite."

I turned from my bowl of cereal and smiled at little Cindy. She smiled shyly, then I wrinkled my face and growled at her and barked.

"Aiiiieee!"

She giggled behind her mother's waist. Her big sister, Sally, frowned. She frowns at everything.

"What is it, Cindy?"

"When can me and Sally bumbee-jump too?"

I stood and caught Cindy under her arms and tossed her in the air, and she squealed.

"Sally and I, sweetheart. And it's *bungee*-jump. Would you like to . . . ?"

She nodded big, but Mrs. Tewks's eyes got really big.

"I'm sorry, but it's a grown-up meditation, bumblebee. Maybe when your big sister's fourteen."

Cindy exaggerated a sigh and deflated while Mrs. Tewks inhaled and relaxed. I smiled at Sally but she looked away.

"C'mon, girls. Time for school."

"*Até logo, moças bonitas.*"

I waved at them, but only Cindy waved back and replied.

"*Até logo*, Uncle Ashton."

Her Portuguese is coming much faster than most of the adults'. Mrs. Tewks took one of the sets of van keys off the hook by the refrigerator, and the girls fell in behind her.

"Ashton, Ashton, you'll never guess what I dreamed again last night . . ."

Glen keeps dreaming about a monkey with a parrot's tail sitting in a tree over his bed in his old apartment in Chicago. He seems to think it means he might Disappear soon.

"What, Glen? What did you dream?"

"The monkey was green this time and—"

"What are you doing here? No, you can't come in! Ashton!"

I was at the front door before I could think. A man with a camera riding his shoulder was trying to enter my house!

"Aiiiiiiiiieeeee!"

Cindy screamed an unnaturally high siren that made us all wince. I pushed past Mrs. Tewks, and Glen was a big shadow at my back.

"Get the fuck out of here! Who the fuck do you think you are!"

It was only then that I noticed the elegant black man behind the cameraman, smiling at me. To me he always looks like an idealized version of my father.

"Hello again, Ashton."

"Ed Bradley. Hello."

"Can we come in?"

"I do not think that is a good idea, Ed. We are just finishing our breakfast."

"We can wait."

"I do not think that is a good idea."

"Then when will you grant me an interview?"

"I . . . I don't think so, Ed."

"There are some people out there calling you another David Koresh."

I made myself smile at the camera. All I could think about were the millions of people watching me and I hadn't yet picked the lint out of my dreads. Behind Ed was this twerpy-looking asshole frantically scribbling down every word I said.*

"Everyone has his detractors, Ed."

Ed Bradley looked over my shoulder.

"You must be Glen Bullock. Your mother is worried about you."

"Tell her I'm fine, goddamnit! Fine! Why is she always pulling on me!"

I turned from the camera and zapped Glen with both barrels of my eyes. He immediately shriveled.

"Ashton, I think you should talk to me. You are an articulate man. Defend yourself. You didn't talk to me last time, and I understand you were not too pleased with the broadcast."

I wanted to conjure my *axe* to erase the video, then stop Ed's heart and his cameraman's, and the heart of the sound guy and the weasely stenographer hiding behind all of them. Unfortunately he is too famous, and he must have told his office he was going to visit me today. So I just breathed a few noisy times, felt my nostrils sting with the coolness of the morning air, and tried to keep smiling.

"Ed, I'll tell you what. Why don't you meet me at the office? I will be over as soon as I finish my breakfast. And Janice, you better hurry along as well. We do not want Sally and Cindy to be late for school. They are both at the tops of their classes and we would like them to stay there."

Of course I just said that for the camera's benefit. But fucking Ed Bradley just grinned even more.

"We know, Ashton. We talked with their teachers yesterday."

*Yours truly.

263

I wondered if I could turn down to stun, just to scare him out of airing his hatchet job. So I closed my eyes quickly, then reached out my hand as I spoke.

"So I will meet you at the office. I'll call ahead and have them set out some bagels, but I will not be long. You have my word."

And we shook.

"Ow . . . You gave me a shock."

Bradley winced and jerked back his whole arm. I turned my back to the camera and grinned evilly just at good ol' Ed. *Fuck with me at your peril*, I silently beamed at him with the flaming bright whites of my eyes. The little Mike Wallace wanna-be quickly stepped back and slinked away, his tacky gold earring twinkling in the morning light.

June 5th

From the television set: "I'm Mike Wallace." "I'm Morley Safer."
"I'm Leslie Stahl." "I'm Ed Bradley. These stories and Andy
Rooney tonight on *60 Minutes*." " *60 Minutes*, CBS's weekly
newsmagazine, is brought to you by . . ."

"Mute the sound please, Henry. We don't need to hear the
commercials."

I hope this isn't too garbled. My hand is cupped over you as I
mumble live. I don't want the others to hear my running com-
mentary. We're all gloomily gathered around the TV. All of us
but Nikki. Her fucking mother's kidnaped her and won't return
any of our phone calls. We know they've talked to everyone's relatives, including Jill's ex, and sniffed around Santa Cruz for
weeks. The energy of the fear and anger in this room is reaching
an almost audible hum.

"C'mon, everybody—*60 Minutes* did a hatchet job on me
before and I survived it. Yes, it is going to be bad. Yes, it is going
to make us angry, but we have to stay calm and . . . and see if
anything is so wrong in it that we can sue. That is why I'm taking these notes with my tape recorder. This first segment, on

waste in the Department of Energy, looks good, though. Henry, turn it up."

I could give two shits about waste in the fucking Department of Energy, but I just can't stand the silence while we wait for my coast-to-coast character assassination. The folks called, saw the ad in *TV Guide* about today's show. The last time was pretty rough on them. Every relative in the world called up.

Back then the show admitted I'd broken no laws, admitted I had many more fans than detractors, but still, I came off as a sleazy snake-oil salesman raking in money from pathetic, weak-willed middle managers desperate for promotion and success. I've retained two law firms in San Francisco to go over the broadcast frame by frame. Nevertheless, my heart skitters in my chest like a wild rodent. Let me concentrate on my breathing to try and clear my mind of all thoughts till my segment comes on . . .

From the television, Ed Bradley: "You might remember a piece we ran two years ago on Ashton Robinson, the charismatic and wildly successful motivational speaker. Back then, though he had broken no law, we found he was perhaps using some questionable accounting methods and perhaps abusing the trust of his ten of thousands of followers. You might have found him a rogue, but a charming one. But what you are about to see tonight will change your opinion of him forever . . ."

Oh, God, *Robinsontown* is the title written on the screen, superimposed over my own fucking house! The little fucking bit of inner peace I'd just achieved meditating instantly vanished.

"Lydia, could you get me a large bottle of cough syrup, please? One of the ninety-twos."

It takes Mrs. Sandilla a long moment to detach herself from the television and rise toward the wine rack. Just last month I tracked down this small cough-syrup and throat-lozenge factory in Cincinnati that had been abandoned years ago and was about to incinerate its expired stock.

On the screen, from a helicopter, my house squats on the sand, huge and white. The bungee crane angles above it like sculpture, and you can barely make out the platform rising. The camera zooms in from the sky and focuses on Mrs. Landi, quaking, and myself behind her. Mrs. Sandilla jogs back with my cough syrup and I swig, while Mrs. Landi, on the screen, pitches off the edge of the platform and bounces helplessly, a puppet on a string.

Ed Bradley: "No this is not some private amusement park. This is a new *religion,* or *system,* as the owner of the mansion would call it. That's him up on the platform, millionaire motivational speaker Ashton Robinson. Once one of the most successful self-help lecturers in the country, Ashton Robinson has traded all that in for a religion of his own invention called *axe.* And now he's trying to *market* that religion to the same people who once paid for his innocuous, business-minded pep talks . . ."

Now on the screen good ol' Ed's in front of the Hyde Park Days Inn. Ughh! I just chugged too much syrup and almost spit up.

Ed Bradley: "As near as anyone can tell, it all started here in the Majestic Windy City Room of this hotel. Robinson was scheduled to perform one of his routine motivational seminars, seminars for which participants paid *one hundred dollars* for *three hours* of advice. Robinson, uncharacteristically, arrived an hour late, and when he did begin to speak, it was not his usual platitudes about seizing the moment and telling the boss what's really on your mind. Instead, say observers, he began talking about a mysterious *midget from Brazil* who came to him and told him about *axe*, an Afro-Brazilian word meaning 'spirit' . . ."

The fucking Dawbridges now fill the screen, sitting in their tacky living room, shaking as they talk.

Ed Bradley: "Meet Len and Susan Dawbridge, longtime Robinson followers and Chicago-area 'officiators,' Robinson's term for the locals who used to help organize his lectures. Though Robinson would clear upwards of seventy thousand dollars a night, the officiators' *only* recompensation was free admission . . ."

Susan Dawbridge: "My husband and I sensed something was wrong as soon as we picked him up from the airport. Then, when he finally showed up at the banquet hall, his eyes were crazed, his voice—I've never heard that voice from him before. He started talking about Brazilians and this local restaurant he went to and how it changed his life somehow, and everybody was very uncomfortable because they knew he was on something, or something, you know? By about, gosh, by about forty-five minutes most everybody'd left, except maybe a dozen people. We stayed because we just couldn't believe that he'd gone off the deep end. We were hoping he was just drunk and would snap out of it. We really were crushed when after the hotel kicked him out of the hall he just kept going on and on in the bar about, gosh, I really don't know what. But he's such a charismatic person! The night manager came over to maybe kick us out, but he ended up staying with the rest of us till dawn!"

On the screen they cut to a grainy photo of Glen, smiling.

Ed Bradley: "That night manager was Glen Bullock. He'd been working at the Days Inn for just six months. Before that he had committed himself to the Northern Illinois State Psychiatric Hospital after his second suicide attempt, that last time trying to cut his own throat with a Japanese cooking knife he'd ordered from an infomercial."

Oh, no. As the camera pulls back from the photo of Glen's smiling face we finally see he's bound in a straitjacket and flanked by two scowling orderlies.

The others stare as away from Glen as can be. But I look and see him petting that small scar on his neck that I'd always wondered about, mesmerized by his own image on the screen.

On the screen this lady who must be Glen's mother is crying in her cheap and yellowing kitchen.

Kathryn Simmons: "He's got my boy! He's got him. Talked him into quitting a good job and living with that man doing God knows what. It ain't right. It ain't right to take advantage of somebody who sick."

Now those fuckers push in for a close-up on the little old crying bitch.

Ed Bradley: "And this house here at six fifty-four Pinehurst used to belong to Henry and Lydia Sandilla. They attended Robinson's unusual Chicago seminar, and a few days later packed their bags for California, at the paid invitation of Robinson himself. Four months later they sold the house for one hundred and sixty-five thousand dollars and signed over the profits to the personal corporation of Ashton Robinson himself."

"Aaaaaaahhhhhh! Those pig fuckers! You volunteered it!"

Lydia Sandilla: "We did! We volunteered it, Ashton! How dare they . . . ?"

The syrup bottle has been drained, but I just jammed my tongue into the opening for the last taste of it. But I'd be queasy even if I hadn't drained the shit. The PES building now looms on the screen.

Ed Bradley: "And what does Ashton Robinson say to the

charges we've made? The man himself surprised us with an interview . . ."

And there I am, smiling my most winning smile, my dreads jiggling.

Ed Bradley: "Why did you change your message from one of self-help and motivation to this new, what do you want to call it, religion?"

From the television, Ashton Robinson: "I changed my message—Ed—because I realized there is much more to life than job promotions and wealth."

Ed Bradley: "And not because a mysterious midget from Brazil appeared in your mansion?"

Ashton Robinson: "I realize the unusual is hard for some to swallow. You are an intelligent man, an analytical man, a man who only believes what can be proven by scientific theory or in a court of law. I used to be such a man myself. That is why my new system is called the science of religion. Instead of dismissing the faiths of billions of people on this planet, we study them, take what we can from each of them, and apply them to our own lives. It is easy to be cynical, to shut our eyes to the wonders of the world, but it is only halfliving; it is closing ourselves off from the most wonderful parts of existence . . ."

Ed Bradley: "So you don't find it strange that a Brazilian midget would materialize in your home and tell you to found a new religion?"

Ashton Robinson: "Ed, you are not even pretending to be listening to me."

Ed Bradley: "What do you think about the Reverend Sun Myung Moon, David Koresh, or Marshall Applewhite . . . ?"

On the screen I am laughing, and I guess I was more nervous

than I thought, because I keep laughing maybe a little too long. Uh-oh. The camera's now pushing in on my laughing face so close my features distort. Anybody'd look like a fucking psychopath!

Ed Bradley: "Ashton, David Koresh also forbade the husbands that were his disciples from sleeping with their wives so he could sleep with them himself."

Ashton Robinson: "What are you talking about?"

Oh shit. Now they quickly cut to the shadowy outline of a man backlit in a TV studio.

Ed Bradley: "Meet a man who was at the Chicago seminar, then was one of the original dozen flown to Robinson's Santa Cruz, California, mansion. He asked us not to reveal his identity. We'll call him Ray . . ."

Nicholas Fucking Harris.* How the hell did they find him? His voice is synthesized eerily, warbles almost unintelligibly and without gender.

Ray: "I arrived with the rest of the people from Chicago and we were all nervous, but he was such a powerful speaker I think he had us all under his spell. He told us about the midget and how it shape-shifted into a beautiful woman he had sexual relations with, and then he had us all dance in a big room and drink lots of red wine and cough syrup. Soon we were all vomiting and completely delirious. I had come with my new girlfriend, and several of the others were married couples. He talked about tantric sex, this Hindu sex thing, and then he chose my girlfriend and this lady who came with her husband and two kids to have sex with him that night."

Ed Bradley: "Couldn't they have said no?"

---

*Pure conjecture on the part of Robinson.

Ray: "I told you, we were drugged. Besides, you can't say no to Robinson. Nobody ever says no to him."

Ed Bradley: "One woman who couldn't say no was Nikki Kennedy."

Oh, my God. Not Nikki! There she is, gorgeous, behind a screen door to, I guess, her mother's house. Her blouse stretches across her beautiful belly, tight like a sail in a breeze. Now she's edging open the door, hooking just her head outside.

Nikki Kennedy: "Leave him alone! Leave him alone! He's a wonderful man! He's a great man!"

Now some woman in white is putting her arm on Nikki's shoulder. Sweet Nikki jerks herself away, then clangs shut the screen door and slams the real door. I love her!

Ed Bradley: "Though Ms. Kennedy would not talk to us, her mother and father confirmed that she was one of Robinson's closest followers until her mother got her to come back to Chicago by feigning serious illness. They have hired a psychiatric nurse specializing in cult deprogramming to watch her around the clock, fearing she might endanger her own life and the life of the child she carries."

Nikki's mother's ugly face fills the screen. Her jaw pulsates.

Ed Bradley: "Mrs. Kennedy, who do you believe to be the father of your daughter's child?"

Alberta Kennedy: "She won't say, but I'm sure it was that crazy man Robinson! That's why I burnt her credit cards, her wallet. I'll be damned if I let her go back to that . . . that—!"

She's grown! Tomorrow I'm flying there myself to bring her the fuck home. Henry was in the marines. He's gotta know how we can sneak in there and free her.

Ed Bradley: "And then there's the matter of the new audio-cassettes . . ."

Right Here, Right Now

And they cut to me on the show saying ten ninety-five shipping and handling.

Ed Bradley: "In fact, according to the Mail Fraud Project of the Justice Department, normal shipping and handling charges for the set of cassettes, which altogether weigh under twelve ounces, would be no more than three dollars."

Then they cut back to me, trying to charm Ed with my smile.

Ed Bradley: "Ashton, how about it? The Mail Fraud Project of the Justice Department accuses you of grossly overcharging for the shipping and handling of your cassettes."

Ashton Robinson: "I don't know where they got their figures, Ed, but I should know how much it costs to ship and to handle our own merchandise, now shouldn't I?"

Ed Bradley: "One last question. You say you're serious about this spiritual quest. I assume that means you plan to continue *axe* for years. So what about the little Tewks girls, Cindy and Sally, now ages six and nine? How old will they be when you start practicing your *special* brand of meditation on them?"

Shit! Here's where I lost it. On the screen my eyes widen and burn at him like a mad doctor's in a cheap science-fiction movie. I guess, fuck, I guess maybe I thought I could convince him with the full power of my *axe* to abandon the whole exposé. Instead, oh, Lord, what now! The camera is pushing in till the huge screen is just my eyes, the whites of them luminous like a glass of milk in front of a bright lightbulb. The camera holds on them; you can even see the red veins shattered across the whites, the pupils as open as a junky's.

Then the screen abruptly just cut away to the fucking *60 Minutes* stopwatch, ticking so fucking loudly.

A loud commercial for Taco Bell comes on as if my life had not just been ruined. They're not saying anything, my flock, but I feel that something has been broken between us. I am pushing myself out of my chair and, oh! wait a minute, I almost fell. I list as I walk, as if I were on a ship at sea, grope for the walls to lead me to the door to lead me down the hall to the front door and outside . . . [Twenty seconds of silence.] Here it looks just as it looked this morning, only this morning I was on my way to joining the pantheon of the world's great spiritual leaders.

I stumble around and around the fountain. Oh, I just ran into the Jaguar. I am slapping my pants for my keys. I hear them jingle but can't seem to find them in my pockets.

I swing the door wide and fall into the driver's seat.

Jill Lowry: "Where are you going? What are you doing?! I love you, Ashton! Take me with you, like it should've been from the beginning! We'll leave the Chicagoans to answer the questions, but we'll be in Mexico or back on St. Barth's, remember? Please . . ."

I am driving now, I don't quite know how. The spirit drives, I guess, because I don't remember once turning, once braking, but here I am rolling up PCH toward San Francisco. Is there gas? How fast am I going? I could look, but if I am truly anointed, I should know. OK, I *feel* the tank is three-quarters full and I *feel* as if I am driving sixty-three. Let's look. Oh, my eyes focus much better on the road than on these damn British dials that float doubled, tripled in front of me. But there's the speedometer's needle sweeping past the nine of ninety. What a car. Oops. A quick zig and a zag got me right around that truck.

"*Você conhece porquê você vai a San Francisco?*"*

---

*"Do you know why you're going to San Francisco?" With the noise of the highway in Robinson's convertible, our panel of experts could make no conclusion whatsoever as to the identity of this voice. The rest of the exchanges have been translated.

Right Here, Right Now

I wonder how long he's been in the car.

"No. Why?"

"Because you must [inaudible]."

"Look, I tried. They're just not ready. And while we're at it, could you turn into that beautiful woman again? I love her."

"[Inaudible] don't need any more women. You should have concentrated more on meditation than group sex; then you might have Disappeared months ago."

I look up and find myself driving through the streets of San Francisco. How I arrived so fast I don't know, but I must still be driving too quickly because the tires complain shrilly at each corner.

"Where the hell have you been all these months? And why'd you let them do that to me on TV?"

"Unfasten your seat belt."

Now I see it. Up ahead. KPIX, the local CBS affiliate. It makes so much sense. Finally. I know I am accelerating; I hear the rising anger from the engine. The lobby is lit so prettily, a guard is holding the door for a woman with nice legs and huge hair. The road turns but I don't, and now they start to scamper. Bursting through the doors, I like the sound of the glass breaking, love the thrill of driving inside a building; driving onto a ferryboat is a weak cousin of this thrill, but driving onto a plane would be fun. I have never driven onto a train either, but I know that you can from New York to Florida. The elevator banks are coming up. Its doors are just rejoining and the folks inside see me and widen their eyes. I have never driven onto an elevator, either . . .

December 5th*

I've never spent more than a weekend in an American desert. I remember crossing the Sahara on the back of a big truck, going back up to Algeria because my visa'd been denied in Niger. I remember the forever of nothingness, but I also remember the brittle, empty ground, not sand, under the doubled wheels of the truck. I remember the skeletons of cars on the left and on the right, as frequent as highway billboards. I remember imagining Tuareg nomads appearing out of the emptiness moments after a Peugot overheated, stripping it cleanly like piranhas of the sand.

My Mojave rattles with living things. [Cough.] Look anywhere for more than a moment and something small will be moving quickly and so low to the sand. Yet that is all I see. Not one single other man-made structure in the miles and miles of my view. When I'm outside of it too long, I sometimes find myself turning away from the gorgeous desert and staring at one of

*These last two transcripts are courtesy of the Federal Bureau of Investigation and published under their copyright.

these hideous prefab walls just to remind myself that I was once part of a great civilization.

Oh, Nikki had our baby girl. She sends me a new picture of Yemayá each month. I've enlarged a few in the photo lab, and they are all that I have done to spruce up my room.

This is not a bad room. It's prefab and cinderblocks; reminds me of my cousin's dorm at UC San Luis Obispo. I used to make fun of these places. I remember when Stacey Koon and Laurence Powell, the cops who beat Rodney King, were sent here, to my new home, the Boron, California, Minimum Security Federal Prison, and I remember my anger. Hector, the guard of D wing, had just started when they were convicted and says they were unbelievably messy. I used to think that was the only reason he liked me. I keep my room as lean as a surgery theater. But last week he finally admitted he used to be in a gang back in San Diego till his priest made him sit down and listen to one of my early audio courses.

Jill went back to her husband.

My plastic hip is a marvel of mechanical engineering. Doc says I'll even be able to surf again. When I get out, of course. Of course, that is at least forty months from now—DON'T THINK ABOUT IT. Everybody says it's not the past or even the present but *the future* that kills you in prison. Even minimum security. If that high-speed elevator wasn't so high speed they would have tacked several counts of vehicular homicide onto mail fraud and I would *really* have had time to get my *axe* together.

What a crock of shit! I was so rich. I was doing so well. Why'd I have to go crazy and spoil it? Why did other people ever believe me? Dr. Rainer says I can't blame it on the cough syrup. Otherwise thousands of juvenile delinquents every year would turn into cult leaders themselves.

I believed it, though. I believed it even as the hood was starting to fold, even as I felt my body rise out of my seat—especially then. Finally, I thought I'd understood Disappearance and was so looking forward to life on the other side! I remember, just before impact, two lights getting brighter and brighter still, till they merged with each other and then with me. I was sure the lights were the *axe* of Mudamenta as man and woman, ugliness and beauty, merging into their fundamental, universal oneness, till Dr. Rainer suggested they could have been just the headlights of my poor Jag reflecting against the shiny elevator doors as I drove into them. But at that moment, if I had died, I would have died believing.

The first words I understood after I'd come back to consciousness were "Jaws of Life." It opened up my $80,000 car like a can of coffee, and I was lying in a bed in the ICU twenty-four minutes later.

But on the bright side, nobody but me got hurt, and I had a lot of great sex. I want—

Prison Guard Hector Villalonga: "Ashton, your people are here."

"Thanks, Hector."

They're forty-five minutes late. Must have hit traffic. My image in the mirror just stopped me before I left my room. It has been six months, yet I am still not used to no longer having dreads. Cutting them off worked, in that even when I arrived here, even after being on Court TV eight hours a day for four months, as soon as I cut them off, I was practically invisible. *Disappeared*, as it were. On the other hand, this corny-looking man in the mirror I do not recognize to be myself. I walk the halls quickly. I haven't seen my mother in a month. I hear the odd music of Ping-Pong as I round a corner.

Right Here, Right Now

"Hey, Jimmy, Fred."

Bond traders. They'll be out a month before me, and we're already talking about a few business ventures, including a chain of Ping-Pong theme bars. They play three hours every day.

I'll fill you in on what the folks had to say when I get back.

■ ■ ■

I hit the bar to unlatch the door to the outside, and it clanked open noisily, and the cool of the air-conditioning inside left me and was quickly replaced by the pressure of the heat of the sun. My mother, father, and sister hadn't yet seen me and were waiting on the picnic benches. Avon has to stay close to home when Papa's away in case a customer has some sort of electrical emergency. My mother sailed a shiny tablecloth over the concrete picnic table while Allison pulled fried chicken from a paper bag, each piece wrapped in aluminum foil, so out here in this moonscape, they looked like a bunch of fist-sized space rocks. Even from far away, the noises of the paper bag seemed loud to me for some reason. [Cough.] Out came the Tupperware of potato salad, baked beans, and cole slaw. Everyone stopped when they finally saw me. I hurried to hug my mother first, careful of her cane.

"How you been, baby?"

"I'm good."

Allison, as she does every month, looked across the land, the main building, the red mountains, and the row of StairMasters and racks of weights, and sucked her teeth.

"If this is prison, then Halle Berry is a man."

"Shhh. Would you rather see your brother behind bars?"

"But they don't even have a fence!"

"We're miles and miles away from anything. Besides, they trust us."

"Oh, like that doctor that lives down the hall from you, the one who made millions billing Medicare for people that'd already died."

"Shhh!"

Dr. Mahoney was right behind us in the pottery shed. He makes the most amazing mustache cups.

"Mother, want to see a new picture of the baby?"

I handed it to her, and my father and Allison crowded behind her to see too.

"Why, if she doesn't look just like Aunt Sis Ruth."

"She's got more teeth than Aunt Sis Ruth."

My words made my father smile. I hugged him and felt his age in his shoulders, felt how they were thinning with time.

"How's your hip, son?"

"I still have to go to physical therapy once a week, but they say it's even better than a real one."

"Can they do something about that scar on your chin?"

"I don't know. But I kind of like it."

"I'm just happy to see them damn snakes off your head. I don't know what made you stop combing your hair in the first place."

I looked to my mother. She's always rescued me from my father's teasing.

"How are you for money, baby?"

"Between the fines and taxes, Geoffrey says I'm going to have to sell the house. But I've squirreled away a little bit here and there that the courts can't attach. If I'm careful, especially if I live someplace cheap, I should never have to work again. Right now, I'm thinking about Costa Rica."

Right Here, Right Now

Then I had another coughing fit. This desert air is killing me.

"You catching a cold, baby?"

"No. [Cough.] I just haven't shaken that same little thing I had last month. But I'm sure it will go away, somehow."

Mother and Father and Allison all looked at each other up and down.

"They still won't give you any syrup at the infirmary?"

"After everything that happened? They'd rather let my voice box fall off than give me something to soothe this damn burning. [Cough.] Mommy, they just don't care."

"Have you tried lozenges?"

"They don't work on me."

She didn't look at the others and I didn't look at any of the others but her. She frowned as she reached into her purse and pulled out a plastic bottle of something that looked so deliciously thick and red.

"Mama! No! You promised! He's lying!"

My sister can be such a pill. My father was a sphinx.

"I don't want you to get in trouble, baby."

"Don't worry. They love me in here."

Hector went back inside. He's heavy and hates the heat. I quickly emptied a Snapple into the dirt and angled the syrup into the bottle under the table between my knees.

"Now, you just sip it till your cough goes away, hear?"

"Of course [cough], Mommy. I promise."

"I'm just so glad you put all this foolishness behind you. What you need to do, boy, is start going to church."

Later December 5th

"Oh, my God, I'd almost forgotten your beauty."
—[Inaudible.]*
Yes. I likes. I likes. Mudamenta is naked and brown in my little room, and such a joy is invading me. After eight months of near nightly ménages-à-trois, these six months here have been quite a change . . . Oh! [Two minutes, thirty-five seconds of wretching sounds.] . . . I was just moving to kiss her when my stomach convulsed and my head flew to the stainless-steel toilet bowl before I could think the thought. [Inaudible.] I'd love to flush away the smell but don't want to wake the others, so I'll just close the lid.
"[Inaudible] teeth."
I do as she says and brush my teeth, quietly. I swallow, and the backed-up enzymes still burn, so I pull a Snapple out of my minifridge . . . I turn to her and try to kiss her again . . . [Kissing sounds . . . moans.] Wow! Flashes just exploded in my brain.

*Prison authorities put the time around 3 A.M. Robinson is whispering, and even some of his undisguised voice is barely intelligible.

"Don't turn back into the midget, whatever you do."

Damn. I just tried to kiss her again, but she pushed me away.

"Not [inaudible]."

"Why not here? I mean, our choices are kind of limited."

"[Inaudible] can you let them win? Is that what the Israelites in Egypt or the early Christian martyrs did? Or Brigham Young?"

"But my sentence was only half what my lawyers told me to be prepared for. If I keep quiet in here I'll be able to start over again on the outside."

"[Inaudible] I thought you had balls. Don't you want to make love with me?"

"What!"

"Disappear with me and we'll make love between [inaudible] and six times a day."

"You're shitting me."

"[Inaudible] let's go."

"Wait!"

Damn! She just passed through the door and into the hall. I see the beautiful waves of her brown stomach through the small square window in the door, a sandwich of glass, chicken wire, and glass. Of course I have to go with her, but should I leave a note for Dr. Rainer?

No time. I draw my door just open enough to scoot around it, and now here in the hall we take long strides on the balls of our bare feet past the Ping-Pong table, past the bulletin boards and water fountains. Bare feet . . . ?

"Mudamenta, I forgot my shoes."

She turns to me with disdain and looks down at her own nakedness. She is kissing my neck as she unbuttons my jean shirt, pushes it off my shoulders, and unbuttons my fly and pushes my jeans off my hips and steps on them so I can step out of the legs. I push off my underwear myself, and she finally smiles again.

Hector is sleeping in front of his tiny TV. A GutBuster® infomercial is on. It had to be. I look to her for what to do next, and she just looks at me. Wait a second. I've got to be really, really quiet . . .

[Forty-five seconds of silence.]

I just slipped the bouquet of keys off the wall behind his head and am now staring at them. I'd forgotten there were so many.

"Which one?"

"One try. If you chose the wrong key, you will never see me again."

She just passed right through the door. My heartbeat is not letting me think. Calm. Calm . . . I am now making myself stare at the keys, bringing my *axe* into my right hand's index finger and passing it over them; there must be at least twenty. Again I pass my finger over them, but I have not really summoned my full-strength *axe* in months now. Let me be quiet for a second and concentrate . . .

[Two minutes, five seconds of silence.]

The cold of the desert night feels wonderful across my balls. We are walking together, hand in hand, slowly but with purpose, toward the mountains, now just a hedge of black angles between the land and the sky. Bushes scratch my calves, animals made frantic by our approach crackle twigs as they escape. I can't believe I'm finally going.

I feel so strangely tense. "Nervous" doesn't come close to telling you what's really going on inside of me. Do I have to die to get to the Other Side? Do I have to check my consciousness at the gate and enter as pure energy? The sand between my toes, my lingam semierect—are these the last feelings I will ever feel? And what about Nikki, what about my daughter, what about the rest of the world . . . ? Here come the tears. Will I ever know if I've done any good? Yet wasn't Christ just this ambivalent as they were nailing *him* up? While he lived he seemed to have no idea how greatly his legacy would change the world. For me that's unacceptable. IF I'M GOING TO HAVE A WORLDWIDE CHAIN OF CATHEDRALS, I WANT TO SEE THEM! PRONTO!

"Quiet. [Unintelligible] guard is a very light sleeper."

"Sorry. But is it much farther? I can't take much more of this."

She just gave me that look she has that always seems to say, Don't be such a human idiot.

"But why are you giving me another chance? I thought if I were truly ready I was supposed to have Disappeared back when I smashed the car. How do you know I just won't fail you again out here?"

"You didn't fail, silly. We just didn't count on the air bag."

[An owl hoots. Footsteps for twelve seconds.]

"Oh. It's right there. I get it now."

[Footsteps stop. Exactly four minutes later, the tape ends.]

About the Author

Trey Ellis is the author of *Platitudes* and *Home Repairs*. He and his wife life in Santa Monica, California.